The superhorse they had sought to create was complete now. He had become whatever they had made him in their greed and ignorance. The chemicals were part of his flesh, and the magic was part of his soul—no known test could reveal either.

But the great stallion, the Silverlord, knew.

One of the men from the shadows was moving again, quietly circling around the pen toward An Serra. He liked her looks. He ran his tongue over his chapped lips. A soft, silken woman like that might be worth risking the wrath of Lord Gaorlain—and if they were careful, no one would ever know what happened to her. Men who could conceal a huge horse could conceal many other things.

But the effects of their drugs were wearing off. The stallion was no longer immobilized by them. He flexed his muscles and found he had control of them all. His hearing was acute. His vision was clearing—he saw the man sneaking up on An Serra.

I will protect you, the Silverlord said, unheard, to the girl.

The man leaped forward and grabbed her, spreading one callused hand across her face to stifle breath and scream together. And the Silverlord rose onto his hind legs, towering over them, sounding his own scream of defiance. One flinty hoof struck out and sliced the top of the skull from the man holding An Serra almost as cleanly as if a surgeon's scalpel had done it.

Blood poured. *Yes!* thought the Silverlord, remembering.

Tor books by Andre Norton

The Crystal Gryphon
Flight in Yiktor
Forerunner
Forerunner: The Second Venture
Gryphon's Eyrie (with A.C. Crispin)
Here Abide Monsters
House of Shadows (with Phyllis Miller)
Imperial Lady (with Susan Shwartz)
Moon Called
Moon Mirror
Ralestone Luck
Wheel of Stars
Wizards' Worlds

Tor books edited by Andre Norton

THE WITCH WORLD
Tales of the Witch World 1
Tales of the Witch World 2
Four from the Witch World

MAGIC IN ITHKAR (with Robert Adams)
Magic in Ithkar 1
Magic in Ithkar 2
Magic in Ithkar 3
Magic in Ithkar 4

Magic In Ithkar 3

Edited By
Andre Norton
And
Robert Adams

TOR
fantasy

A TOM DOHERTY ASSOCIATES BOOK
NEW YORK

MAGIC IN ITHKAR 3

Copyright © 1988 by Andre Norton and Robert Adams

A TOR Book
Published by Tom Doherty Associates, Inc.
49 West 24 Street
New York, NY 10010

Cover art by Steven Hickman

ISBN: 0-812-54709-8   Can. ISBN: 0-812-54710-1

First edition: October 1986
First mass market edition: September 1989

Printed in the United States of America

0 9 8 7 6 5 4 3 2 1

CONTENTS

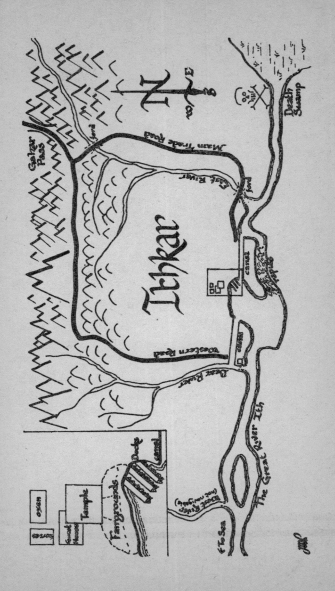

PROLOGUE

Robert Adams

The Three Lordly Ones are said to have descended in their sun-bright Egg and come to rest on a spot near to the bank of the river Ith. The priests of their temple reckon this event to have occurred four hundred, two score, and eight years ago (and who should better know?). Though the Three never made any claim to godhead, they now are adored as such, and for at least four centuries, many pilgrims have come on the anniversary of the day of their coming to render their worship and to importune the Three to return.

The Three are said to have remained on the spot of their descent for almost a generation—twenty-one years and seven months—though they journeyed often in smaller Eggs that, it is told, could move far faster than even a shooting star and so bore them in only a bare day across snowy and impassable mountains, across stormy and monster-infested seas, to lands that most folk know only in fable.

Since not even the learned priests can fine down the exact date of their coming closer than a ten-day, pilgrims came and still come all during this period, and centuries ago, the Ithkar Temple and its denizens lived out the rest of each year on the donations of the pilgrims, the produce of the temple's ploughlands, orchards, and herds, plus whatever edible fish they could catch in the Ith.

But wheresoever numbers of folk do gather for almost any purpose, other folk will come to sell them necessaries and luxuries. Pilgrimage Ten-day at Ithkar Temple was no different. Each year succeeding, more and more peddlers and hawkers gathered around the temple, the more astute arriving before the start of Holy Ten-day, so as to be well set up for business upon the influx of even the first-day pilgrims. Of course, other sellers, noting that these merchants always appropriated the best locations, began to plan their arrivals even earlier to claim these spots for their own. Within a few more years, most of the merchants were in place a full ten-day before the beginning of Holy Ten-day and many of the pilgrims then began to come earlier, in search of the bargains and rare merchandise often to be found at Ithkar Fair, as it was coming to be called far and wide.

Now, in modern times, the Fair at Ithkar has lengthened to three full ten-days in duration and still is extending in time even as it increases in size.

Nearly seventeen score years ago, the then high priest of Ithkar Temple, one Yuub, realized that the priests and priestesses of the shrine were mostly missing out on a marvelous source of easy, laborless income. He it was who first sacrificed the nearer gardens—betwixt the temple enclave and the river-lake—and made of them three (later, four) campgrounds for the merchants and tradesmen, so that they no longer surround the temple on all sides as in the past. He it was, also, who first hired on temporary fair-wards—local bullies and old soldiers—to maintain order with their bronze-shod staves, enforce the will of the priests, and collect the monies due for the marked-off shop-spaces during the fair.

As the Temple at Ithkar waxed richer, successors to old Yuub continued to improve the temple and its environs. A guest house was built onto the northwestern corner of the temple's main building in order to house the wealthier and nobler pilgrims in a greater degree of comfort (for which, of course, they were charged a more substantial figure than those who bode in tents, pavilions, or wagons or who simply rolled in a blanket on a bit of ground under the stars). A guest stable followed shortly, then a partially roofed pen for draft oxen. The next project was a canal to bypass the terrible rapids that lay between the East River's confluence with the river Ith and the Harbor of Ithkar.

Two centuries ago, a high priest arranged to have huge logs of a very hard, dense, long-lasting wood rafted down from the northern mountains, then paid the hire of workmen to sink them as footings for the three long docks below the lower fair precincts, these to replace the old floating-docks which had for long received water-borne pilgrims, fairgoers, traders, merchants, and the like. Now these docking facilities are utilized year-round by users of the main trade road that winds from the steppes up the northern slopes of the mountains, through demon-haunted Galzar Pass, then down the south slopes and the foothills and the plain to the Valley of the Ith. Southbound users of the main trade road had, before the building of the docks and the digging of the canal, been obliged to either ford the East River well to the northeast, prior to its being joined by tributaries and thus widened, then

11

to follow a road that led down to a ford not far above the Ith, or to raft down the East River, then portage around the rapids and falls.

With the great success of the temple or eastern canal there clear for all to see, the great noble whose lands lay just to the west of the lands of the temple in the Ith Valley had dug a longer, somewhat wider canal connecting Bear River to the harbor and its fine docks, charging fees for the use of his canal and, through arrangement, sharing in the commerce-taxes that the temple derived from year-round use of its docks by the transmontane traders, hunters, trappers, and steppe nomads who tended to use the Bear River route rather than the main trade road.

Before Bear River was rendered navigable by an earth-quake that eliminated the worst of its rapids, the folk who used it had come down into Ith Valley via the longer, harder western road rather than the eastern through well-founded fear of wide-ranging denizens of the Death Swamp.

Many long centuries before the blessed arrival of the Three, it is related, a huge and prosperous city lay on the banks of the Ith somewhere within what now is deadly swamp but then were pleasant, fertile lands and pastures, vineyards, and orchards. But the people of this city were not content with the richness of the life they enjoyed, so they and other cities made war upon another coalition of lands and cities, using not only swords and spears and iron maces and bows, but terrible weapons that bore death from afar—death not only for warriors, but for entire cities and lands and all of their people and beasts. It was one such weapon as these that destroyed the city, rendered all living things within it dead in one terrible day and night, left all of the wrecked homes and empty buildings not destroyed outright clustered about a new lake created by the weapon, a long and wide and shallow lake with a bottom composed of green glass.

In those long-ago days it was that lands surrounding the destroyed and lifeless city earned the name of Death Swamp, for many of the most fertile of the former city's lands had lain well below the usual level of the river Ith and had been protected from riverine encroachments by miles of earthen levees, but with no care or maintenance of those levees, spring floods first weakened them, then breached them and inundated field and farm, pasture and vineyard and orchard. Within a very short time, reeds waved high over expanses that once had produced grain-crops, while monstrous, sinuous shapes wriggled through the muck that had so lately been verdant pasturelands filled with sleek kine.

Monstrous beasts, kin of the mountain dragons, dwelt in many swamplands and in as many near swamp wastes—this was a fact known to all—but the denizens of Death Swamp were not as these more normal beasts, it was said, being deformed in sundry ways, larger ofttimes, and more deadly. It also was said that the Death Swamp monsters were of preternatural sentience.

Descriptions of the Death Swamp monsters were almost all ancient ones, for precious few ever deliberately penetrated the dim, overgrown, terrible place that even the Three had warned should be avoided, adding that there were other places akin to it in lurking deadliness hither and yon in the world, sites rendered by the forgotten weapons of that long-ago war inimical to all forms of natural life.

Of the few who do brave the Death Swamp, fewer still come out at all, and many of those are mad or have changed drastically in manners of thinking, acting, and speech, and seldom for the better. The sole reason that any still venture within the lands and waters surrounding that blasted city is the extraordinarily high prices that wizards will pay for artifacts of that ancient place, many of which have proven to be of great and abiding power. And magic is as much a part of this world as the air and the water, the fire and the very earth itself.

The fair precincts are surrounded by palings of peeled logs sunk into the earth some foot or so apart, and those entering the gates must surrender all weapons other than eating-knives. Be they merchants or traders, they and the wares they would purvey must undergo questioning, weighing, and scrutiny by the fair-wards and the wizard-of-the-gate, lest spells be used to enhance the appearance of shoddy goods. Some magic is allowed, but it must be clearly advertised as such in advance and it must be magic of only the right-hand path.

Those apprehended within fair or temple precincts practicing unauthorized magic, harmful magic, or black magic can be haled before the fair-court. The high priest or those from the temple he appoints then hears the case and decides punishment, which punishment can range from a mere fine or warning up to and including being stripped of all possessions, declared outlaw (and thus fair game for any cheated customer or other enemy), and whipped from out the precincts, naked and unarmed.

The Ithkar Fair is divided into three main sections, each of which is laid out around a nucleus of permanent shops and booths; however, the vast majority of stalls are erected afresh each year, then demolished after the fair. Most distant from the temple precincts lies the section wherein operate dealers in live animals and in animal products—horses and other beasts of burden, hounds and coursing-cats, hawks, cormorants and other trained or trainable birds, domestic beasts, and wild rarities, many of these last captured afar and brought for sale to the wealthier for their private menageries.

In this fourth section, too, are sold such mundane things as bales of wool, hides, rich furs, supplies for the hunter and the trapper. Here, also, are places wherein performing animals can be shown and put through their paces, offered for sale or for hire to entertain private gatherings and parties of the well born or the well to do. Of recent years, quite a number of all-human performing acts have taken to auditioning here for prospective patrons:

The westernmost section of the main three houses craftsmen and dealers in base metals—armor, tools, and smaller hardware of all sorts and descriptions. Once the folk dealing in the sundries of wizardry were to be found here as well, but no more. Farrier/horseleeches are here, as are wheelwrights, saddlers, yoke-makers, and the like.

The middle section of the main three holds dealers in foods, clothing, and footwear. Here are weavers, tailors, embroiderers, bottiers, felters, spinners of thread, dealers in needles and pins, booths that sell feathers and plumes, metalcasters' booths with brooches, torques, and arm- or finger- or ear-rings of red copper or bronze or brass or iron. Cookshops abound here, some of them with tasting-booths from which tidbits can be bought, some of them offering cooks and servers for hire to cater private parties or feasts. Also to be found here are the dealers in beers, ales, wines, meads, and certain more potent decoctions, with the result that there are almost always more fair-wards—proud in their tooled-leathern buffcoats and etched, crested brazen helmets, all bearing their lead-filled, bronze-shod quarterstaves—in evidence about the middlemost section.

The easternmost of the three main sections houses the

workers in wood and stone—cabinetmakers, woodcarvers, master carpenters; statuette-carvers to master masons. Dealers in glassware are here to be found, candlemakers, purveyors of medicinal herbs, decoctions, scented oils, incense, and perfumeries, potters of every description and class, and lampmakers as well.

In this section one may purchase an alabaster chess set and, a little distance farther along, an inlaid table to accommodate it. Here to be seen and examined are miniature models of the works of the master masons and carpenters, with whom contracts for future work may be arranged; likewise, custom furniture may be ordered from the cabinetmakers.

Within the outskirts of the temple complex itself is a newer, much smaller subsection, centered around the temple's main gate. Here, where the ever-greedy priests' agents can keep close watch on them and on their customers, are the money-changers, dealers in letters of credit, public scribes, artisans in fine metals and jewelry, image-makers, a few who deal in old manuscripts, pictures, small art treasures, and oddities found or dug out of strange ruins or distant places. Here, also, are those who deal in items enhanced by magic.

There are a few scattered priests, priestesses, mendicants, and cultists from overseas or far distant lands who worship other gods and are allowed to beg in the streets of the fair. They are, however, strictly forbidden to proselytize and are kept always under strictest surveillance by the men and women of the temple. One such alien god is called Thotharn, and about him and his rites of worship some rather odd and sinister stories have been bruited over the years: a committee of the priests of the Three is conducting secret studies of this god and his servants, while considering banning them from the fair.

Since all who legally enter the fair or the temple must surrender their weapons at the gates and swear themselves and their servants or employees to be bound by fair-law and fair-court for the duration of their stay, the well-trained, disciplined, and often quick-tempered fair-wards, armed with their weighted staves, seldom experience trouble in maintaining order.

The bulk of their work takes them to the middle section, with its array of pot-shops, or to the outer fringes of the enclave, where gather the inevitable collection of rogues, sturdy beggars, bravos, petty wizards, potion-makers and witches, would-be entertainers, snake-charmers, whores, and, it is rumored, more than a few assassins-for-hire.

And now, to all who have paid their gate-offering, welcome to the Fair at Ithkar.

THREE KNIVES IN ITHKAR

Gareth Bloodwine

They were only wood, she explained to the guards again and again. Toys of painted lath unsuitable for cutting even butter, and obvious even in the dark.

"Care to try your luck? For you, the first throw's free. No, I'm not the prize, ha ha, you handsome devil! Who's next now? Don't be shy, step right up—"

Jorn balanced the slender, flimsy blade in his hand, staring at the rotting straw of the target, trying to keep his eyes off Salisa. The crowd of lowlifes and slumming dandies shouted coarse mockery and encouragement by turn as he squeezed the gaudily painted blade with sweaty fingers and lifted it to his ear. The first had fallen, but, miraculously, the second had actually remained impaled within the crudely painted circle, daring him to win the prize with a second successful throw. Salisa laughed with the rest, bending forward ever so slightly to give him a glimpse of her large, ever-so-distracting bosom. How easy to ruin their aim. And Jorn craved her, craved her with a passionate, obsessive love he did not dare express. She was too dangerous, her laugh an instrument of death by scorn. If he could get past that, past his failures at the game, then, then maybe . . .

The air was filled with stale ale breath and the smoke of burning goat-weed. Jorn glared about him as he was jostled, then, in a split second of calm and clarity and comparative silence, stilled himself as best he could and snapped the feeble thing forward. The crowd hushed, watching as it spun through the air and then pushed its way into the fetid straw.

It stayed where it was put, but the other knife was not so secure. The touch of the third in the straw loosened the second, which drooped and sagged and finally fell with a nasty clack to the beaten dirt of the gamester's floor. The crowd exploded with jocular derision as Salisa scooped up the coins of the wager and held them aloft. Her entertainer's smile fastened on the hapless Jorn, and she waited for him to throw down yet another notched Ithkarian farthing.

Jorn was in love. Salisa looked on a face so full of longing and pain that it was impossible to maintain the pose of a cheap huckster. Their eyes met, and the raucous sounds around them became a distant shell, isolating them. Jorn couldn't speak; his mouth opened, but there was nothing, nothing to say that Salisa didn't know. She shook her head slightly and, in pity, leaned forward to tell him with a glance, Later. Come back later when the others have gone, and we'll talk then. No more than talk, but that, at least, will be yours alone.

Jorn hated the enforced cleanliness of his foster father's stall, where he sold herbs for flavor and for health to the middling prosperous and the very well off. The tyrant was constantly harping on the one note: Clean! Cleaner than that! Who'll buy if the scale is dirty, if the parchment wrapping scraps are stained, if the costly glass and glazed ceramic pots are dusty, if your fingernails are filthy? So Jorn washed and dusted and polished and shined and learned what his father was willing to teach of herb lore. The old man was stingy with his knowledge, but a lovesick boy was hardly the kind of pupil to warm the heart of a man whose reputation in his craft had spread the length and breadth of Ithkar and beyond.

Thus it was an especial good fortune for the boy when he discovered the secret cache: a wooden chest beneath the sacks he never moved from laziness. The old man never dreamed that Jorn might seek solace from his tormenting love in work. And so, on the fourth day of the fair, when the old man was at the temple, gossiping and promoting his wares at the invitation-only party in the courtyard, Jorn, terrified of his own audacity, opened the chest and found the pale gray-green leaves unlike any others in the pots and flasks of the public shelves. They glowed with their own faint light as he held them up in the curtained darkness, barely bright enough to throw faint shadows into the moist green gloom. He even pounded his head as hard as he could, but he could not think of the name of the leaf nor of its virtue, though special its virtue must be. It reeked of magic, of such power that even the old man must be terrified of it. This was the stuff of the highest sorcery, no mere hedge-witch charm. It had to be priceless.

There wasn't much of it, but a few of the leaves were broken. Surely one little piece wouldn't be missed. One little piece wouldn't be too much to trade for a chance to achieve his heart's desire in a life of toil, frustration, servitude, and endless humiliation.

There was only one person in all the fair that Jorn knew well enough to approach. At the sign of the Snug Bung he gripped his threadbare cloak around his bony shoulders and walked in as though he were one of the habitués. It wasn't hard to recognize Wazzan in the back, lecturing to a tavern wench as if she cared for anything other than the copper that was always forthcoming.

"An' that's why the reeves won't give your boss a hard time, even if he holds out on them. They need the trade more than they need chump change from him, see? Hey!" He pushed the girl aside. "Whaddayou want, boy?" The girl, undaunted, sat up and flowed around Wazzan's shoulders. "Speak up. If you haven't got anything to say, beat it! I've got important business to transact."

"Me too, Wazzan. Something you might be interested in." Jorn tried to look cagey.

You never know. The reprobate reached under the wench, who stifled a squeak as she jumped in the air. Wazzan turned on his most charming smile. "Come back in ten minutes, all right?"

She rubbed her tail and calculated what the drunk was worth compared to her dignity, and decided it was all right. She kissed him on the cheek, sneered at Jorn, and slid away into the noisy darkness.

"This better be good," Wazzan said, settling himself into the wooden booth. His one brown-spotted, useable hand reached for the mug of ale and tremulously enmeshed the handle.

"I have something you might want to buy," said Jorn. "A rare herb from my father's coffers."

"You stole it."

"Better a wizard like you should have it than the priests who bleed us dry, whatever they pay."

The hand jerked, and the warm bitter ale splashed into Jorn's face. "Don't ever call me that!" the old man wheezed. "My days of magic are over, and good riddance! It never brought me anything but misery, and besides"—he reached forward—"this place is crawling with those staff-toting thugs. Now tell quietly what it is you've got, or I'll throw you out of here with my good hand myself!"

Sweat appeared on Jorn's forehead. "Maybe this isn't the place—"

Wazzan fixed him with his stare, one of his few remaining specialties. The priests could not snatch him for merely having eyes in his head. Jorn sat still and reached for the little pouch. The elderly mage grabbed it and, turning to the wall, pulled the leather string. At once the faint radiance lit his face. Subdued, he studied the tidbit of foreign plant for a moment. His eyes went to the boy's eager face.

"Do you know what this is?" he asked.

Jorn nodded, his ignorance plain.

"Do you know that merely possessing this, you would be hanged with no questions asked?"

Jorn swallowed and nodded again.

Wazzan pulled the drawstring with his teeth and glanced around the tavern. No one had seen. He cupped the precious pouch with his good right hand and the festering lump of scar that remained of his left and appraised the boy.

"All right. What do you want?"

"For the herb?"

Wazzan put on his professional face, which was stiff from unaccustomed use. "No, you idiot. What do you want from me, what manner of spell is it? Surely you wouldn't have come to me if it weren't for my . . . special skills.''

It was hard to say, an admission of failure. ''I want a girl. I want Salisa. You know. The three daggers.''

Wazzan's smile began as professional indulgence, but he couldn't keep it from turning into a loud guffaw. ''Ho, ho, my boy! You don't aim too high, do you? Salisa! By the Three, you want to have that saucy, tasty lioness love you? This is too rich!'' Putrid wine-breath chortles sprayed Jorn.

Faces turned to see what had ignited the old drunk, but all they saw was a young boy burning with shame, shrinking into himself. Jorn stood up and snatched the pouch from Wazzan's grip.

''You crave her for yourself, don't you? As if she'd have anything to do with a burned-out shell of a man like you—''

''She wouldn't. And why should I care when the girls here take care of me as pleases me just fine? But Jorn''—he quieted and leaned forward again—''what would she want with a boy? Especially a clumsy amateur thief who'd be found out in an hour? Especially considering the offers she's turned down?''

Jorn whirled to leave, but the wizard's good right hand sprang out to clamp his wrist. Unexpected strength forced the boy into his seat.

Wazzan leaned so close their noses almost touched. ''There's no way that woman will ever consider you short of magic. It's plain to see. And here you've been, talking to me in sight of half the brass-hats of Ithkar Fair. So after you waltz off with the most desired woman in this quarter, and that gobbet of phlegm who sired her wakes up and realizes that his only child is under a spell, and runs to the temple to complain, who do you think those stinking priests will come for?''

Wazzan held up his left hand—a mangled thumb, the rest of the digits burned off at the base; the result, a smelly, dripping, red, festering scar. "I'm lucky to be alive. This is what they left me after my last attempt to help some needy soul. Take my advice, Jorn. Put that—thing back where you found it. Do it now. Life is short, unless they want to give you a little souvenir to remember them by. I never forget them. They won. I'm not going to face pain or death or both because some pretty fluff's gotten your blood up. Save your coppers and buy a girl who looks like her, and scream Salisa's name in her ear and give her everything just once, to finish it off. And then go find someone else to love, who can love you."

Jorn held up the pouch. "Isn't this worth anything?"

"I don't know what you're talking about. Hey, Clannia! Come back over here! The kid's leaving!"

There was still too much light in the sky for roisterers to begin gathering at gamesters' row when Jorn went to collect his precious, private moment with Salisa. The smells of a score of different cooking pots drifted in the strange emptiness between the painted signs and raucous challenges. Nothing could distract Jorn.

At the sign of the three knives, Jorn hesitated, afraid to face his love. Within he heard a paroxysm of hard, moist coughing and a muttered curse. Salisa's father.

"I can't take much more of this," he said. "I can barely lift a full mug to my lips anymore."

"Oh, Father," came a voice, softer than Jorn had ever imagined. "You get this every year."

"Look at me, I'm so thin, so thin. . . ."

Jorn rapped on the heavy post by the tent-flap. In a

moment she was there. Salisa's face was a mask to spite all Jorn's hoping. She motioned him in.

"My father, Tuberc," she said. The gray-faced man held up a bony hand.

"Forgive me for not getting up," he said. "I'm not well."

Jorn nodded. "So I've heard, sir. I'm the herb-master's apprentice. I've brought something for you." He reached into his shirt for a small packet. "It's mountain lungwort. It'll make the coughing briefly worse, and then it will be over."

"Couldn't get much worse than it is. Thank you, son, and thank your master, too. Generosity's a rare, sweet thing at Ithkar Fair."

Jorn turned to Salisa. "You make a tea with it. Not too strong, though."

"You are too kind. Come with me." Jorn followed her to the little open plot behind the tent, where she did her cooking.

She wore only a simple tunic of homespun, belted with rope, washerwomen's clothes, but even so she was magnificent. He watched in silence as she filled a small pot with water and hung it from an iron hook over the embers. The red glow lit her cheeks and made Jorn wish he were a poet instead of a tongue-tied fool.

"You don't have to be afraid of me. I don't bite."

"I . . . I wish I could . . ." He blushed, ashamed. "Your father is very ill," he said.

"He's dying and he knows it. He wanted to see me married, but it's impossible. Who'd take care of him if I went to be a wife?" She went to Jorn and put her arms around him, and his knees almost failed. She felt it and said nothing. "I know you like me. I would have met you even if you didn't bring your gift. It was very thoughtful. You can't know how he suffers."

She met his eyes and then, hers fluttering closed, leaned forward and gave Jorn a kiss. He felt her breasts press against his chest, and his hands found her waist. Salisa gently pulled away when she felt it was time.

It gave him courage. "How I've wanted just that—a pure kiss from you. Oh, Salisa, for years I've—"

She pulled away with a gentle laugh that had none of her hardness in it. "Jorn, my little friend for so long. Did you know that on the first day a captain of cavalry was here, waiting for the game to open, who had waited a year to try to change my mind again? Just because these are big"—she cupped her breasts in her hands—"he'd spoil his chances by courting a gamester's daughter. I know how to wiggle for the crowd, and now I've caught you, too!"

"What about your chances? Is this what you want to do for the rest of your life?"

"No. But when that captain becomes a general, will he want a gamester's daughter who's no longer young and pretty to be at his side? When he goes to court?"

"What about a life as an herb-master's lady? Travel, respect, more than a comfortable living—"

Salisa shook her head and stirred the tea. "Your master's learned how to live a fine life without a woman in it, and anyway he's too old for—" Suddenly she dropped the spoon and turned to the young man. She watched his earnest eyes search her face. "Jorn, oh, Jorn. Don't even think it. Please. I would never hurt you, you know that—"

His heart cramped as though it were glass and her words were flying rocks. "Is it so impossible, so ridiculous?"

"You're the little boy I've met here every year since—"

"Yes, and I can remember when your chest was flat, too! So what?"

"I'll know the man when I meet him, but you'll always be the herb-master's boy to me."

"Please!" He hated himself for pleading. "Don't make me give up all hope!"

She went to him and touched him again, and he shivered. "Jorn, I'm really fond of you, and I really am grateful for your help with Father, but you have as much chance of becoming my lover as you have of winning the knife game."

It jarred him. "What did you say?"

"You can't win the knife game. It's the way they're weighted. They always fall out." She looked at him wonderingly. "After all the money you've lost, didn't you figure it out?"

"But you do it all the time!"

"It's a trick. You'll never get to use the daggers I throw."

Jorn shut his mouth. It had never occurred to him that she was capable of cheating.

"Now that you know," she said, "I won't let you play anymore. And tell everyone; they'll still line up for a chance to beat me at my own game and watch me bend over to pick up their coins."

So she was a fraud. It didn't make any difference. "Salisa, I love you. You must give me at least a chance!"

She sighed, the beginning of the end of patience. "I love you, too, in my way. So you can have all the chances you want—at the game. And you've paid for them. I'll slip you coin to bet with; it'll build up the clientele—"

"And if I win, will you be the wager?"

Salisa laughed, her old hard laugh. "Why, sure, Jorn. And if you lose?"

"That's certainly no more than you've always expected."

"It's a deal." He couldn't make his feet move to take him from her presence. Laughing, she gave him one of the flimsy, painted weapons carven of scrap wood to take and practice with; more mockery.

His mind was open to her as if he spoke aloud. "If I give you one more kiss," she asked, "will that make it easier?"

She knew the answer. Well, after all, he had brought the herb to still her father's disease. Salisa stepped back and, with a rough motion, pulled off the tunic and stood there in a thin muslin shift. Sweat and work had molded it to her body. It cost her nothing in pride, honor, or virtue to share an embrace with him. She smiled and held open her arms. As he clung to the treasure of his affections, Salisa comforted herself with knowing that even though his sleepless nights might stretch out for months, at least for this one moment, she had completely satisfied his desire.

Jorn waited on his foster father in the bored way he always did before going out for the night. The herb-master was again invited to the temple; he was to be escorted to the upper precincts, a distinct honor, and he was in a jovial mood. He tossed a freshly minted silver coin at his boy and sauntered out to meet his guides.

Silver! It wouldn't be enough tonight. Jorn knew where the strongbox was hidden, all of oak and steel. He had long since been trusted with the key. The old fool left layers of jumbled coins lying loose in there. A single gold coin, just like that terrifying bit of magic greenery, that's all; not enough to be hanged for. . . . Jorn sweated with each squeak of the twisted hempen ropes that held the awning, and the rattle of rodent feet that scurried through the darkness with their stolen crumbs.

At last it was done, the casual disarray rearranged just so, even the dust smeared back where trembling fingers had clawed it off.

Wazzan had taught the boy well. He crept through the lanes of the craftsmen's quarter, occasionally hearing the hammer blows of some sturdy worker eager to finish a commission. It was common enough to hear the sounds of work in the quarter all through the night.

He barely knew the smith Klovik, who came from some distance downriver. His work was sturdy but no match for the artisans who came to earn their year's wages in a month; yet he seemed always busy and had plenty to do. Jorn found him still at work, alone. The boy had kept his face muffled and looked a proper beggar with his tent-flap pulled around him for a cloak. The fair-wards had had no call to stop him, and he was sure he had been unobserved.

Klovik cocked a curious eye at his young acquaintance.

"Up to no good. Never any good if a disguise is needed."

"You know I've never hurt anybody."

"Wish it, maybe, but not doing it. Not stupid, this one." His hammer rang on the anvil as a piece of horse harness took shape. "Not a social call."

"I need you to make something."

Klovik kept heating, hammering, waiting.

"Three things."

"Costs three times as much. No discounts. So? You tell or I guess?"

Jorn reached into the folds of his clothes and brought out two pieces of painted wood, tacked and glued together to resemble a dagger and painted with gaudy colors.

"You want weapons? You madman. We hang by the same

30

rope. If this no joke, get out and I do you a favor and forget I ever saw you.''

"Klovik, no one saw me come here. You didn't even recognize me yourself! I've got to have them!"

The smith was a big man; the wooden thing was a child's toy in his hand. "What is this you have to have? Who for? Whose ribs?"

"Not so loud, not so loud! Please!" Again, the whining note he hated. "You don't recognize it?"

He turned it in the forge light and studied the ragged jags of faded red and blue and green. "No."

"It's from a stall in gamesters' row. The woman who owns the knife toss—you know, put your money down, hit the target, and collect double—told me herself that it's a cheat, you can't win, these things always fall out of the target even if they manage for a moment to stay in—"

Klovik stared hard at him. "She robs people, the wards don't care?"

"She is very beautiful, and, and . . . and I'm in love with her. That's why I've got to win! I have to! It's the only way I'll ever have her!"

"You love a liar? Better to marry the gibbet."

"Please, Klovik! Will you help me?"

"You mad, and a fool. And after?"

"I'll throw them in the Ith." They stared at each other, each trying to believe what they heard. "I promise you."

Slowly the big man asked, "What you pay?"

His heart pounding for the certainty and danger of it, Jorn handed him the gold piece. Klovik saw that it was real. He tossed it back.

"Where you steal it from?" Jorn stammered, looked away.

"Take it back tonight where you got it. Fool. I help you fix the cheat for nothing." He turned back to his work.

"Klovik, if there's anything I—"

"Do nothing for me. Fix the cheat, that's all. And if you get caught with weapons, forget you ever heard of me. Now get out. Back tomorrow, bring paints with you and we match this one. Go!"

The day was particularly balmy, with the faintest of hay-scented breezes to freshen the airs of Ithkar Fair. The heralds went about the lanes and great boulevards of tents and booths to tell of the processional, when genuine relics of the Three Lordly Ones were to be shown to all who cared to see. The taverns made ready to broach their sweetest ales, their strongest meads, their strangest liquors and liqueurs. The jewelers unlocked their most fabulous treasures, and the wealthy decked themselves in their richest raiment. All day the crowds flowed and jostled this way and that, the loud jollity tinged with the faintest haze of hysteria. At terce the priests began their circumambulations, the low resonance of the temple bells shuddering the afternoon, the sweet incense from their scores of censers intoxicating the very air itself. The mixture of reverence and giddy energy pulsed through the fair and gave it a life of its own, as if it were a living, breathing creature, and all the people there felt it so.

No apprentice could stay and work on such a day, and Jorn was no different from the rest. The three knives were snugly tied to his belly, so that it was painful to bend forward, but it didn't matter. They felt fine in the hand, and he had confidence. Even the fair-wards—and there were so many of them about!—could not make him feel afraid. He tipped his cap to those he knew and sauntered down the ways with the rest of the fair folk.

Salisa's hair glowed from endless brushing. Her dress was snug and flattering, as if her luxurious figure needed flattery, but it amused her to be as disconcerting as possible. Her father rested in his bed, able to sleep at last. Poor Jorn, she thought. It would be so much easier if I could be in love with him. But I'm not. Oh, if only my captain will be here!

Jorn skipped about, thrilled with nervous energy. Once he noticed himself clenching and unclenching his fists, wet fists, and stopped it by an act of will. He calmed himself with a word, then danced again as though he weighed nothing, so happy he felt, as though the prize were already his. "Salisa!" he shouted to no one in particular, and wended his way through the throng, waiting for the evening dark, and the game.

Gamesters' row was beginning to fill, with tosspots and revelers and fair-wards, with the rich and their private guards, the less rich in disguise, the poor with their begging bowls, and the rogues with their schemes and quick eyes for misfortunate opportunities. Salisa pulled the ropes that stayed the flaps of her booth and made ready to put the three knives into action. In seconds, the regulars began to drift toward her, and she began all the usual automatic banter. The targets had been freshly painted with the vegetable dyes she could afford, and the little "knives" were likewise spruced up for this special festival night. All but one—and then she remembered where it had gone, and she felt an instant of guilt for the boy who knew nothing of love except in his imagination.

A cocky bravo stepped forward and tossed a large silver coin on the counter. "I'll try for it," he said.

Salisa picked up the piece. "Good sir, I haven't the funds to cover this, yet. Perhaps a little later—"

"Why, if I win, I'll take it in trade!" he shouted, and the crowd loved it. Salisa smiled and tried to blush, and pocketed the coin. He was charming. She gave him one of the slightly heavier wooden knives. He held the blade in his fingers and prepared to throw it.

"Hey there!" came the huge voice of a fair-ward, and a yellow gleam flashed down. The bravo gave a yelp as the brass-shod truncheon smashed into the wooden knife and scattered the flinders to the ground. "I'll have you before the magistrate for threatening with weapons here!"

"Now, see here, my good man—" the bravo began, but he was drowned out by the spectators, who came to his defense. Somehow the fair-ward had missed this booth before, but he was no different from the others when Salisa cast the oldest spell known upon him.

"They're all wood, you say?"

She smiled and spread her arms apart, then bent forward ever so slightly. "You couldn't cut butter with them. Here, try me." She reached a bare arm forward and leaned a little closer.

"It's plain to see you're not hiding any others," said the fair-ward, and the crowd roared its approval. The bravo pushed up to the counter. "Good maiden, my turn now, if you please?"

Salisa blew him a kiss and stationed herself for his best vantage. One landed flat and fell. Two hit point on but bounced off. Three sank in a bit, then drooped and fell. "Rather like you with that little fluff last night, eh, Anders?" The bravo laughed and, arm in arm with his buddies, waltzed off to new amusements.

New revelers shoved in, trying for a close-up look at the beauty behind the counter and a chance for their money with their skill at playing the game. They laughed, and the coins flew across the boards into the gamester's coffers.

Jorn was in among them now, pushing forward with the rest. Some would try once or twice, rarely more, and then move on. Even the fair-ward tried his hand, a free play for a kiss, and didn't win. He stepped back, and Jorn twisted his way to the counter, a wicked grin frozen on his face.

Salisa met his eyes and felt a coldness down her spine. But she kept up the cheery patter and, as she had promised, slipped him a copper to place on the betting space.

"Jorn, my old friend, come to try it again? Two to one for you, you're my best customer. Hey, friend, don't hesitate now. . . ."

"For coin, Salisa? For mere coin?" He raised his voice, and some of the folk turned to hear him. "It's easy for you, no?" And he threw the wooden things as hard as he could, one, two, three; they clattered to the ground. "You told me it can't be done. Can't be done, Salisa? Surely it can! It's too easy!"

"Jorn, what's the matter? Is it too much drink?"

"I've never been more sober. Put the knives down, Salisa. I'm ready to play the wager you promised. For you. Are you ready?"

Those who were near silenced to hear this tale long abrewing come to its end, with the throbbing noises of Ithkar Fair surrounding them, isolating them. Salisa nodded, sad that the boy had so pathetically snapped. If he must insist on being publicly spurned, so be it. She handed him the knives.

He stepped back to prepare his throw, but the moist ground

made him slip, and he fell on his face. Such awkwardness was no new thing for him, and they all knew it. But on the ground, he had his brief second to grab the metal blades from their hiding place and push the wooden pieces under the drape that hung from the front of the counter. The crowd had closed over him, smothering him, but they parted as he rose, ready to play, the knives held steady in his hand. The blades' fresh paint gleamed luridly in the lantern light.

One. The blade sank into the target up to the hilt. Two. It wobbled as it sailed across the booth to strike home at an odd angle, but it did not fall. Three. With reddened eyes, the target blurring with every condescending, patronizing sneer he had ever endured, he threw as hard as he could. The blade whistled through the air and plunged straight in. The rotted hay of the target bale teetered on its spindly legs of reed and fell over, coming apart in a fetid mush. The crowd went berserk and tried to lift the boy to their shoulders, but he wriggled free. "Salisa!" he shouted. "Salisa!"

The woman paled. He had won. In a daze, she bent to the ruined target, felt for her knives, and instantly discovered the secret. She stood with the massive things in her hands, all painted with her colors.

She was not afraid of him. "These are not mine," she said. "Take them."

"I'm not interested in the knives, Salisa. To the Ith with them, and this whole booth, too. I beat you, and you're mine, you hear me?"

But the fair-ward was interested in the knives. He picked one up and saw that it was steel. A genuine weapon. He spun around to face the woman.

"So you do have real knives with you!" He lifted the huge

staff and held it above his head. "Not to move, understand, or I'll smash your head in!"

"They aren't mine! This lovesick puppy brought them—am I to blame for that?"

The fair-ward turned to Jorn, trapped by the dense crowd and unable to flee.

"Who would carry a knife like that, let alone three—all painted up like a gamester's cheating tools and made to the same design?"

The fair-ward frowned. "Cheating tools?"

"Have you ever heard of anyone winning?"

The brass-hat turned back to Salisa. "Woman, is this so?"

Salisa smiled and relaxed. "Of course it is so. How else could we earn enough to return next year? And who has come here and not been entertained to the value of the coin he put down, and got less than his money's worth? Jorn could not have won unless he brought his own knives, which of course I do not allow. And as you pointed out, I have no place to hide three knives at all."

The fair-ward whirled upon the boy and grabbed him by the back of the neck. "At the temple we'll see if you have other weapons hidden! Come on!"

Jorn shouted, "But the challenge! It says only to throw three knives!"

Salisa laughed, a hard and weary sound. "So it does, Jorn. All right. You've won."

Jorn was completely powerless, dragged like offal before the fair-ward. Success and failure were so mixed that he had no idea what was happening. Eventually he was stood before a temple magistrate and made to tell his story, which was not believed. And then they took him to the scaffold, where his offenses were proclaimed: each of the knives was a separate offense, so this was the third time for all. He was right-handed, that was plain, so with the tongs they grabbed his right hand and laid it on the block. As the hooded one stepped up, Jorn finally realized what they were going to do to him, and he began the pleading and whining he had mastered; but there was no mercy in them, only cold, mechanical efficiency. The hooded one stroked the stone over the crescent blade, one side and then the other. Jorn wept and begged, and as the hooded one stood and stretched, Jorn screamed and thrashed and pulled against the iron until the skin ripped. The hooded one lifted the great axe, and then it came down with a splintery thump into the wooden block; white-hot needles piercing to the spine, screaming, his chest a rack of pain and tremors in his bowels; then the hot iron to stop the bleeding, and the tar, unimaginable pain; then rough hands to throw him down the scaffold stairway to the mud, and still more echoes of pain and solitude.

The hand of an assassin was nailed still quivering to a rough wooden beam of the gallows, next to the others, and there it remained.

He must have slept, for it was dark when he was again aware. The pain had lessened a little, but not much. He was aware of hunger, vaguely, and his filthiness. He pulled himself to his feet and looked down at his arms.

It was true.

Jorn knew how short was the way to the stables, but it seemed to take forever to drag himself there. The stableboy was frightened of his appearance and did as he was told, dousing Jorn again and again until the stink was gone. One must prepare to go calling, he thought to himself. And when his toilet was finished, he set off for gamesters' row.

Salisa had not fared well in the rumors that flew through Ithkar Fair. Her game had had at least a semblance of honesty, even if a moment's reflection was all that was required to see through it. And the lovesick boy, mutilated by the magistrate's decree when everyone knew how timid and harmless he was . . .

Jorn staggered down the ways and lanes, his feet directed by hidden memories. Folk occasionally noticed him, and thought on the tale, and stood aside for him. Jorn never saw it.

It was the middle of the evening on gamesters' row: overheard conversation revealed that two days, not one, had passed since the evil thing was done to him. Everywhere was gaiety, except for one space that everyone shunned. Jorn moved there and saw, alone in a booth and ignored, Salisa, his beauty, and a challenge to throw three knives that no one would accept.

She stared at Jorn and at the horror where his right hand had been. In only two days, his face had gone gaunt and pinched and pale.

"The herb-master—" she said.

"Who?" His voice was a dry rasp. His eyes remained fixed on her face. There was nothing to say.

She took him by his hand and led him into the tent.

"No one will come here anymore," Salisa said. "You beat me at my own game." She helped him to sit on her pallet and helped him pull his wretched clothes off. "The herb-master sent word here. He told me to tell you that a bright mind and one hand were all that's needed to master herb lore."

Jorn shivered, naked and cold, as Salisa brought a thin blanket for him. It seemed to take hours to get just one thought together.

"What do I need," he finally asked, "to master you?"

Salisa watched him. The blanket would never be enough to warm him. She stood and peeled off her tunic and then the thin gown underneath. Under the blanket he felt like ice, but she pressed as much of him into her warmth as she could. A frozen hand touched hers and gripped it, and she felt tears against her breast. It pleased her.

"Not three knives, that's for sure."

WERE-SISTERS

Ann R. Brown

Dereva tossed back her graying hair and lifted another tray of venison pastries out of the way of the chopping block. There was an untamed lightness in her agile body as she balanced the tin sheets on top of the other trays at the end of the wooden counter. Before the opening of Ithkar Fair the following morning, there was much for her to do: mince and spice the meat from the deer she'd pulled down in the forest a few leagues from the town; roll out circles of dough; fold and seal each pie; and fry the pastries in a caldron of lard. Dereva had hoped that her younger sister would be of help to her, but Lila only paced the confines of the booth and growled.

Lila's yellow eyes gleamed. "I hate this—how can you bear to be around all these humans? They stink of perfume and soap and soft living." She snatched a hunk of deer meat and gnawed it with her white teeth.

"Don't let the customers see you eating it raw," warned

Dereva calmly, rolling the dough with a deft hand. She was only a few years older than her fiery, red-haired sister and had once been just as wild, but responsibilities had steadied her.

Lila paced restlessly from one side of the booth to the other.

With the tip of a copper knife, Dereva sealed the edges of the dough semicircles. Nothing in the booth was made of iron. Even the trays and kettles were either copper, brass, or tin.

"Here, help me fill these pastries," suggested Dereva. "There was no point in your coming with me if you're only going to sulk. Let's get ready for the opening, and then we can take the rest of the night off."

Lila uttered a short laugh that sounded like a bark and shoved aside a rolled-up canvas awning.

"You only want to see if Gervys the hunter has come this year," Lila mocked. Her good humor returned, and she began to spoon meat into the center of each dough circle. "How can you like a human man who trapped you?"

A smile lit Dereva's sun-browned face. She was a young woman still, despite the streaks of gray in her glossy chestnut hair. "He released me as soon as I turned into a woman. It's just a tiny scar on my ankle."

The work went much faster with Lila's slapdash assistance; and before too many hours had passed, they were ready for the first day of the fair.

With a sigh of relief, Dereva ripped off her apron and stretched her arms upward in a gesture of freedom. "You're free until tomorrow morning, Lila, but don't think of going on all fours or I'll crate you and ship you back to Wolvendale on a pack mule."

The wild young girl laughed and embraced her sister briefly.

"You weren't always the motherly type, Dereva. I remember when the elders were always calling you before the Circle of the Law for howling all night and running with strange packs."

"Unlicked cub!" taunted Dereva as the girl darted through the curtain and was gone into the night.

Stepping out into the cool evening, Dereva allowed the breeze to fan dry her sweating face and hair. It felt good to be free of the confines of the cramped stall, and also free of the responsibility of watching over Lila, at least for a few hours. Sometimes her watchful care was galling to them both. Next year perhaps she would leave the reckless girl back home in the forested peaks of Wolvendale. Lila didn't belong in a populated district like Ithkar. Dereva didn't like the town, either—the crowding, the smells, or the press of noisy humanity. But she had disciplined herself to bear these gatherings during the past ten years; and the silver she carried back to the dale would last her kin the whole year.

She set out with a free-swinging stride through the rows of silent pavilions and stalls that displayed such tasty delights as marchpane, gingerbread, suckets, florentines, fritters, and star-gazey pies. Dereva hummed a tuneless song as she strode down the twisting alley.

"Bitch!"

The cry of hatred made her whirl, her green eyes glinting.

The same coarse voice roared, "Why don't you stay in Dogdale with the other dogs?"

Dereva's keen eyes recognized the fat oaf leaning over the counter of his cookshack, and she choked down a red wave of fury. She wanted no trouble with the fair-wards, priests, or townspeople of Ithkar.

She retorted, "Are you making your pies with cat meat again this year, Otrok?"

The corpulent baker spat into the dust. "Sorceress. Witch. Why don't the priests arrest you?"

"You were drunk, Otrok. What you believe you saw was only your sodden imagination," stated Dereva through her teeth.

"I saw you!" he screamed, and hurled an iron ladle. Dereva dodged, and the metal didn't touch her. "I saw you! Five years ago I saw you change!"

Dereva lengthened her stride and soon left her competitor's screams behind. Out the northern gate in the palisade she hurried, Otrok forgotten. Before her loomed the massive domes of the temple, which shut out half the night sky with its vast ramparts and towers. But it was to the huddle of tents beyond the stables that she ran, her heart slamming erratically. Her eyes, which saw so well in the dark, scanned the rope corral of horses but saw no sign of the big gray stallion of Gervys. Many seasonal workers for the temple and the fair pitched their tents on the green hill behind the stable. Toward the light of a flickering campfire she raced. Standing guard over the rough encampment was a retired fair-ward. Dereva recognized him by his battered helmet.

"Frey—I seek Gervys. Is he here?" she panted, holding her side.

The grizzled old veteran scratched his unshaven chin. "He delivered the wild boar and chamois the high priest ordered for his feast, and then disappeared. He said Thunderer had picked up a pebble in his hoof. You know how Gervys feels about that horse, missy. Maybe he went back to the hills."

Bitter disappointment froze her heart. Gone. She'd missed him. And it would be a long year before she'd see his smiling eyes again. Slowly Dereva walked on to the crest of the hill and gazed over the roofs of Ithkar to the distant jagged mountains. In one of the far-off hidden valleys was her home. Sudden depression wrenched her, and longing for the countryside. This town was stifling. Perhaps this would be the last fair for her, and the folk of Wolvendale would have to seek another means of earning silver.

At length she turned and walked back through the encampment, descending the hill toward the palisade.

"How's your ankle?" a deep voice queried.

She lifted her head and took a long breath. Beside her strode a tall man in leather, his rugged face smiling.

Dereva couldn't speak for an instant. Then she asked, "Have you caught any more ladies in your traps, Gervys?"

"I couldn't be that lucky twice," he replied, and slipped his arm around her waist.

"I thought you'd gone back to the hills," she remarked unsteadily.

Warmth and amusement tinged his deep voice. "Now is that very likely? Would I go without giving you a chance to turn me down again?"

She nuzzled his strong shoulder, inhaling the scent of his leather jerkin and vest and the man himself.

In a low voice Gervys said, "I think about it all the time, the two of us roaming the greenwood and the purple moors, tramping side by side, lying under the shade of an oak to rest when the sun is high, hearing the skylarks singing. I think about the two of us sitting outside our tent at night, watching the stars and talking softly to each other in the darkness. Sometimes it's so real to me I can almost see you in the light of the campfire. How many more years are you going to make me wait?"

Dereva turned her head away. The words were hard to speak. "You know I still have a responsibility to Lila, even if you say I baby her too much. I can't desert her to hunt with you."

Gervys paused for a moment, fighting for control, and then deliberately lightened his tone. "We'd make a great team. Thunderer packs the wild boar out of the hills, but he can't help me pull them down."

"I always knew you only loved me for my teeth," Dereva said lightly.

"Is that what you think?" he answered rather roughly, and fell silent.

Her long strides matched his as they strolled companionably back toward the northern gate of the palisade, pausing for a time to admire the sunrise that tinted the horizon with streaks of gold and crimson.

Then the noise and bustle of the market rose around them again. Vendors and peddlers were preparing for the first day of business, unrolling striped awnings, arranging trestle tables and benches, and lighting charcoal braziers. Some of the vintners stood idly by, sampling their own wares. The passersby were a blur of undefined shapes to her as she trod back toward her booth. Only the man at her side was real.

Dereva pushed open the curtain of her foodstall and found devastation.

Caldrons lay empty, their contents spilled. Trodden into the dust were trays of pastries. Tools had been scattered and flour shaken from sacks. Into the spilled flour had been traced one word: "bitch."

Dereva screamed with inhuman rage and raced outside to see a fair-ward advancing with Otrok, whose arm was bandaged.

She snarled, and her lips drew back from her teeth.

"Dereva, don't. It won't help," cautioned Gervys, and he gripped her arms, hiding her paws within his vest. Slowly she allowed her hands to return to their human shape. But there was nothing human about her green eyes now. They had the glare of a wild creature.

"There she is, Officer," blustered Otrok.

The coarse voice sent shudders of hatred down her back. Gervys tightened the grip of his encircling arms.

"That bitch sister of yours wrecked my shop, and nearly tore my arm off. I'll have her shot like a mad dog, or if she changes back into a woman, I'll have her hanged."

Then, when he saw the glare in her eyes, and the power of the man who accompanied her, Otrok stepped back to shelter himself behind the bulk of a glowering fair-ward brandishing a metal-tipped staff.

The fair-ward said grimly. "This man claims your wolf attacked him and destroyed his property. We caught the animal in a net. It appears to be untamed and vicious."

Otrok whined, "That wolf you caught is this woman's sister. I demand they both be handed over to the inquisitors on charges of black sorcery."

Gervys stepped forward and faced the burly, irritated fair-ward. His voice held authority. "This man is drunk as well as malicious. The wolf was left to guard Dereva's property, and he startled the animal when he was tearing up this cookshop." With one arm Gervys pulled back the curtain, and the ward gazed at the wreck of Dereva's booth.

"Let's inspect the animal," ordered the scowling ward. "If it's mad, a sword thrust will finish the matter."

Gervys tightened his clasp around Dereva's shoulders to

47

prevent her from giving herself away. Rage quivered through her whole body.

They heard the infuriated howling of the wolf long before they reached the guardhouse at the eastern end of the fair-grounds. Guarded by two wary sentries, the wolf lay entangled in a rope net within an iron cage that was used as a portable lock-up. Her yellow eyes were completely bestial.

"The iron— it's hurting her," Dereva moaned.

"Kill it, officer—it's rabid," demanded Otrok, licking his cracked lips.

To the fair-ward Gervys spoke, in the tone of a man accustomed to being heeded. "Let me in the cage and I'll prove the animal is tame."

To Dereva's startled protest, Gervys murmured, "Stay out of this, or the officer will suspect a connection between you and the wolf. Lila won't injure me."

But the hunter's rugged face was rather white as he walked with long strides toward the iron cage and grasped the barred door. The wolf thrashed madly within the net, gnashing her teeth and flinging saliva from her snapping jaws.

"Open the cell, Eiger," ordered the fair-ward. Gingerly one of the guards unlocked the barred door, and Gervys stepped inside the cage, latched it behind him, and knelt beside the maddened beast. He laid his hand lightly on Lila's flank through the net, and the animal twisted in fury, snapping.

"I'm going to untangle you, Lila. I'd appreciate it if you wouldn't tear my throat out," he murmured, and whistled a slow tune to himself as he found the edge of the snare. The thrashing head of the wolf thrust up, and her fangs raked his hand through the mesh. Gervys drew a harsh breath and concealed his bleeding hand inside his deerskin vest.

Dereva saw the slash of Lila's fangs and heard Gervys's

indrawn breath. She raced forward, ignoring the jagged waves of nausea and pain that shot through her body as she neared the cage. She gritted her teeth and forced her arm between the bars, stroking the shoulder of the infuriated beast.

"Lila—easy—easy," she gasped.

Gervys pulled the net free. The animal staggered to her feet, and the hunter saw his death in her baleful eyes. Then the wolf turned her shaggy head toward Dereva and thrust her hot tongue against the woman's reaching hand.

Gervys closed his eyes for a second, then said to the sentries and fair-ward, "As you can see, the animal is tame, and was merely guarding the property."

Unlatching the cage, Gervys stepped out, leaving the door unlocked but closed. He didn't trust Lila within sight of Otrok.

He supported Dereva, who had almost passed out from the pain of the cold iron, and led her away from the cell. To the fat baker, Gervys said grimly, "Collect your things and be gone within the hour, or the customers will be eating pies made of your face."

"He's threatening me, Officer!" Otrok whined.

"I want all of you off the grounds before the gates open," ordered the ward. "I'm banning both of you from this year's fair. Anyway, I got sick from those cat-meat pies you sold me last year, Otrok."

The baker protested loudly as he waddled after the two sentries and the fair-ward. "Those tarts were made of the finest veal!"

"Well, I found a whisker in mine," declared the ward as the guardhouse door closed behind them.

Gervys swung open the barred cage door, and the wolf leaped down to the ground. Away from the cold iron, she regained her strength at once and frisked around Dereva playfully.

Dereva dropped to her knees. "Can you understand me, Lila?" The wolf nodded her shaggy head.

"Go on back to Wolvendale on all fours," she ordered. "Don't stop to raid chicken coops or chase sheep, and avoid farmhouses. Do you hear me?"

The wolf seemed to grin, and the sharp face had a look of the human Lila. The forested crags of the mountains were where she wanted to be.

Dereva stroked the animal's hairy shoulder. "And you really should thank Gervys for rescuing you."

Saucily the wolf flipped her tail. She'd never have any use for humans. With a low howl of joy, Lila loped toward a gap in the palisade and headed out toward the distant mountains.

When she was gone, Gervys asked gruffly, "You're not going with her?"

Dereva stood up and stretched luxuriously. "I've babied Lila long enough. I'm beginning to think you and I might make a great team."

Gervys's stern face lightened magically.

"I've waited ten years for this," he exclaimed, and his arms went around her. They kissed passionately, and then the hunter laughed to himself.

"What's so funny?" Dereva chided.

"There's something I'd like to know," said Gervys, raising one eyebrow.

"I don't turn around three times before I sleep, if that's it." She grinned.

"If a canine ages seven years for every human year, are you really a woman of thirty-five or a wolf five years old?"

"Catch me at the right time of the full moon, and maybe I'll tell you," she teased.

They walked out of the noisy fairgrounds and kissed again under the wide sky, then turned toward the fresh green countryside without looking back at the narrow streets and stuffy houses of the town of Ithkar.

THE MAGIC CARPET

James Clark

It was the second day of Ithkar Fair, and Gorahdan, dealer in carpets and rugs, was in an excellent mood. Much of his good humor was due to the high quality of the merchandise he was offering for sale this year, and some of the mood could be attributed to the small keg of ale at his side. He had begun tapping it in earnest, and it was an excellent brew. Still, his cheerfulness extended beyond these reasons. He was happy simply to be in Ithkar.

There was no city like Ithkar at fair time.

Gorahdan knew this to be true, but he had speculated for many years without coming to a satisfactory answer as to why. Perhaps it was the presence of so many pilgrims, come for the festivals at the Temple of the Three Lordly Ones. Or the fair laws, which forbade the bearing of deadly weapons. Or the prohibition on the use of magic. Or even, though Gorahdan sincerely doubted it, the attendance of so many lords and ladies. *Something* made Ithkar a city without equal.

It even extended to the sounds of the city. There was a melody in those sounds that the merchant had never heard in a long life of travel. The rumble of countless feet, the blend of voices that always reminded him of the sea, the sharp cries of others hawking their wares, and the squeaks and rattles of passing carts. No temple chorus or lord's entertainers had ever made more beautiful music. Of course, he was careful never to make that claim aloud. The lords and the temple were his best customers.

In such pleasant musings did Gorahdan while away the second morning of the fair. No customers interrupted him, nor did he expect any. His clientele were the powerful and the wealthy, and they would find him soon enough. Sipping from his flagon of ale, he reminisced pleasantly about his days as a caravan driver. That was how he had first come to Ithkar. Looking back, they seemed romantic and adventurous.

The merchant was still in his exalted mood when a large man, dressed in the uniform of a squad leader of the fair-wards, ducked into the stall. It was Daven, a man Gorahdan had cultivated as a friend for many years. "Fair day to you, Daven," called the merchant, chuckling at his pun. "I hoped you would not let another day pass without dropping by. How have you been this past year?"

"Well, Gorahdan, well. The Sky Lords have blessed me with another son, and health for all my family. I would have stopped by yesterday, but the first day of the fair is our busiest time. I sometimes think that merchants are the pettiest people in all the world." He rolled his eyes.

Gorahdan laughed. "Tell no one I said so, Daven, but you're right. We scrabble for every advantage and every half-copper to be had. It's in the blood, I suppose. Bah.

What foolishness is this to talk of between old friends. Sit, sit, and I'll show you I've not wasted all my time since arriving in Ithkar.'' He produced another flagon and began to fill it from the keg.

The fair-ward laid aside his weighted staff and sat on the floor. He breathed deeply, sampling the rich aromas of high-quality dyes. ''Your carpets are of high character this year.''

''Even I would agree with you, my friend,'' the merchant said with a smile. ''But allow me to be the proper host. Join me in a cup of this most invigorating ale. I purchased it yesterday, and it would please me greatly to introduce you to it.''

Daven drank deeply, lowering the mug with a sigh. ''An excellent brew, indeed. Fully worthy, I'd say, to be offered at the fair. But what of you? Have your travels enriched your purse? And what of the world?''

''The world is still there, for the most part.'' Gorahdan chuckled. ''Oh, an odd kingdom or two has fallen to some conqueror, or some ruler was murdered in his bed. And more than a few travelers have been waylaid by bandits. But on the whole, the world is much the same.''

The fair-ward shook his head. He had never traveled more than two leagues beyond the limits of the city, and he found such news hard to comprehend. These things happened seldom in Ithkar. Still, he asked more questions, and Gorahdan answered. Most interesting were the doings of wizards.

For a dealer in carpets, Gorahdan was a superb storyteller. He beguiled Daven with tales of strange deeds and stranger people, wars, wizardry, and even of business. Through it all, though, he was careful to give no hint of how he himself had done. Gorahdan was a cautious man. He kept Daven so enthralled that he never even noticed the omission.

Relating the affairs of the world was thirsty work The keg was much emptier when the recital finally ran down. As he drew another flagon, the merchant shook his head. "It is a great pity, Daven, that I can find ale of this quality only at Ithkar Fair. Compared to this, what they serve at inns and alehouses in other lands is tepid stuff indeed. Did I not know of the fair laws forbidding magical merchandise, I would suspect a touch of sorcery in the brewing."

The fair-ward nodded. "I've had suspicions from time to time, it's true, but not often. The penalties are too severe. Confiscation of goods and belongings, and sometimes even outlawry. Few but fools would risk it. Do you not remember what happened to Hanibar last year?"

"The vintner? I know him, but I recall nothing special about him."

"Ah, then I've news for you. He was summoned before the fair-court on the last day of the fair, accused of selling two casks of spelled wine to Lord Servin. The casks were spelled, sure enough, and two more like them were found among his stock. The court confiscated all his wines and named him outlaw. He escaped Ithkar by the thinnest of margins. There were rumors that he was aided by followers of Thotharn. There were also rumors that he was aided by an eastern wizard."

Gorahdan pulled at his chin. "I knew none of this. I left the fair early last year." Shaking his head at the folly of men, he piously called upon the Three Lordly Ones to grant mercy to Hanibar and wisdom to those who sought to break the laws for gain. Daven joined in the prayer.

The merchant guided the conversation to more pleasant topics. He produced small gifts for the fair-ward's family, insisting that it gave him joy to give, which it did. He honestly liked Daven, but it was not any less a calculated policy to make him a friend. For a traveling merchant, friends among local authority were uncommonly valuable. Gorahdan cultivated many such in his wanderings. He had always considered it a wise business practice.

They talked until the fair-ward, saying he had neglected his duties long enough, stood, placing the merchant's gifts in a belt-pouch. He retrieved his staff and was about to leave when the first customer that Gorahdan had seen entered the stall. Daven nodded to his friend and moved back out into the crowd. Gorahdan, affecting a rolling seaman's gait, went to greet his customer.

On close examination, he recognized the man as one Zyk, apprentice to the wizard Lyrtran. Gorahdan had a fine memory for those able to afford his goods, though neither man had ever patronized him in the past. In fact, for a wizard as powerful as Lyrtran was reputed to be, the merchant could recall nothing about him save that he was powerful, wealthy, and paid his debts promptly. Of course for Gorahdan the last was the most important. He needed to know nothing else.

He stepped forward, bowing. "Welcome, Wizard Zyk, to the finest collection of carpets and rugs ever seen at Ithkar Fair. Carpets for the floor of a harem or the walls of a king's hall. Carpets of a soothing single color or of the most intricate and beautiful pattern. Carpets and rugs of any weave or size. You have only to tell me how I may serve you, Wizard Zyk."

Zyk, however, paid no attention to the merchant. Lips moving silently, he prowled among Gorahdan's stock. Here and there, he would stop to finger a carpet and then move on. Gorahdan let his patter trail off and watched, hiding his growing amazement behind a fixed smile. This was strange conduct for a customer. This was even strange conduct for a wizard.

Lyrtran's apprentice finally worked his way to the rear of the stall and paused in front of a pile of rather average carpets. Here he became excited, yanking up the top three, one by one, and throwing them aside. The fourth, Zyk treated much differently. The young wizard froze for several heartbeats before reaching out a hesitant hand to caress it. He looked, for all the world, like a man gentling a skittish colt.

Puzzled, Gorahdan watched silently. He was an astute-enough merchant, but he could see nothing special about this carpet. He recognized it easily enough. It was from a bale of exotic carpets from across the Western Sea that he had purchased scarcely an hour before the ship that had carried him to Ithkar had sailed. He had had no chance to examine his hasty acquisition before the *Snow Bird* had berthed. He had opened it for the first time the previous evening. By luck, only three of the carpets in that bale were even as low as average in quality. This was one of the three, and, by the Three Lordly Ones, the merchant could find nothing exciting about it.

Such was not the case for Zyk, however. He turned to Gorahdan, bowing and touching a hand to his forehead, a gesture from the mysterious east. "I salute you, merchant. Hiding such a valuable carpet so openly was a stroke of genius. Had I not been sensitized by my studies this morning, I would never have felt it as I walked by. And your tongue does not wag loosely, either. There has been no hint that a flying carpet would be for sale at the fair. You are, I believe, Gorahdan, the carpet dealer?"

The merchant nodded absently. He had always believed that in every merchant's life would come an opportunity that, if properly handled, would ensure a life of wealth. And the idea that this was his opportunity had struck him with the force of a thunderbolt. The fair had already gathered most of the wizards and great lords of the land. Offer them the carpet at auction, and they would be like wolves in winter. With trembling knees, he strove to answer in a normal voice. "Yes, Wizard Zyk, I am Gorahdan, dealer in the finest merchandise. How may I serve you?"

"In the matter of this carpet, of course."

"I'm sorry, but that item of merchandise is not for sale at this time." It sounded weak even to the merchant.

Zyk's face became a mask. "You would not accept an offer now? No. I see not. How could you? It's been over a hundred years since the last flying carpet was seen. Imagine the uproar when you announce the auction."

The last was an arrow launched in the dark, but it was rewarded. Zyk saw the merchant's face twitch as he thought of the heights to which the bidding could go. Naked greed burned behind those eyes.

The young wizard turned back to the carpet. He held his hands over it and muttered a spell. A ripple moved down the carpet's length, followed by another. Then it lifted slightly into the air. Gorahdan laughed, clapping his hands. Marvelous. Wonderful! It still looked like an average example of the weaver's art, but it was much, much more. The merchant could hardly restrain himself from dancing.

Zyk eyed his handiwork approvingly, then turned to the merchant. "I go to fetch Lyrtran, my master. Accept no offers until we return, and things will go to your advantage."

"Of course, Wizard Zyk. It is my fondest hope that I can make Lyrtran a satisfied customer." He bowed the apprentice from the stall.

Humming, the merchant examined the carpet again. He marveled that it could look so ordinary. If Zyk had not left it suspended in air, it would bring no more than a silver coin or two. But it would not do, he realized, to leave this valuable carpet hanging in the air for any passerby to see. Theft was not unknown at the fair. He must hide it.

Grabbing two corners, Gorahdan tried to fold it. It was like trying to fold a board. He tried again, exerting his strength to the full. Nothing. Frowning, he pulled the carpet to the center of the stall, where it hung in the air waist high. Again and again he tried, but every effort was futile. He could not even crinkle a corner.

Angrily, he began to wrestle the thing around, even trying to crush it in a bear hug. Trying to crush a rock would have been as easy. The merchant's face turned red, and exertion made him grunt like a rutting bull.

Finally, exhausted, he slid to the floor and lay there, panting. He was defeated. He tried to catch his breath, glaring all the while at the stubborn carpet. He was still on the floor when Daven, followed by two of his fair-wards, ducked into the stall. Gorahdan waved weakly at his friend.

But there was no friendship in the squad leader's face. He took in the flying carpet with one glance, then pointed his staff at the prone man and thundered, "I arrest you in the name of Ithkar Fair. Men, take him into custody."

As the fair-wards gave the carpet a wide berth, the merchant lifted a beseeching hand. "Daven, old friend, this is ridiculous. You know I'm no magic user. I couldn't cast a spell to curdle milk, let alone make a carpet fly. Come, have some ale and forget this nonsense."

"No friend of mine would sell magicked goods at the fair!" Daven roared. His two men jerked the carpet dealer to his feet. "You go before the fair-court, and may the Sky Lords grant you mercy." He reached out and pulled Gorahdan from the grasp of his men. "Bring that along," he ordered, indicating the carpet with a nod.

The rest of Daven's squad was outside, and they all formed up and marched off toward the temple. Daven, stone-faced, led the way, gesturing the curious aside with his staff. Gorahdan came next, surrounded by four men who hustled him along. Last were two fair-wards, gingerly pulling the flying carpet. For the first time, Gorahdan began to be truly worried. He had finally remembered the story of Hanibar—the very story Daven had told him so recently. He felt ill.

If he had listened to the crowd as they passed, he would have felt even worse. They were all abuzz with speculation about his crimes. Many of them knew the carpet dealer and had known him for years. They were men he had been on good terms with sometimes for more than a decade. But their guesses as to the nature of his crimes ranged from being a votary of Thotharn to being a sex murderer, with the carpet as evidence of the deed. And they mentioned the possibilities calmly, too, as though they had known all along. Gorahdan, fortunately, never heard a word.

The march to the temple passed quickly. Almost before he could blink, the merchant found himself facing two judges (one priest, one wizard to signify the seriousness of the post), listening to Daven pronounce the charge.

"—accuse one Gorahdan, dealer in carpets and rugs, of offering for sale at Ithkar Fair a magic, flying carpet." That brought a murmur from the spectators that was quickly silenced, and another, louder one when the carpet was brought forward. The fair-ward paused for a long moment, letting the carpet speak of its own illegality as it hung three feet in the air. "Acting on anonymous information, I took my squad to the stall of Gorahdan, where I found the merchant and this carpet, which bears his mark. My duty was clear, and I arrested him, to place him before the court."

The judges leaned forward, studying the carpet and Gorahdan. Ialfen, a temple priest, was impassive. But the other, a wizard named Strakh, was dumbfounded. He peered at Gorahdan's carpet in some consternation, then turned to the priest and started whispering urgently. Ialfen nodded often.

When Strakh finished, the priest turned his full attention to Gorahdan. "Have you any defense against this charge?"

The merchant looked at Ialfen's cold, hard eyes and knew it was futile. The priest was old and dry, and only too aware of the value of Gorahdan's stock, never mind the flying carpet, which would be forfeit to the temple. There would be no escape from this.

But trying would certainly not hurt; the situation could not get any worse. With a deep breath, he began, "Honored Judges, I beg the mercy of the court. I am but a humble seller of carpets and rugs. I had no way of knowing that a magic carpet was among my merchandise. I command no magic to test such things. In fact, I still would not know if an apprentice wizard named—"

Ialfen held up a hand to cut him off. "Speak to the point, Gorahdan. The possible crimes of others are no defense for you."

He inclined his head. "Of course, Your Honor. Then my plea must be ignorance. I had no knowledge of the magic properties of the carpet." It was over. Gorahdan had hoped to distract the judges with Zyk's use of magic to activate the carpet. It had been a faint hope, dashed in infancy. Ruefully, he realized who had provided the anonymous information to Daven that sent the fair-ward to his stall.

Ialfen conferred with his fellow judge. It took very little time.

"Gorahdan, your guilt is obvious. Your ignorance is no defense, and we have only your word for that, anyway. The laws are explicit: no article for sale may have its normal properties enhanced by magic. A flying carpet is certainly that." Ialfen shook his head. "You brought this carpet to Ithkar Fair to sell it; it bears your mark. The court has no choice. But we will be as lenient as possible. All your goods are confiscated, and I name you outlaw. You have until sundown to leave Ithkar in safety. This trial is over."

The fair-wards almost dragged him from the courtroom, shoving him out into the streets of Ithkar. Blinded by tears, the merchant stumbled along. Twenty years of hard and honest labor, destroyed in a morning. The crowds parted before him. News had traveled fast. People watched him silently, and from as far as they could manage. Anything else might tempt the Three Lordly Ones to visit them with a similar tragedy.

Gorahdan slowly regained control. And noticed the man who paced at his side. It was Zyk. "You," he blurted, drawing back a pace.

He bowed. "My master wishes to see you, merchant."

Gorahdan started to sputter an angry reply but swallowed the words. Anger was useless. What kind of revenge could a carpet dealer take on a wizard? "I do not wish to see Lyrtran, but there is little else to do. Lead on."

Zyk took him to a pavilion near the outer boundary of the fairgrounds, politely holding open the entrance flap for the carpet dealer. Inside, Gorahdan automatically appraised the large chamber he found himself in. Rich, but not gaudy. Lyrtran had taste, and only the finest would appeal to him. It was too bad he had nothing to show the wizard.

"Please wait here," Zyk said, "while I fetch Lyrtran." He disappeared through an opening in the far wall. Gorahdan passed the time wondering why he had come. He was still pondering idly when Zyk returned with Lyrtran.

"Greetings, merchant."

Gorahdan replied in kind.

Lyrtran immediately came to the point. "I've heard much, today, of your troubles, Gorahdan, and you have my sympathies and apologies. My pupil was overzealous and will be disciplined. But his actions are my responsibility. His meddling, and its results, have placed an obligation on me in your behalf. I must repair things as best I can. So I have booked you passage aboard the *Snow Bird*, which sails downriver at sunset. In addition, I have placed all the merchandise from your stall aboard her, too."

The merchant was stunned. He could feel nothing; too much had happened. He had gone from uncounted wealth to the depths of poverty and back to affluence while the sun rode across the sky. He stammered thanks to Lyrtran, the Sky Lords, and even to Zyk.

The wizard stopped his burblings with a raised finger. His face grew stern as he said, "Remember well the lessons you've learned today. Zyk reacted to your greed. He saw that you had no idea of the value of the magic carpet. We could have cheated you, but we would not have. You, however, tried to cheat us.

"Our knowledge without the carpet was worthless. Your carpet without our knowledge was worthless. There are obligations beyond the coin. Using our knowledge to gain a true idea of the value of that carpet placed an obligation on you which you tried to ignore. You can see the results."

Gorahdan listened humbly. The words were true enough. He nodded. He could see the depths of his folly.

But there was something, still, that nagged at the edge of his mind. A tiny doubt that would not go away. His merchandise, that was it. It would take a day or more to pack his carpets for shipment. How had Lyrtran managed it in less than an hour? Gorahdan had the awful feeling that the wizard had used his magic to accomplish that feat. And even as far out as the pavilion was, they were still within the fair, where the use of magic in any form was forbidden.

The thought was more than frightening, it was terrifying. Gorahdan had just been convicted of using magic, and the court had confiscated his goods and named him outlaw. What would the penalty be if they learned of this? Why, he had circumvented the first penalty completely by the use of even more magic. "Did you use magic?" he asked in a hushed voice. The wizard nodded, smiling faintly. The merchant was suddenly very interested in boarding the *Snow Bird*.

But there was one last question to ask. "Wizard Lyrtran, what of the flying carpet? You didn't send it to the *Snow Bird*, did you?" He was afraid the answer might be yes, and he was afraid the answer might be no. And he wasn't sure which he was more afraid of.

Lyrtran smiled. "No. I'll buy it from you." He pulled a purse from his robes, the largest and heaviest Gorahdan had ever seen.

"But the temple confiscated it. I don't have it anymore."

Tossing the purse to the merchant, he nodded. "True, but you have a moral claim which I choose to honor."

Gorahdan slowly tucked the purse away. "Very well, but I don't know how you'll take possession."

"I've already taken care of that." The wizard made a summoning gesture, and the carpet drifted through the opening in the far wall.

The carpet dealer bleated.

Lyrtran laughed. "There is more magic than the wizards of this land understand."

For Gorahdan, this was the final straw. He looked wildly around, expecting fair-wards to be bursting through every entrance. But no one was there, and he bolted from the pavilion as though Thotharn himself were at his heels. Nor did his pace slow until he was aboard the *Snow Bird*. But even on the ship, he did not draw an easy breath until sunset, when she slipped away from the docks and rode the current downstream.

Gorahdan watched Ithkar fall safely behind, sighing with relief. Thinking over the events of the day, he decided he was well out of the city. He was not even dismayed over lost opportunities. Running afoul of the law and mixing in the affairs of the powerful were worth a man's life. This time, he had been lucky. He thought about the bales in the *Snow Bird*'s hold.

Sunset was a dim red glow in the west, and Ithkar was far behind now. Gorahdan, leaning on a rail and looking aft, vowed never again to buy merchandise without examining it first. No matter how good the price. He felt a cool evening breeze on his face and thought again of the bales in the hold. It was time to start planning his next stop. There were far worse things than not being wealthy.

THE AMIABLE ASSASSIN

A. C. Crispin

"Please hold a moment, Master Renkath, while I read this back to you," said the youth with the shaggy brown hair, squinting at the ragged rectangle of parchment. "It would never do for me to make a mistake. For your own weaponry, that's one gold-hilted sword with an eye-agate set into the pommel, one dueling knife hilt bound with silver wire. For your assistant, one dueling knife, hilt inset with jade. No sword. For your two bravos, one iron-bladed pikestaff apiece, one plain-hilted sword each, and two common dueling knives. Correct?"

The gem master nodded curtly, shifting from one foot to the other in his impatience. Evening was stealing through Ithkar Fair, and the smells of food and sounds of revelry were enough to make any newly arrived traveler grudge the necessary but boring business of checking his weapons. "Correct, Alven lad," he said, his deep voice issuing from a

cavern of mustache and beard so thick and black they nigh
hid his lips, until one almost wondered if he'd spoken at all.
The last gleams of sunset doubly reddened the huge garnet
brooch securing his dusty ebon travel cloak. He was a massive man, thick of shoulder, thigh, and waist. Even the
jewel-encrusted rings studding his short, powerful fingers
were bulky.

"Well then, Master Renkath, here is your receipt and your
bin number in the weapons house," Alven said, extending a
quill-marked parchment with one hand while filing a copy
under "R." "As you know, you must next stop by the
wizard-of-the-gate to have your wares inspected. A mere
formality in your case, sir, but . . ." He trailed off with a
shrug. Master Renkath had been coming to Ithkar Fair for the
four years Alven had served as weapons clerk and was
known far and wide for the excellence of his gems—he had
no need to enhance questionable goods with magic. Still,
rules were rules. He gave the merchant his best professional
smile. "Enjoy your fairing, master, and good business to
you."

"And to you." The man nodded courteously before turning away, followed by his thin-flanked, sallow-cheeked assistant and the two hired bravos, both looking as though they
felt insufficiently clothed without their weapons.

Alven hurried to place the collected arsenal into the assigned bin. He finished just as the final crimson curtain of
sunset was yielding to night blue. The fair gates were closed
until dawn on the morrow—those arriving late would have to
bed down beneath the wooden shelters of their traveling
wains or, if they had come afoot or riding, beneath the stars.

Now for a passing glance at the new Quintka animal show
that came in today, he thought, then a quick sup and an ale at

the Joyous Goblet. I'll be home in time to help with the ironing. Mother can't possibly object to *that*. After all, I worked hard all day.

But he couldn't help feeling uneasy about his decision.

"Good evening, Alven!"

Alven turned from locking up the weapons house at the cheerful hail, breaking into a wide smile as he saw his visitor. "Jenilyn! What brings you out so early? On your way to an evening's work? If so, 'twill be his money's worth he'll be getting. The sun just now set."

The dark-haired young woman with the gray skirt and silver bodice lacings laughed heartily. "No, your mother sent me to fetch you, Alven. She wants you to hurry home so you can take over in the laundry while she picks up a few coppers telling fortunes."

Her bright black eyes crinkled with rueful amusement at his grimace. "Sorry to be the bearer of unpleasant tidings. But unlike you, 'tis the easy job I'll have this night, for the captain of the fair-wards has hired my time to go afairin' with him. By the time the second wicks in the torches are lit, he'll be happily drunk, and I'll not have had to give him more than a kiss or three!" She tossed a small pouch expertly, her eyes gleaming at the audible clink. "I wish they were all earned so easy, m'dear. If they were, I'd change this silver skirt for a golden one before two more years had passed."

Alven sighed. "You certainly deserve the best of things, Jeni, the pick of rich merchant husbands. If I had any money, I'd—"

"If you had any change to jingle, you'd probably turn out just like all the others, with their beery kisses and sticky-hot hands. I'd rather you remained poor, so we could continue friends," she said, her usually lively expression softening, becoming grave. "You're a good fellow, honest and loyal even to that mother of yours. I wouldn't want your head put awry in some crazy scrabbling after gold. You're a nice, kind lad—"

"Nice!" he burst out, turning away from her, waving long arms whose wrists poked out of the patched sleeves of his overjerkin like bones from a half-eaten drumstick. "Nice! By the Three, I get so sick of that word!" His voice rose to a mocking squeak. " 'Be a nice boy, Alven, and iron these shirts for Mistress Vell. Be sweet, Alven, and starch these collars. Watch what you say, Alven my son, or I'll do a little private conjuring that'll give you a taste of life as a water roach.' " He slammed a bony fist into his palm, grinding it there like a pestle into a mortar. "Sometimes I—"

"I know," Jenilyn sympathized. "I know. Most lads would have gone off awandering long since. No wonder they call you Alven the Amiable. You have the patience of a *klessen*."

"More likely the stupidity," growled the young man, straightening his collar, then finger-combing his hair with stabbing motions. "Any man—any man worthy of the name, that is—would've stood up and dared her to try her nasty little spells long since. If I were a *man*, I wouldn't be buried here at Ithkar the livelong year, scrubbing the sacramental robes for the temple priests; I'd be here only for the fair, then gone the other eleven months, off roving, seeing the world. I've never been farther than a spit beyond the twice-cursed gates!"

Grabbing up his cap, Alven jammed it onto his head, turning away from the weapons house. His strides came long and angry, and since he was a tall youth, Jenilyn was gasping for breath by the time she caught up to her friend. "Alven, wait! This is the wrong way—"

"No, it's not," he growled, skipping adroitly around one of the brass-helmed fair-wards, armed with his long, bronze-sheathed staff. "I've been working since dawn, and by the Three Lordly Ones, I deserve a bite to eat before I start in again! I'm for the Joyous Goblet. Can I buy you a drink, Jeni?"

"No, thanks," she said, stopping to smooth her mahogany curls, tumbled from her rush after Alven. "Kenyon Treegirth is expecting me, and he's a man I like to keep on my side." She giggled. "Or on my back, as the case may be. Enjoy your dinner, Alven. I'll stop by tomorrow, to make sure you're still in your proper shaping."

"That's kind of you, fair lady." He swept his cap off his head and bent his knee in an ironic bow. "If I am indeed a frog, promise me you'll carry me down to the canal and let me live out my life on the reed banks. Who knows but that I might find a green-skinned, bulgy-eyed damsel to ease my plight?"

Jenilyn was still laughing as she disappeared into the jostling, festive crowd of fairgoers. Alven entered the Joyous Goblet, standing in the doorway a moment for his eyes to adjust to the dimness. As it was still early, the ancient dark-timbered common room was sparsely populated, with only a thin bluish haze of smoke to sting the eyes. He waved at Qazia, the tavern-keeper, and she waved back cheerfully, automatically drawing a mug of Alven's favorite ale, plunking it down on the oaken bar.

As he made his way over to claim his brew, he spotted a familiar bulk sitting at a nearby table. "Master Renkath! Enjoying your fairing, sir?"

The heavyset gem master and his spare-shanked assistant turned at the hail, then the merchant waved Alven and his drink to the seat opposite him. "Why, it's young Alven! How goes it with you tonight, lad?"

"Fine, master," the younger man replied, taking a quick swig from his mug as he sat down.

The three men exchanged a few pleasantries as Alven sipped his ale. The merchant had shed his concealing cloak in the warmth from the hearth, and suddenly Alven caught sight of a tantalizingly familiar shape swinging against the velvet overtunic covering his barrel chest. The youth frowned, his eyes narrowing as he strove to make out the shape of the pendant the gem master was wearing. It was a six-pointed star with green—

"Master Renkath!" Alven gasped. "Where in the name of the holy Three did you get that pendant? Who sold it to you? And, most importantly, how long have you been wearing the thing?"

"This?" The gem master's thick fingers moved toward the heavy silver-plated star with its six points, each containing a bright green drop of some glassy substance.

"Don't touch it!" Without thinking, Alven seized the merchant's hand, dragging it away from the pendant.

"Impudent fool! Let go my master!" Pryden, the assistant, made a lunge for the younger man. Alven used his other hand to pin the skinny wrist against the table in a wrestling hold that made the man halt, gasping.

"On your peril do not touch the pendant, I beg of you, sir! Please, answer my questions!"

"Why, I bought it three days ago from a man who passed my wains on the Main Trade Road. He had a paltry few gems he was coming to sell, but this was the only thing with any appeal for me," the gem master said, obviously puzzled and beginning to be a little alarmed. "Why, what is it?"

"Thank the Three!" Alven whispered, nearly limp with relief. He released Pryden, who sat rubbing his wrist sulkily but not daring now to speak. "Unless you have scratched yourself with it—you haven't, have you sir? . . . Then it hasn't been on your person long enough to cause harm. That is a Killstar, a very exotic and deadly weapon. I've only seen one other come through Ithkar in the time I've been working as weapons clerk."

With infinite care, Alven lifted the pendant from around the man's thick neck. "See these stones? They're the danger. Green glass, mined, they say, from the bottom of the Death Swamp. If you'd worn this around your neck for several weeks, you'd soon begin to vomit, then bleed beneath your skin, and your hair would fall out. Finally death would come, and from what I've heard, it would have been none too soon for you."

Master Renkath was looking pale beneath his beard. Alven lowered his whisper even further. "If scratched by one of the points, the victim's fate is the same, though it may take a little longer. Six weeks, at the outside." The passion of a scholar lecturing on a subject he knows intimately colored Alven's voice. "Truly the perfect assassin's tool—deadly and untraceable. And disguised as a piece of jewelry, a man or woman could wear it almost anywhere, then use it to slay outright, if that became necessary."

"This bauble—a weapon?" Pryden was plainly skeptical of this last claim.

"For an expert, yes. Watch."

Detaching the pendant from its chain with infinite care, Alven stood up, turning toward the hand-knife target hanging on the wall across the half-empty room. His fingers flicked so fast they seemed naught but a blur of silver and green, then the Killstar thudded hard into the scarred board and sank deep, quivering.

"That, of course," Alven said quietly, "is the direct way to use it." Carefully he went to the target, pried the deadly bauble out, then wrapped it in one of the red homespun napkins off the nearest table. When it was swathed to his satisfaction, he lifted the target off the wall. "Not safe to leave it there," he explained to the stunned gem master. "Someone might brush the spot where it landed with his fingers, and if he had an open sore or cut . . ." He shrugged eloquently.

"I'll make you a new target, Qazia," he called to the tavern-keeper. "I'm afraid I split your old one."

"You never miss, lad," the woman called back, "but this is the first time you've halved my target. Your aim is getting deadlier by the moment."

Alven grinned, flattered. Picking up the mug of ale that Master Renkath had motioned the tavern-mistress to refill, he gulped its bitter coolness gratefully. "Thanks for the drink, sir."

" 'Tis little enough, lad. I'm still shaky thinking what might have happened if you hadn't been so alert."

Alven smiled. "I'm just glad our paths happened to cross tonight. I'll just turn your little bauble over to the captain of the fair-wards on the morrow, with my report. You should stop by to speak with Kenyon Treegirth yourself. He'll probably want a description of the rogue who sold you the thing. Perhaps he can be traced, and your money recovered."

The gem master made a brushing-away gesture. "A few coins are nothing compared to my life, lad! I'm eternally in your debt."

Alven modestly shook his head and, still carrying the Killstar and the contaminated target, made for the door.

Ithkar Fair roared and screeched and jostled around him as he emerged, the sounds, smells, and crowds as sudden and tangible as a slap across the face. He paused outside, feeling the effects of the ale he'd gulped. He'd best buy himself something to eat at one of the vendor's stalls, or he'd be tipsy, and nothing escaped Mother.

As he hesitated, trying to decide between a barbecued *klessen* leg and a venison pasty, something tugged at the edge of his jerkin. Alven started, turning, to find a dark-cloaked figure beside him.

The Joyous Goblet's eaves overhung the stranger, casting his features into flickering, bright-edged shadows in the torchlight. The youth's hand went immediately to his coin purse, but it was still there. The figure chuckled. "Wise youth. But I'm no cutpurse. I saw you in the Joyous Goblet, lad, and I've some dirty linen that won't stand a public laundering, so I need the services of someone like you." The man paused, peering upward into Alven's face, brightly lit by the torches snapping in the night wind. "Is it true you never miss?"

"Well . . ." Alven shrugged modestly, stepping closer, trying to make out the features hidden beneath the rough-woven hood. Absently, he thrust the cloth-wrapped Killstar into the breast pocket beneath his overjerkin. "Let's just say I don't miss nearly as much as I used to."

"And humble, too." The man chuckled again. "Do you work the fairgrounds regularly? I've not seen you before."

"Oh, yes," Alven said. "We've been doing a brisk business for the temple priests for years now. And, of course, when the fair comes each year, we've more than we can handle."

"Well, well, who would have thought the priests of the Three Lordly Ones would soil themselves so?" The stranger snickered.

Alven thought of the mounds of temple robes, sacramental hangings, surplices, and body linen he and Mother toiled over, washing, bleaching, and pressing. "The priests are no cleaner than anyone else," he assured the hooded man. "You'd be surprised some of the things they get into. But you mentioned that you have work for us? We do the best, quickest job in all of Ithkar."

The man nodded. "Aye, well, I hope for your sake your claim is true, for I have a job to challenge the toughest. But who is this 'we,' lad? Do you have a partner?"

"My mother and I are in business together," Alven explained. "She's has far more experience than I . . . after all, it's been her life's work."

"Your *mother?*" The stranger sounded a bit taken aback. "Well, they say some of the best have been women. . . ."

Alven was beginning to feel a little muddled and wondered if he'd missed something. The ale was singing in his veins, making his head feel as though he'd held his breath underwater too long.

"But no mind," the man continued. "Do you guarantee your work?"

"Of course," Alven said a little indignantly. "We specialize in the cleanest—"

"Shhhh! Keep your voice down!" the man hissed, and Alven closed his mouth, his cheeks hot as the torchlight over his head. He peered down again at the man, trying to see his face, but caught only the narrow-bridged sheen of a jutting nose beneath the hood. He couldn't make out anything of the man's eyes and abandoned the effort with a shiver.

"Sorry," Alven muttered. "When can I pick up—"

"Nay, lad. I'll bring the work to you. But we've yet to settle on a price. Standard wages acceptable?"

"Well . . ." Alven was beginning to feel *very* dizzy indeed, but his mind cleared a trifle as he heard the clink of coin in the stranger's purse. "If you need the work done quickly, this is our busiest time. It will cost you more. Twice standard," he said, feeling somewhat audacious but justified. They really *did* have a huge workload due to all the pilgrim ceremonies at the temple.

"Sounds reasonable." The man pressed the coin purse into Alven's hand, then glided back farther into the shadows. "I'll bring your target by this spot tomorrow, just at sunset. You'll know the high priest by his height, and by this sign. . . ." A perfectly featured but leering countenance molded from dull, beaten gold glimmered faintly on the breast of the man's robe for a second. "Remember, you guaranteed your work. . . ." This last sentence came but faintly to Alven's ears. The youth blinked, and in the space of that tiny motion, both the amulet and the stranger were gone, melting into the darkness as though they'd never been there at all. Not even a scrape of sandaled foot against hard ground betrayed the man's passage.

"No, wait!" Alven called, plunging into the alley—only to trip and fall headlong over the remains of a small woodpile. The fall made the ale slosh sourly in his belly, and for long moments he thought he and it might part company. When his dizziness finally abated, he found that he was still clutching the purse of coins. It was heavy. Too heavy.

Cautiously, Alven climbed back to his feet, staggered out into the torchlight, then peered into the purse. He almost dropped it, so great was his shock when he saw the gleam within.

Gold! There was enough gold in the leathern sack to raise two copper skirts to gold skirts in the space of a single night!

Oh, no! Alven thought, considerably sobered. His ale-muddled suspicions congealed into a hard, cold certainty that he had gotten himself into terrible trouble. Nobody paid this kind of money to get his laundry done.

The man must have watched the little byplay in the Joyous Goblet and drawn the wrong conclusions about Alven's line of work from his knowledge of exotic weapons like the Killstar. The cloaked stranger's reference to "dirty laundry" was naught but a slang term for a man he wanted dead—a man he'd just paid Alven a year's wages to kill.

And he was supposed to come by this spot tomorrow at sunset to see whom it was he was supposed to—what was the correct term used by assassins nowaways? "Dispatch?" "Relieve of all ills?" "Assist in shedding his mortal guise?" Alven found that he was giggling shrilly and managed to gain control of himself only by mentally listing all the types of weapons he knew that could be used for bludgeoning.

What else had the stranger said? "You will know him by his height and by this sign. . . ." and then he'd given Alven a glimpse of an evilly smiling, chiseled face. The youth had seen those golden features before . . . but where?

As Alven concentrated, frowning so furiously that some of the passing fairgoers glanced at him askance, he finally remembered—and, remembering, nearly burst into hysterical sobs instead of laughter.

Thotharn, the forbidden god! The lord of evil! Oh, fine, Alven, not only do you unknowingly accept a job to murder someone, you can't even pick an ordinary person; you have to choose a priest of Thotharn! Stupid, stupid, *stupid*! Mother had had the right of it all these years. He, Alven the so-called Amiable, deserved nothing better than life as a water roach. . . .

Still cursing himself in half a dozen tongues as well as thieves' argot, Alven finally summoned enough presence of mind to smooth down his clothing and hair, then begin walking. His lagging steps automatically took him in the direction of home—the tiny shack adjoining the temple's massive laundry. He concentrated on looking as normal as possible when he ducked his head to enter the living and eating area.

"Where have you been, you worthless lad?" His mother cuffed him sharply even as she set a plate of *klessen* stew before him. "You come dragging in, filthy and sour-faced, smelling of cheap ale, while I've been here trying to keep food in our bellies and a roof over our heads! Don't just sit there like a mooncalf—eat, eat!"

Alven picked up his spoon.

She began gathering up her palm cards, her bone needles, and her skin herbs, still fussing. "I hate to think of all the coppers I've missed while I stayed on, minding the fires beneath the soaking vats, mixing the lemon rub for the white acolyte robes! I ought to give you a taste of life as a barnacle!"

"Right now, that sounds very peaceful," Alven mumbled around a mouthful of the hot, flavorful stew.

"What did you say?" she demanded suspiciously.

"Nothing, Ma." He sighed, tearing a chunk of bread off the barley loaf she pushed toward him.

He barely noticed when she gathered up her brightly fringed shawl and went out, still scolding. His mind was too busy turning over the possible alternatives.

I could go to the fair-wards, make a clean breast of everything, he thought. But they'd surely take the gold, and Treegirth would likely dismiss me for trafficking with one of Thotharn's chosen.

He could also keep his mouth shut, hide the gold, and hope the short priest was too wary to seek him out when he didn't appear tomorrow evening. Somehow, he doubted that he'd live long enough to spend any of his unearned "fee," though. Thotharn's chosen weren't noted for their forbearance and forgiving natures—especially toward someone who'd had the misfortune to become privy to knowledge of their internal power struggles. The dark god's priests were rumored to possess awesome and uncanny powers. Life as a water roach would probably be a boon by comparison.

Even if he sought out his "target" and confessed all, the high priest would most likely express his gratitude by ordering Alven to dispatch the smaller priest. And afterward, even supposing he could accomplish that feat, he'd be marked for death himself, as a turncoat. . . .

Or—

—he could attempt the deed. . . .

And surely be slain in the doing. Alven had few illusions as to his ability to best one of Thotharn's high ones with ordinary steel. At least that way I could hide the gold in the house where Mother would find it, he thought gloomily. It'd keep her comfortable for the rest of her years. . . .

Somehow none of those alternatives seemed at all appealing. But at least if he confessed all to the captain of the fair-wards, he might still be alive to hear his mother's opinion of her idiot son . . . and hear it, and hear it. . . .

On the other hand, death definitely had its points. . . .

Alven scraped his plate, then scrubbed the dishes. After

checking the robes that were soaking in the huge laundry tubs, he threw himself down on his narrow cot, so tired that even his eyelids ached. Sky Lords, he thought fuzzily, help me decide what is best to do. . . .

He shut his eyes, falling into a near doze, his mind running the conversation through his head over and over. Why hadn't he realized what the man was talking about? What exactly had he said? He'd guaranteed his work, mentioned a fee, and—

"Oh, *no!*" Alven found himself on his feet, racing toward the door with his heart threatening to bound from his chest. I told him I had a partner! I told him I worked with my mother! If the high priest gets wind of any of this, he'll come looking for both of us!

He had to find her; then, together, they'd go to the fairwards. Even if the brass-hats locked them both up, a night in the temple dungeon was preferable to what Thotharn's high priest might do. Rumor held that they had spies everywhere, some of them not human. It was said they could eavesdrop on conversations through the eyes and ears of spiders, or vee-lizards, or almost anything small that crawled. . . .

Alven bolted through the laughing, bustling crowd of fairgoers, gulping for air as he zigged and zagged, trying desperately to find the shortest path through the throng. His mother usually frequented the wineshops and drinking booths. He checked so suddenly he almost pitched onto his face as he spotted a familiar gray skirt and silver laces straining across a well-filled bodice. "Jenilyn! *Jeni!*"

"Alven?" The woman turned away from her bull-chested escort, her professional smile fading like morning mist as she saw the youth's face. "What's happened? What—"

"Mother! I have to find her! Have you seen her?"

"She was over by the Joyous Goblet—"

"May the Three reward you! Bring the captain, quick!" Alven was off again, his words trailing behind him like threads on the night breeze.

He reached the tavern and paused outside for a second, desperately trying to steady his breathing. He mustn't panic her. . . .

Then he went in.

The smoky darkness inside was filled with a din of laughter, singing, and squeals from the barmaids. Taverngoers jostled each other, slopping drinks and food grease everywhere—the floor beneath Alven's buskins was by turns sticky and slippery. He began elbowing his way across the room when he spotted a familiar shawl. As he neared his mother, he saw that she was talking earnestly with a massive, black-bearded man—Master Renkath!

"Mother!" Alven called, putting his hand on her arm. "We have to—"

"Well, if it isn't Alven!" his mother said, beaming up at him. "The gem master here was just telling me why you were late to home. Why didn't you say—"

"We have to go, Mother, right now!" Alven tugged at her shawl, trying to keep his panic from breaking free. "I'll explain—"

The words died in his mouth as his narrowed eyes penetrated the blue haze of the tavern to make out a small, shadowy figure sitting at the back table. There was a glint of gold on the chest.

"Oh, no!" Alven grabbed his mother by the arm and swung her about, heading for the entrance. She squawked and flailed at him like a small, colorful hen, demanding to know what he thought he was doing . . . didn't he realize that Master Renkath was in their debt and wanted to—

Ahead of them the door opened, and Jenilyn, dragging a muzzy and uncomprehending Kenyon Treegirth, appeared. "Treegirth!" Alven shouted, beckoning to them. "Over here! I want you to—"

Behind the captain the door was hurled back on its hinges with a dull boom. The torches flickered in their sconces, and the wildly dancing shadows revealed—then hid—a tall, dark shape looming in the entranceway. A universal gasp rippled around the room, and Alven was aware, with part of his mind, that the revelers were melting away out the back door like snow beneath a hot sun. Before he could do more than blink, there were only a handful of people remaining.

Even Qazia, who was hardly a wilting bud of helplessness in the face of danger, dived behind the bar and stayed there.

The tall figure's voice grated across the room as a long arm lifted in a dark sleeve to point. "Is that the one you saw plotting, bravo?"

Only then did Alven notice the grizzled, scarred face of the bodyguard who stood beside Thotharn's high priest. "Aye, sir," the bravo said. The tough old mercenary shivered visibly as the cowled head turned to look down into his eyes. "That be the one, sir. The little one, wearin' the hood."

Alven's knees sagged as he realized, for the first time, that the high priest was pointing *past* him, to the small man in the back.

"The truth, maggot-spawn." The grating voice was all the more sinister for its calm. "Speak."

The small man writhed, tiny noises erupting from the back of his throat; then his struggles ceased abruptly, and he rose to front his accuser. "Aye," he said tonelessly, "I paid an assassin to kill you. They said he never missed."

"Which one?"

Alven felt his insides heave and prayed that he wouldn't disgrace himself as the small man swung toward him, his finger jabbing the air like a bony blade. The youth barely managed to step away from his mother in time for the incriminating digit to indicate him alone.

"Die, then," the high priest intoned, his hand closing around the golden image of his god.

With a squeal and a jerk like a lanced pig, the little priest tumbled over. They all stared in horror as the body began to melt, as though consumed by fire from within. A faint stench of decay reached Alven's nostrils; then it was gone.

And so was the small priest.

"Is this the man you saw talking with him?" The high priest indicated Alven to the bravo.

"Aye, sir. He took the sack o' coins."

"Very well. Dispatch him. He will offer no resistance."

Alven heard strangled cries from his mother, Master Renkath, Jeni, and Treegirth as they all struggled to move, patently helpless beneath some restraining spell Thotharn's chosen had cast. The bravo drew his hand knife, grinning as though he truly loved his work, and walked toward Alven, who stood frozen, waiting for the immobility to strike him, also.

But it didn't.

Struggling to comprehend the fact that he could still move, Alven lifted one hand to stare at it wonderingly; then, as the bravo came in with a low upward slash designed to disembowel an opponent, he leaped back, rolling away under the table.

As he did so, something hard poked his breastbone, and he remembered the Killstar that he'd thrust into his overjerkin pocket! Frantically he scuttled away as he dragged it out, still in its red napkin, careful even in his haste to keep from touching the green-starred points. Then it was free of the cloth, and in his hand. Alven rolled up to one knee, sighted, then sent it spinning across the tables.

It was a perfect cast. The bravo went down with a final, hideous gurgle as the Killstar buried itself in his throat.

There was a long, shocked silence as Alven and the high priest looked at each other across the room. Then the tall man reached up to grasp Thotharn's image. Alven tried to meet his end bravely, open-eyed, but his body wouldn't obey his mind, and he cowered back, covering his hands with his eyes.

Twenty heartbeats later, he peeked through his fingers, to see the high priest, frowning with effort, make a magical pass through the air, chanting softly.

Nothing happened this time, either.

With a bellowing roar, the high priest thrust the gold image of Thotharn at the youth, his face darkening visibly with strain. As he concentrated his energies, Alven saw Master Renkath stir; then his mother dropped to the floor in a faint, and Jenilyn blinked.

Alven crouched on the greasy floorboards of the tavern, waiting—and waiting . . .

And *waiting* . . .

Until Jenilyn, with a darting motion like that of a stooping gyrfalcon, grabbed one of the massive pewter ale tankards off the bar and brought it down on top of the high priest's head with a *thunk*. Ale sheeted down the tall man's face as he staggered, blinking; then the tankard connected with the top of his skull again, and he fell, to lie unmoving on the sodden floor.

The next few minutes were chaotic. A sobered Kenyon

Treegirth bellowed to the nearest fair-ward to fetch the most powerful wizard in the temple's employ and the magistrate on duty. Thotharn's chosen, stumbling between his guards, his hands bound behind him with a blessed vine, was taken away. For practicing dark magic within full sight of witnesses, he faced having to drink Lethe-water, which would deprive him of the memory of how to use his powers, as well as permanent exile from Ithkar Fair and its environs.

"Alven, lad!" Master Renkath clapped the youth on the shoulder with a vigor that made the slighter man wince. "You saved me again! You and this quick-witted young lady! I can never repay you!"

Hastily, Alven introduced the gem merchant to Jenilyn as he helped his mother sit up. "Alven?" She patted his face as though not believing he was really there. "Are you all right, son?"

"Fine, Ma."

"But, Alven . . ." Jenilyn's dark eyes were puzzled as they all sat down at one of the tables Qazia was busily righting. "How were you able to move, when we couldn't? And why didn't you melt away, like the little man?"

"I don't know." Alven shrugged.

"Let me try something, son." His mother's gaze sharpened, then she touched his face and began muttering under her breath. They all waited for long moments, then she took her hand away. "By the Three, I would never have believed it! Magic has no effect on him! He's immune to spells!"

"I am?" Alven was stunned. He'd never heard of such a thing. Finally, as the idea penetrated, he began to chuckle weakly, finally giggling like a fool. "And to think," he gasped, "all these years I've worried about being turned into a water roach, or a newt! Who would ever have thought it!"

As the tears ran down his cheeks, his mother, too, began to laugh.

When they could talk coherently once more, sitting over a mug of Qazia's best, Master Renkath grasped the youth's arm with his big, beringed hand. "Alven, you're obviously a lad with many talents," he began.

"Do you know how useful somebody like you could be to me? Not only as a bodyguard, but to learn the gem merchant's trade? One of the constant problems I have in my business is guarding against jewels that have been enhanced by magic to appear a better quality than they are. *You* would be unaffected by such spells. Would you consider traveling with me as my bodyguard and apprentice?"

Alven gaped at the black-bearded man, then hastily closed his mouth and sat up a little straighter. "To see the world outside Ithkar's gates has been my fondest wish. I will travel with you, and gladly."

"Alven!" his mother protested. "I need you here! You can't just go off and—"

"Yes, I can," the youth said calmly. "And I'm going, Mother. But only if Master Renkath will advance me half my first year's wages before we leave."

"Done!" the merchant said, opening his purse.

"With this"—Alven spilled the coins out onto the table—"and this"—he dug the dead priest's gold out of his jerkin—"you won't have to labor in that laundry from dawn to torch lighting each day, Mother. Before I leave, I'll see you set up in a snug little cottage in the country, with a cat to keep you company and some hens to scratch beside your doorstep. I'll be back every year for Ithkar Fair, and I'll bring you half what I earn. You'll never have to scrub another piece of underlinen again—except your own."

"But—"

"I'm going, Mother," he repeated, and after a second she sighed, resigned, then went home to pack.

"It's settled, then," said the gem merchant, rising to his feet. "And now, since it's nearly dawn, I'm heading for the guest house and a long-delayed sleep."

"It's nearly time for me to report to work," Alven said, then, realizing, grinned. "I don't have to go," he said. "Treegirth will have to find someone else to check weapons from now on."

"Speaking of our noble captain"—Jenilyn grimaced—"he forgot to pay me."

"Well, since you were the one who actually felled the high priest, we can't have you go unrewarded, either, my dear," Master Renkath said, twisting the gemmed ring off his little finger and handing it to her with a courtly bow. "I admire a quick-witted woman. Have you ever considered traveling beyond Ithkar's bounds?"

Jenilyn smiled, sliding the ring (it was still too large) onto her thumb. "I don't know," she said, eying the gem merchant measuringly and evidently liking what she saw, for she smiled again. "I never thought about it."

"Think, my dear," said the merchant, offering her his arm with another bow. "You'd look lovely in gold, you know."

The former weapons clerk of Ithkar Fair stood outside the Joyous Goblet, watching them walk away together in the pale pink light of dawn, thinking with a smile of mountains and rivers and deserts . . . all the places he'd never seen, that now lay ahead of him. . . .

Just as Jenilyn and Master Renkath turned the corner out of sight, she glanced back at Alven, and one dark eye closed in an unmistakable wink.

GUARDIANS OF THE SECRET

Ginger Curry and Monika Conroy

The toadish face of the wizard-of-the-gate squirmed as his weary eyes followed the path of the bloody sunrise, inching its way up, shoving away another tired night. Waning to light, the night crept back to its primordial hideout. The freshly scrubbed peaks looming over the fair city of Ithkar, damp from a recent rain, gaped their frozen greeting to the first rays of day.

The gnomed figure of the wizard slouched against the gate as he observed the spectacle of a new day at the fair. His eyes rested momentarily on the license fee officer and the squad of fair-wards. Pink from lack of sleep, his heavy lids kept sinking down over eyes that could not stop seeing. Flashes of fragmented pictures formed, jarring him once again into opening his eyes. To what body did the aged female face he saw each night in his dreams belong? And why the feeling of uneasiness associated with her? He knew that soon she would answer his questions, for she was headed for Ithkar.

As the sun gained in strength, its warmth cleared the wizard's mind, chasing the remnants of his nightmares into the abyss of the darkness.

He nodded off for a moment. When next he awoke, a scabrous yellow cart, drawn by a brown horse who was already crunching tufts of grass from the ground between bit and teeth, was stopped before the gate to Ithkar. The wizard's glance shifted from the horse to the woman making the familiar transaction. After placing a few copper coins on the officer's palm, the woman seated on the wagon took the paper assigning her place in the compound and stuck it into a pocket.

Eyes that had been disinterested suddenly focused. The wrinkled old woman was dressed unfashionably in a leather jerkin and cotton skirt. Sturdy wooden clogs completed her outfit. Ancient, almost forgotten pictures fell into place. Lisandra the perfumer! Of course! The last time he'd seen her was nearly a century ago—he'd been a child. Something had happened to her in Ithkar. Something that was whispered about but never spoken aloud. When she had left the fair, her beauty was dulling. Eyes known for their luminescence were now dark—because she was blind. It was rumored that she had been chosen to become the guardian of the secret.

The wizard motioned Lisandra closer, and she nudged the horse, which immediately pranced over to the wizard. The woman absentmindedly stroked the animal behind its ear. What had seemed to be a worn-out work horse was, up close, a shaggy but otherwise thoroughbred racehorse. The wizard stored the anomaly away on a special shelf in his mind as he greeted the woman.

"Lisandra! You came back!" He leaned closer to see if she was still blind. His gaze encountered blue untroubled eyes that could not focus.

"Yes, I am back."

Her voice had a husky, pleasant timbre to it.

"Why?"

The old woman answered simply, "The time has come."

Feeling uneasy without knowing why, the wizard stalled. "But you're rather late, aren't you? Only three fair days remain."

"I have traveled along many roads, and I was not certain that this was my destination until I arrived."

Puzzling over her meaning, the wizard became more wary. But the old woman had done nothing wrong—yet. She had not used her magic scents to deceive. As to what she was planning . . . Her aura was much too strong for him to penetrate—alone. Still, as he watched the perfumer and her cart disappear into the crowds, he became anxious enough to search back through aged images for a clue as to why Lisandra had returned to the fair. Coming up with nothing, he wondered if it was possible that she had come merely to sell her perfume. He shook his head. The air about him vibrated strangely, like the gathering of storm clouds before the fury of the wind breaks loose. But he could not attribute its source to Lisandra. He decided to let it simmer for a while. Shrugging, he settled back against the gate to slumber until another fairgoer arrived.

The noonday sun shone benignly upon the pandemonium of people, animals, and wares on the third to the last day of the fair. The odor of foreign foods and spices wafted about, engulfing the multicolored inhabitants, causing them to eagerly anticipate the new fares.

The city was much more alive than when last Lisandra had been in it, throbbing with sounds that were both unfamiliar and enchanting. She guided the horse to her assigned position between ten pillars at the edge of compound two. The animal stopped before Lisandra could command it. Dismounting, Lisandra stroked the horse, the feel of his velvety fur as satisfying to her as the sight of a sunrise is to a portrait-maker.

She whispered, "I know, my friend, you need no command. As always, you anticipate me." The animal snorted and shook its mane.

Lisandra made the cart ready for business, pulling down one side to reveal crude shelves jammed with casks of differing sizes and colors of fragrances. The fingers of her left hand played over the rows of bottles until they found the preselected purple vial containing her most exquisite perfume. Dropping it into a skirt pocket, Lisandra picked her way slowly through the groups of people to the temple entrance.

As she climbed the marble steps, she sensed the wizard's presence. Although she was relieved that he was close enough for her to keep track of, she could not allow him inside her aura, so she expended a little of her store of energy to strengthen the field.

Moving between twin pillars into a gigantic hall, Lisandra was conscious of her slow pace as the clunk, clunk of her clogs drew the curious stares of the dozen or so fellow worshipers.

At one time she had thought her patience to be an asset. No more. Now she thought her inherent deliberations to be more a matter of body over mind than patience. Outside Ithkar she had meandered across the steppes and over the mountains, letting the surroundings condition her thinking.

Creeping in the vastness of wilderness, loping among the hustle bustle of fair tradespeople, and dragging once again in the atmosphere of lingering temple pilgrims, her thinking processes altered accordingly.

Resisting the languor, Lisandra hastened to place the purple vial of perfume, her offering to the Three Lordly Ones, into the outstretched hands of a fair-ward. She must not allow atmosphere to fool her into believing excess time remained to confront Thera. Of the three tentative successors she had chosen years ago, Thera was the only one left. Call it patience or call it cowardice, when it came to inflicting pain on others, Lisandra always procrastinated. And yet she knew that change would not come about without pain. The other two intendeds had died before she could bring herself to . . . She sighed, knowing full well that by sparing them a few moments of discomfort, she had cost them their lives.

She had tarried too long. She had only 'til fair's end, three days, to succeed . . . or fail. And she was beginning to feel the weight of her 110 years.

As Lisandra turned and hurried from the temple, she felt the presence of Thera scraping the edges of her field for a weak spot.

Lisandra sent her eclectic sight toward the prober. It showed her a wooden-latticed portico overhead where Thera was observing a peasant making what she felt was a paltry offering to the gods. The young woman's lips curled in distaste as she wheeled about and descended into her personal suite in the students' dormitory.

The eclectic sensor followed, hovering over the priestess, gathering details that would aid Lisandra in the future. The young woman was studying her image in a full-length looking glass. Hair, the color of burnished copper, was piled atop

Thera's head and held at bay by a ribbon. The subtle gemgreen hue of her dress reflected the color of her eyes. While practicing a demure smile, she looked the part of a priestess studying the Three Lordly Ones instead of what she was—a secret follower of Thotharn. Then the image changed. The corners of Thera's mouth twisted into a cruel smile, her head went back, and she burst out laughing. A few strands of hair floated loose, and in wild abandonment, Thera loosened the green tie and shook her hair rapidly from side to side. Finally she realized that if any of her teachers should see her admiring herself, they would dismiss her from the study group.

After swiftly retying her hair, Thera applied a pale makeup which restored her studious air. She completed her toilet in preparation for sight-seeing in Ithkar. The green dress, indicative of her rank as apprentice student of the Three Lordly Ones, rustled as she swept from the room.

Calling the eclectic sight to her, Lisandra strode back to her cart. There she arranged small bottles in the front rows and larger containers toward the back. Then, removing a drab vial from the middle section, Lisandra replaced it with a multifaceted, lead-crystal flask filled with a rose-scented fragrance.

She had just taken up her position in a makeshift chair with her eyes shut and her face and body relaxed—as if she were asleep—when the voice she was waiting for drifted into her ears.

Lisandra's head jerked up, and she began to call out in a husky voice, "Perfume! A fragrance to please everyone and to accomplish anything. Replenish your husband's desire; entice your lover to . . ."

In a tone of voice rich with the confidence of youth and beauty, Thera asked, "Old woman, what can you do for me?"

Laughter broke out amongst the small group of friends that had encircled the perfumer and the priestess.

"My dear," replied Lisandra, her fingers deftly uncapping the vial positioned adjacent to her red crystal one and dabbing the scent of apples upon Thera's wrist, "I only pray that I may have a fragrance delicate enough to complement your regal bearing and attire."

Before Thera could answer, the old perfumer shook her head, muttering, "Much too wild. Perhaps this one?" Her fingers trailed over the red bottle to a pale blue one flanking its opposite side. From this container she smeared several drops on Thera's left cheek.

Thera's nose wrinkled at the odor of cinnamon, and her eyes followed Lisandra's fingers to the stained apron where they were dried.

As Lisandra reached out to choose another sweet bouquet, Thera jumped back a step. "No, no, old woman! You have no nose for what pleases me," she said, snatching up the rose vial and dampening both inner elbow folds with the cloying sweetness.

"Now this, old woman," said Thera, dropping a few coins on the shelf, "is more fitting, don't you agree?"

"Whatever pleases you, my dear," muttered Lisandra under her breath. She chuckled.

Corking and dropping the vial into a pocket, Thera wandered off, chatting and giggling with her friends.

Lisandra waited patiently until the priestess had left the area before closing up the cart for sleep and beginning her meditation. Thera's faith in herself was very strong, and Lisandra would need all her strength for the upcoming battle of wills. Integrity of conviction was necessary, for a lukewarm faith will remain weak while evil converted to good has the toughness of a sword tempered in flames. Somehow Lisandra had to convince the power-hungry girl of the importance of becoming a guardian who lets the secret be tapped but who will die trying to prevent its unfolding. Or . . . Thera must die because after absorbing the knowledge of Thotharn, she might become powerful enough to analyze the secret by herself.

Just before Lisandra entered the peace of deep trance, a pounding upon the side of the cart alerted her to the wizard's presence.

"Lisandra," called the wizard, "I feel that you have entered Ithkar for false reasons, and therefore, I should report you."

Without rising, Lisandra sent her voice through the tiny window near the top of the cart. "It is too late for you to interfere."

His shrill voice rising another octave, the wizard shrieked, "*You* will think it is too late when the fair-wards come marching in to drag you from Ithkar."

Lisandra sighed, knowing she must give him more information—or he would make good his threat. "I have chosen my successor. The process has started."

"Successor to what? Do not talk in riddles, Lisandra. I warn you."

"Why, successor to me, of course. Thera shall be the next guardian of the secret of the Three Lordly Ones." She wished she had the sureness of her words.

Her eclectic sight showed her the blanching of the wizard's face and the repetitive squeezing of his chin by his right hand. In spite of his obvious reluctance to cause any disfavor with the gods, however, he continued the interrogation, demanding that she open the cart and step out.

Lisandra groaned, knowing she could tell him no more. She would have to resort to magic, and there would not be enough time to replenish it. If only she had not used so much on the other two novitiates. Regretfully she implanted the image of the eldest and most powerful of the Three Lordly Ones into the wizard's mind.

Standing out against the fast approaching dusk, an iridescent blue shaft of light emanated from Agor's face and struck the ground at the wizard's feet. Jumping back and choking down a cry, the wizard commanded, "Stop it, Lisandra! I believe you. For two days I will not intrude in your quest. But if you are still here at fair's end, I will notify the fair-wards."

Evening drifted lazily in upon the city like the slowly falling veil of a woman disrobing, muting the many sounds and slowing down the frantic pace of the people.

Thera was sauntering through the animal compound when she felt her back shiver violently and begin to hunch. Using her magic, she forced herself straight again. Within seconds she was bent even more. A sudden fear that she had not experienced since childhood squeezed her ribs, making it difficult to breathe. Why was this happening to her? Why now, when she was so close to leeching the power of the Three Lordly Ones?

A passing man gave Thera a lingering look. She was used to the admiring glances of men, but the pity in this stranger's eyes made her want to hide. Like a wounded animal she crept along the shadows of wagons, makeshift shelters, and houses until she was back in her room.

She stared in disbelief at her image in the mirror. For a few moments she was an orphan again. A hunch-backed orphan around whom the other children were forming a circle and chanting, "Hunchback! Hunchback! What's your dirty deed? Hunchback, hunchback, what makes you face the dirt?"

It can't be happening. It cannot be happening to me. It's not fair! Unheard moans issued from her mouth.

Wasn't she one of the chosen ones? Hadn't she, little by little, taught herself how to use the magic to straighten her defective frame? Unbidden, the thought struck her as it had when she'd first realized her growing powers. *Is somebody helping me?* Unanswered as before, the question dissolved in her anger.

Damn it! She could not stand to see the pity on people's faces. Why should they pity her when she pitied no one? Pity made you weak.

Hour after hour Thera forced herself through the painful beginning exercises, calling on her magic to help. But each time she let up for an instant, her back curved slowly and resolutely until she was again facing the wretched floor.

Finally, exhausted, she crept into bed.

When she first awoke the next morning she had forgotten the events of the night before. She jumped out of bed and nearly fell on the floor from the lopsided weight. Again she expended much energy in trying to overcome the defect. Revolted by and ashamed of her deformed figure, she closeted herself all day in her room.

By afternoon, she had decided that the wizard whose many advances she had spurned was getting even with her. Impatient, but relieved at finding an answer, she waited for the obscurity of night before confronting the wizard-of-the-gate at his private quarters.

Challenging him, she yanked off her cloak, turned her back to the wizard, and demanded, "Look at me! Look at what you have done to me! How could you be so cruel—I thought you liked me.''

The wizard's frog eyes grew larger, expressing his shock. He spun her around and shook his head wildly, saying, ''No, no! I would not twist this lovely body that I have longed to possess.''

Thera felt her anger growing out of control. Her lips curled and her eyes expressed her disgust at his physical appearance. Her voice dripping venom, she said, ''Were I to remain bent for a thousand years, I would never let your talons near me!''

Squeezing his jaw, the wizard said, ''Think, Thera. Who has greater power than you? Not me!'' The premonition and uneasiness he had felt the day before suddenly returned, and all the many fragments became one picture of awesome proportion. ''Wait! I think I know who did this monstrous thing to your beautiful body—Lisandra!''

''Who?''

''Lisandra, the perfumer.''

Thera's mind flashed back to the temple, to the ugly old lady whose link to the Three Lordly Ones she had sensed earlier in the day. That afternoon, she remembered, she had bought a crystal bottle of perfume from her. Connecting the two events, she seethed with anger. ''I will destroy her! No one—not even Thotharn, who lusts after me—will I permit to touch my body.'' Brushing aside the wizard's offer to help, she rushed away.

Immediately upon leaving the wizard, Thera felt a relief of weight and realized she was suddenly standing straight once again. To her surprise, she felt extremely weary. Her emotional discord must have drained her more than she had thought. Too sleepy even to talk with anyone, she returned to her suite and plunged naked under the warm quilts.

While Thera slept the deep sleep of very early childhood, Lisandra's psychic fingers eased through the newly formed enactive memory until she located the information the wizard had supplied Thera. Gently, as if erasing a penciled error from onionskin paper, she brushed away her own name. Thera would find her soon enough. But first she must be initiated. How painful or deadly the rites would become would depend solely on Thera.

But knowing how well the girl would resist, Lisandra sighed, simultaneously wishing there were an easier way and knowing there never had been and there never would be.

Dawn was a vampire lover kissing the slumbering city awake as Thera sat up screaming from images of mud-caked bodies oozing blood from every pore and silver flakes falling from dismembered limbs as they floated eerily through a greenish-purple sky.

Beads of perspiration formed on her upper lip and forehead. And in place of her usual calm demeanor were trembling hands and a puckered brow.

She stood before the window willing the soft breeze to cool her mind as well as her face. After a while she felt almost normal. The nightmare images had faded into forgotten demons of the night. Under control once more, Thera performed her usual morning tasks and left her suite. As always, her outward appearance was serene and beautiful.

Sauntering toward the trades compound, Thera was horrified to notice that each person she encountered was wearing or growing macabre living masks. At first she was struck by the novelty of it. But by the fifth image she was seething inside at her inability to control it.

Sometime between late afternoon and sunset, the lady time who cools tempers and soothes worries as she brings the workday to an end caused Thera to discover that if she covered her eyes with her hands, the terrible visions that had plagued her all day would disappear. Her mind raged to find their cause, but no answer came forth. Patience was not part of her, she thought. Not since the day magic became hers. Was she maybe projecting her uneasiness from the nightmares onto the fairgoers? What else could it be?

Finally the gross features made her so anxious, she felt she would surely strangle the next one she saw. Instead of going to the study room, as she had intended, she swiveled about, hands over her eyes, and slunk back into her suite.

There she tried to discover the reason for the hallucinations. She shook her head at the futility of it. Like leaves adjusting to seasons, the faces constantly shifted, never staying the same long enough for her to get a hold on them. It was almost as if someone were using her impatience against her.

How foolish, she thought, springing from her chair and going to the mirror to reassure herself that at least her beauty remained the same. Then, for the first time since she had claimed magic as her own, a feeling of helplessness began to build in her. Horror reflecting from her eyes, she watched an ever-shifting pattern of distorted features. The change began on her left side, spreading so slowly that one change melded into another until her whole face looked like a wax caricature deliberately placed too close to the heat of a fire. Each change was accompanied by an intensifying pain as tissue stretched and eventually split, exposing the raw flesh to the air.

Thera did not know how long she watched the parade of strangers in the glass. When her powers had no lasting effect on the grotesque reflections, a coldness spread through her mind, freezing her thoughts and keeping her from the madness that called to her.

Night was squatting once again upon Ithkar when Thera began to feel that the walls were closing in on her. The chill in her mind was replaced by panic. She had to get out before the room smothered her. She flung a shawl over her head and draped it about her lower face and shoulder before bolting from the room. She did not stop until she reached the edge of the animal compound. Panting, she felt a strange kinship with the animals that she had never felt for her own kind. She inhaled the odors of their food and excrement and shared in the wildness of their coupling. For a few moments she felt safe. Suddenly the combined desire of the caged cats for freedom screamed from their throats in one cascading emotion.

And Thera knew terror.

Screaming like an injured animal, clamping her eyelids with her hands to shut out the monstrous faces, not seeing her surroundings, she ran into a surging group of merrymakers that linked her in their chain. A living chain that swung first one direction, then another as it wound itself through the square.

Breaking free from the chain, Thera cowered into the first alley she came to. She thought she was alone until she heard an asthmatic breathing a few feet away. The man moved closer to her, and she stepped back in shock. He looked like the deformed young man from her village, the one with elephantiasis. She could have helped him. He had asked. But who had helped her when the children had taunted her? ''No one,'' she said, clenching her hands into fists.

She jammed her fists into her pockets. When the right hand came out holding the vial of perfume, she knew who her adversary was. Without glancing back at the misshapen man, Thera hurried in search of the one person who could answer why.

Lisandra did not sleep this night; she sat waiting for the inevitable. Soon it would begin. And soon afterward she would know if she had won over a successor. She hoped she had chosen the right one. She had tried to conserve her strength for this encounter. And now she tried to block uncertainty from her mind. She had made her pilgrimage to the Shrine of the Three Lordly Ones, and there was nothing left to do to prepare. If only she did not have to divide her power in an effort to veil the soon-to-be encounter from the fairwards and wizards, she would be less worried over the outcome.

As if it were an aroma of perfume, Lisandra sensed the fury and anger that was coming toward her. As it got closer, she marshaled the forces of the Three Lordly Ones. She would not need the eclectic sight in these tight quarters. If the outcome weren't so crucial, she would have eagerly awaited the clash of wills, as she had many others in the past.

The voice licked her ears like flames from a fire.

"Old hag, where are you hiding?"

Lisandra had time to think, At least my method of hiding is better than hers, before thick waves of rage surrounded her, almost hurling her from her chair.

"In front of you," Lisandra whispered. "Remove your shawl and look at me."

The soft rustling indicated to Lisandra that the young woman had obeyed her. The next sound Lisandra heard was the strident, pain-laden scream reverberating off the buildings that stood silent watch like soldiers at attention.

"Close your eyes!" Lisandra commanded.

Thera choked out an angry reply between sobs of pain. "I'll report you to the council of wizards for what you did to me."

Lisandra smiled to herself. "No."

"I won't let you get away with what you're doing to me."

So softly were the next words spoken that Thera had to hold her breath to hear them.

"What am I doing to you?"

"It's the perfume you made! I know it is. It makes me see ugly, vicious faces."

"My dear, all the perfume does is to reveal your dark side."

Thera held her palms against her ears to mute the unacceptable words. "No!" she shouted. "I'm not like this! I'm a priestess who serves the Three Lordly Ones. I'm good."

"Are you really?"

Lisandra knew this was her last chance to awaken decency in Thera. Marshaling all her strength, the aged one searched Thera's mind to find the one thing that might make her vulnerable enough to understand. Deeply hidden beneath forced forgetfulness and pain, Lisandra found the bitter secret, and as a new dawn rose, Lisandra reluctantly made it come to life again in Thera.

Her voice as cold as the river Ith in winter, Lisandra said, "Open your eyes, then, girl."

"Mommy! Is it you, Mommy?" Tears streaming from her eyes, Thera looked down at the tiny boy clutching her dress. Squeezed by the huge water-filled head, his eyes were slits. But there was a beatific smile on his face as he said, "I love you, Mommy. Why did you kill me?"

Thera fell to her knees, sobbing and hugging the boy to her. This could not be the baby she had killed at birth. It must be an illusion. Oh, if only she'd been blind then; she would not have listened to the taunts of others. Why had she allowed shame to overcome her? Eyes closed, she screamed out in pain. Feeling a release of pressure, she opened her eyes and saw the boy was too weak to stand. He lay on his back, his brown eyes bound to hers through a love she had never known. Crying hysterically, Thera took the massive head into her hands and kissed it.

After many long moments her grief lost its painfulness. She felt a presence beside her. Glancing up, she saw the pain on Lisandra's face. Once again they entered the circle of every woman who has ever squeezed a baby from her womb.

Lisandra and Thera were drawn close in their pain. Too weak to cast off the countless minds straining to fuse with hers, Thera finally realized that this sharing of pain was good, for it brought love into the world. Immediately upon thinking this, she began to tingle all over, and a sensation like countless fingers massaging every inch of her body told her that pain, at least this pain, also brought integration. Why had she fought this feeling before? She lifted her eyes to Lisandra and was shocked to witness the rapid aging of the old woman. She was dying.

Thera brought out the vial of perfume. "Why did you put a spell on me?"

With her remaining strength, Lisandra held the lead-crystal bottle up to the light. The first red rays of sun that were fingering the square brushed the vial gently. The rays broke into myriad colors that shone upon Lisandra. Bathed in this soft light, Lisandra's wrinkled face was beautiful in its serenity.

Lisandra whispered, "I am the guardian of the secret. But now you must guard it against discovery from unworthy ones. My time has come to return to the Three Lordly Ones. You are the one who will succeed me.''

Thera was stunned into momentary silence. Then, gathering her wits about her, she said, ''Why pick me if you think I am evil?''

''Because, my dear, your powers are so much stronger than anyone else's. Once, a long time ago, I was like you. And time's laden years will teach you goodness and patience— as it did me.''

Thera began to think of the power she would have. Then she weighed this against the shriveled, blind old woman before her, and she shivered. ''I will not spend the rest of my life like you. I shall discover the secret by myself.''

Lisandra said, ''No. Madness will grip you first.''

''Thotharn will help me,'' Thera said viciously.

''No! I picked you. You will and must succeed me,'' Lisandra said calmly.

Smiling, Lisandra dropped the vial to the floor, breaking it. The scent rose like steam and within a second fused with dawn's sun. A white cloud enveloped Thera. Though it seemed to Thera to last hours, a gentle breeze arose within minutes and dispersed the cloud.

Thera opened her eyes but could see nothing. A voice seeming to come from everywhere and nowhere said softly, ''Trust me, my little one. You will live up to your task.''

A calmness she had never known before permeated her bent body. Suddenly the fragments of her life coalesced into an awareness of the totality of life's meaning. Peace was hers at last. She was now the guardian of the secret.

As a yellow cart approached, the wizard was shocked that the aged, hunchbacked figure was that of his beloved Thera.

Nearing the gate, she paused for a moment and smiled directly at him.

The wizard whispered, "Good tidings, Thera."

As he watched the perfumer and her horse pass through the gate, he was astonished to see three rings of varying shades of blue light surrounding horse and driver. As they pulled away, the three rings merged into one soft blue glow that encompassed them.

The wizard blinked. When next he opened his eyes there was only the vastness of space. They were gone.

THE BEGGAR AND HIS CAT

Gene DeWeese

Beggars, I have often been told, cannot be choosers, but I have made choices far too often for me to subscribe easily to such a belief. I even chose, in a manner of speaking, to become a beggar. True, the choice was between that and starvation, but it was a choice, you must admit. Unless, of course, you choose to disbelieve, which is certainly your right, Your Lordships. After all, I did not say that *only* beggars may choose, eh?

And my four-legged friend here, he, too, has made his choices, more than most have made in their lifetimes, I daresay. He seems to have chosen to follow me, for instance, though only the Three Lordly Ones know why, and I hope that I will not cause offense if I confess that I sometimes have my doubts even about them. There have even been times when the trek from one village to the next has loomed longer than I at first believed, that he has chosen to bring me food, carrying a squirming, squeaking bundle of fur carefully in his mouth and depositing it at my feet. The fact that I do not fall upon it and devour it as he has done with its predecessors seems to puzzle him, but it does not discourage him. I suppose he imagines he has simply not found something to my taste. Which is, I must admit, quite true.

And I—I chose some time ago to journey to the great Ithkar Fair, though I knew I would not likely be allowed within its borders proper, to mix with the merchants and artisans and other even more exalted personages. That did not greatly concern me, however, since I had been informed by those who had journeyed to past fairs that even the outer fringes are an experience not to be forgotten. The pickings, they said, are even more splendid there than on the busiest street corners of most villages at that or any other time of year.

And these probable restrictions on our movements concerned my friend even less. With his four-footed stealth and slit-eyed cunning, he knew he could not be held back by mere humans, even those such as yourselves with priestly authority and finery. He has, I imagine, had a most agreeable day and night, what with the morsels that, by intent or accident, find their way from the fine tables down to his more earthy level. I suspect that, had he fetched me a few of those in the same way he offered me those tiny creatures of the field and forest, I would have been sorely tempted to accept.

But, alas, he brought me nothing, not even his companionship, during those hours. Not that I would ever censure him, certainly. There was, after all, no leash upon him, and he was as free to choose then as when he first chose to accompany me. And there were doubtless many things to occupy him, others of his own kind, for example, such as that fine creature there in the door with its silken fur and curious eyes. And there are times, as I am sure Your Lordships are aware, when the lure of such companionship is not to be denied even to the humblest of creatures.

As for my other friend—

Ah, I see from his scowl that he does not appear overly comfortable with my choice of words. My acquaintance, then? Yes, that would be better, I agree. It certainly would be better than those names by which he first addressed *me*, I assure you, when in truth we were perfect strangers.

But as I was on the verge of saying, I cannot speak for him, whether he be an acquaintance or a friend or even a stranger. I can speak only of what I have seen and heard and been subjected to, though for me that is quite sufficient. I only hope, Your Lordships, that it will be the same for you, and that when you have heard me out, I will be rendered guiltless in this unfortunate affair.

My first sight of this man—he asserts his name is Arkola, and I have no reason to doubt him—was less than twelve hours ago when he set upon me like a madman while I was engaged in nothing more offensive or magical than attempting to find an unoccupied patch of ground on which to rest during those few remaining hours until dawn. Though I am not normally a nocturnal creature, I had not sought rest earlier because, in keeping with what my informants had told me, the pickings were indeed excellent here at the fair, and the sights most wondrous. Though many of the hangers-on were a trifle surly and did refuse me, many did not, and even of those who refused me, none were overrough in their manner of refusal. Thus I had eaten better that day than any other day in recent memory. I had even been afforded the wherewithal for a few spirits. Nothing as fine, of course, as those splendid wines and ales that can be found within the borders of the fair, but to my own taste it was veritable ambrosia, and I must admit that my head was in something of a fog, albeit a most pleasurable one, as I searched for a resting place. I earned a few curses as I stumbled over those already retired for the night, but none seemed upset enough by my clumsiness to offer blows. Or perhaps they, like myself, were in something of a fog and hence either incapable of violence or simply not inclined in such directions.

But my acquaintance here, the merchant who calls himself Arkola, was very much inclined.

"So!" he shouted into my face as he took my poor garment in his hand and virtually hoisted my feet from the ground. "It *is* you! I have you at last, thieving sorcerer!"

I tried to disengage myself, not alone because of his words, but because of his breath as well. My own, I know, is foul, but it is a foulness to which I have grown accustomed and which therefore no longer troubles me overmuch. His, however—

But of course, Your Lordships. I understand. Such details are not relevant, I agree, and I will not trouble you with them further. I will only state that, regardless of his claims, I did not recognize him, and I still do not. I thought he must certainly have mistaken me for some villainous person who resembles me in some small way, or perhaps he was simply mad. There was certainly a look of madness in his eyes and the strength of madness in his hands. I have known madmen in my day, though none with his peculiar brand of madness, so I am sure you can understand my reasons for struggling.

"Who are you, sir?" I asked, though I may not have phrased it so properly in the heat of the moment.

"My name is Arkola," he said, shaking me in his fury, "as you well know!"

Well, of course I did not, but I could see, even in my mildly besotted state, that he was not open to a rational discussion of his beliefs. Even so, what could I do but state my own ignorance of his meaning?

But that, as you may have surmised, was not satisfactory. He neither loosened his hold nor changed the formidable set of his features. He merely turned me in his grip and directed my quaking gaze toward a nearby spot on the ground. To my surprise, there in a darkness lit only by the distant torches of the fair, was my friend, my four-footed companion of this last year. He seemed none the worse for his recent absence, nor even the slightest bit regretful, though I fancied I could discern a touch of apprehension in his eyes as he gazed unblinkingly at my captor and myself. Perhaps he sensed the danger, as wild creatures are known to do, or perhaps it was my own fright that was reflected there.

"Do you deny," my captor near shouted, gesturing toward my friend with his free hand, "that yonder creature is the selfsame one you stole from my household in Audris only this past summer?"

At that point, Your Lordships, I began to realize that, even though this man was indeed mad, he may not have mistaken me for another. For I had indeed been in Audris at the time he claimed. And it was indeed during my sojourn in Audris that my four-footed friend first attached himself to me. But steal him? Never, Your Lordships, I assure you! I am a beggar, not a thief. If those I approach choose not to heed my pleas, I say no more.

And how, I ask you, could one such as myself steal a creature such as that? I have no house in which to imprison it, nor even a cage or leash, so it is free to come and go as it wishes, now as always.

The truth of the matter is, this poor creature was quite literally hurled out through the door of some fine home in Audris to land, trembling, at my feet as I chanced to be passing by. Accustomed as I was to being treated in such a way myself, I of course paused to offer what comfort I could, kneeling down and stroking its fur. Before I could do more, however, a man and woman appeared in the door. They were dressed in a manner befitting the house, which is to say, most well and expensively, but their shouts at each other would have done justice to two like myself battling over a discarded crust of bread. I remember nothing of what they said, if I apprehended their meaning at the time. I only remember their fury, which seemed directed not only at each other and the creature one of them had just pitched into the street, but at everyone and everything in this world and the next. The woman, I recall, gestured toward the animal as she screamed, and the man turned from her, his face seeming purple with rage, and stalked toward where I still knelt with the animal.

I knew not what his purpose might have been, but I knew from sad experience that such anger cannot portend well for such as myself. Hence I scrambled to my feet and was gone, scuttling down the street and through an alley as rapidly as I could, not once looking back to see if I was being pursued. It was only when my breath gave out, and then my legs as well, that I paused. Neither the man nor the woman, I was overjoyed to see, was anywhere in sight.

The animal, however, was only a few yards distant, sitting quietly and watching me. He was not even, so far as I could perceive, breathing hard, and as I looked at him, he came slowly toward me and began to nuzzle at my legs.

Now I swear to you, Your Lordships, that that is all I did. I will admit that this merchant Arkola might indeed be the man from that fine house, though I would never in my life swear to it. That other man was well fed and florid of face, while this gentleman is lean and pale and not nearly as richly dressed, but for all I know, they could well be one and the same. And, since he claims to have recognized both the animal and myself . . . well, how am I to deny it?

But that is *all* I can in good conscience admit to the possibility of. I did *not*, as he so angrily stated, scoop the animal up in my arms, nor did I, as I ran, hurl magical curses at him. In my somewhat less than robust state, I barely had the strength to carry *myself* away from those angry shouts. I certainly could not have borne the extra burden he claims, nor would I have had the breath to shout *anything*. Had I known magical spells, I would have used them to lend wings to my feet, nothing else, but alas, I knew none then, nor do I now.

If I did, I assure you, I would not have submitted as I did when he came for me last night, nor would I be here before you. I would—

Yes, Your Lordships, I heard his charge, that even though I may not have cradled the animal in my arms as I ran, my magic bound it to me, forcing it to follow my retreating footsteps. But I ask you, could even the most accomplished of wizards cast *two* spells simultaneously? One to force a recalcitrant animal to race after me, and yet another to bring ruin and calamity on the head of a merchant whose very name I did not know? And do I look as if I have magic at my beck and call? Would I dress as I do, in little better than rags? Would I linger on the fringes of the fair, among others such as myself, or would I have long since cast the spells necessary to raise my station in this world?

And would I have allowed this furred creature whose destiny and movements he claims I control—would I have allowed him to come face to face with the one from whom I stole him?

No, I have no magic, I fear. And I have my doubts that even magic would be sufficient to control this creature. As I have stated before, Your Lordships, he is as independent as any human I have known, and I suspect he has followed me only because he recognizes in me a kindred soul, one who sups on the scraps the rest of the world discards and who yet finds occasional small reasons for rejoicing.

As for this man's woes, which he claims with great bluster are the fault of my spell, I can do little but deny it. I have never been a merchant, though in years long past I have worked for such as he. Worked for them and then been cast aside, I would add, just as my four-footed friend seemed to have been cast aside, and often with equal roughness. His perfumes, he says, have lost their allure. Some even developed a scent more suitable to a gutter than to a gentle lady's person, he says. If I were he, Your Lordships, as of course I am not, I would look not to some stray beggar glimpsed during a moment of anger, but to those from whom I obtain my ingredients. Or I would look to my instruments, whatever they might be, that I employ in the manufacture of what I sell. Or even to myself. There is, after all, the matter I alluded to earlier, Your Lordships, the fact that the fumes that emanate from the good Arkola's mouth could not be fully disguised by the strongest of his perfumes. But, truly, I know nothing of such matters, and even less of magic.

Yes, I realize that, even as Your Lordships' esteemed

representatives came upon us, I was indeed chanting and cavorting and making strange gestures in the air, but I assure Your Lordships it was not what it seemed. I was simply defending myself to the best of my ability.

No, not by magic, Your Lordships, even though I understand that such a use is permitted under your gracious rules. What happened was this, if you will allow me to continue.

As I have already given account, this merchant who calls himself Arkola set upon me without warning. It seems that he had spied the animal his wife had expelled from their house a year past—expelled it over his objections, he now claims, although if that person I saw was indeed he, there seemed to be no love lost between himself and the animal. Nor, I daresay, between himself and his wife, who is, he claims, no longer with him. Whether he blames that on my sorcery as well, he has not said.

Very well, Your Lordships, I will continue apace. This gentleman spied the animal and recognized it as his own and then followed it as it made its way back to me. Then, with a grip so tight as to make my head spin, he told me this mad tale, of how I had, for no explicable reason, stolen the animal from him and, even as I ran, cast a spell upon him, a spell that soon brought his ruin.

I denied it, of course, as I deny it now to you, but he would not listen. He would have nothing but that I lift the spell. Which, as Your Lordships will easily apprehend, would be a most difficult task for one who has not so much as made the acquaintance of even the lowliest of wizards.

But what could I do? There was blood in his eye, and there would surely be blood on his hands—blood that had once coursed through my own veins—if I did not attempt what he commanded. To cry for help would have been less than useless, for who would take sides with one such as I? To resist, I had already discovered, was useless, for his strength was more than a match for mine. As I was dragged through the sleeping crowd and then past the shuttered stalls of the fair itself, I came to realize that my only chance to escape whole from this seeming madness was to pretend to acquiesce to his demands. I could not, of course, cause his perfumes to lose their stench, any more than I could remove the stench from his breath, but as long as I continued the pretense, I could at least count myself among the living.

Hence, once he deposited me in front of his own stall, its wares fully displayed and yet untouched by either purchaser or thief, I began my charade. Claiming that the removal of a spell was more time-consuming and more difficult than the casting, I took my time and studied his merchandise, even sampling those he said were the worst affected. And as I did, I took heart, for the odors did not, in truth, seem all that different from those that my nostrils had experienced in the past when fine ladies stepping down from their carriages paused to bestow upon me some small measure of largess.

Perhaps, I reasoned, the stench of which he so bitterly complained was not in his wares, but in his mind. And his own breath, which was no illusion, could surely have driven prospective purchasers to flee, regardless of the quality of his merchandise. Or his own sharp tongue, if what had assaulted my ears in those few seconds on the steps of his home were typical of what it produced.

Therefore, if he could only be convinced that the spell had been lifted, when in truth it had never existed, the true aromas might once again become apparent to him. His other difficulties, if indeed they existed outside my own desperate imaginings, would not be remedied, but if he were enabled to once again apprehend the true scents, that might be enough to persuade him to release me in no more a battered state than I had already achieved.

Thus, as Your Lordships can well imagine, my performance lacked nothing in boldness. My hands wove arcane patterns in the torchlit darkness, and my voice called upon the Three Lordly Ones and Thotharn and all the others, both real and imagined, that my poor mind could summon up.

And that, Your Lordships, is the end of my tale and my defense, for that is where your esteemed representatives came upon us. I, for one, was overjoyed at their arrival, even though their manner was justifiably harsh and their accusations strong; for I knew that, once I was allowed to present my humble story to Your Lordships, justice and common sense would prevail, and I would have nothing to fear.

Ah, my friend, it is good to be beneath the open sky once again, is it not? And it is good that you still choose my company over those with which you disported yourself at the fair.

But might I ask you to be a trifle more wary in future times? I know it is foreign to your nature to bend to another's will, but I feel we would both gain advantage were we to keep both the city of Audris and the person of Arkola at a modest distance. Even though Their Lordships appeared to believe my protestations of innocence, I doubt that the unfortunate Arkola was overly impressed. And, though he was declared outlaw and therefore fair prey for all who might feast upon him, I have little doubt that he will extricate himself in due time. And beyond the precincts of the fair, he may well, if given the chance, attempt to renew our acquaintance, a prospect I do not cherish in the slightest.

But tell me, my friend, is it possible there was a grain of truth buried in the good Arkola's seeming madness? Not that I myself have come to believe in those foolish chatterings that spouted so volubly from my desperate tongue, nor do I truly attach any magical significance to the spastic gyrations with which my limbs sought to accompany them. No, those were indeed no more than what I told Their Lordships, chance inventions designed solely to preserve my own hide.

But you, my friend, you are perhaps a different matter. If the unfortunate Arkola is indeed the one whose wife pitched you into the street, and if his story of this last year is to be believed, then truly his fortunes have turned precipitously downward, beginning with that very day. And since I know that *I* was not the cause, I must look elsewhere—if, of course, a cause indeed exists.

And my own fortunes, though not to be compared with those of the estimable Arkola before your sudden departure, have certainly been much improved during those selfsame days and months. It seems that I have suffered fewer indignities than in previous years. Fewer indignities and fewer injuries offered by those who are offended by my mere presence or by my simple requests for the use of some small item for which they themselves no longer have need or use. Fewer nights when my belly has growled with hunger, certainly, unless my memory is playing me false.

And the way you peer at me now, I do not recall the like of such a gaze from other four-footed creatures, not even others of your own kind. Are you amused at my ramblings, my slow-wittedness?

Could you be a talisman of sorts, a living repository of minor magics bestowed upon you by your past associates, before the lamentable Arkola? Does luck travel with you, leaving its obverse in your wake?

Or could there be more? Could you be more knowing and more devious than I give you credit for? Your finding of your former companion, who was only one merchant lost among endless throngs of such men—was that sheer chance? And was it sheer chance that his eyes were so sharp as to spy you out in the shadows? Was it sheer chance that his feet were so swift and sure as to carry him unerring in your wake as you darted between legs and under tables and through stalls?

And was there an air of smugness even more pronounced than usual about your furred features when Their Lordships' minions laid hands on us both? And do you think I did not observe your casual-seeming attention to Their Lordships while we stood before them, waiting for their judgment? Yours and that of your other friend that I spied peeping through the door more than once during the telling of my tale? Were those merely your normal disdainful observations of we lesser creatures with whom you deign to associate on occasion? Or were you perhaps . . .

Ah, I see you tire of this discussion. You are restless once again, as am I. And we should be on our way, true enough. The unfortunate Arkola, though declared outlaw by Their Lordships, will doubtless emerge with his life and more than sufficient strength to throttle either of us, were he ever to lay eye or hand upon us.

And do you have a preference as to the more attractive compass point? Away from the road to Audris, I have little doubt, but beyond that—

Ah, so *that* was the source of your restlessness, another struggling morsel you wish to lay at my feet? Is this your way of rewarding me for my part in the downfall of the miserable Arkola? Or perhaps your way of objecting to my worthless speculations, your way of proving that you are, after all, merely a cat?

Ah, well, it matters not. I have the feeling that, no matter what your true nature, we two may be bound together for some time yet to come. Bound by choice, I hasten to say, with which we are both so richly endowed, are we not, my friend?

FLARRIN RED-CHIN

M. Coleman Easton

Flarrin the basket-weaver fingered her purse solemnly as she watched the crowds stream past her stall. Since arriving at Ithkar she had three times reduced the price of her wares, but business continued to be slow. Most fairgoers, it seemed, had brought their own baskets with them. Flarrin noticed two nomad women strut past, balancing their loads on their heads. With a professional eye, she studied the graceful lines and the evident strength of their hampers. These dark-eyed women had no use for Flarrin's cruder work.

A neatly dressed townsman slowed and approached the cookstand with which Flarrin shared space. The customer fumbled for his purse while trying to hold several bolts of cloth he had tucked under his arm. Flarrin wondered how he would juggle his purchases while he devoured his grilled sausage; surely he would not lay them on the muddy ground.

"Two coppers!" the young woman shouted suddenly while

she held out a broad-mouthed basket. The townsman shrugged. "One and a half!" she suggested. To her relief, he nodded.

Better to sell at any price, she thought. She watched the satisfied customer licking grease from the fingers of both hands while his cloth rested safely in the basket at his feet. Then she glanced at the grizzled beard and tired eyes of her friend Jejnon as he stoked the fire under his grill. The two vendors had come down the Western Road together from their small mountain village, Jejnon because he made the trek every year, Flarrin because she was leaving her birthplace forever.

The basket-weaver turned to seek a new prospect in the crowd. Her voice was growing hoarse after a full ten-day at Ithkar. She smoothed her simple skirt, straightened her slim frame, and tried to put a cheerful expression on her face. "Two coppers!" she shouted again. A limping woman raised her eyebrows but walked on. "One and a half!" The woman was already out of earshot.

Flarrin's chin began to itch in its customary painful manner, and she thought once more about the potion-makers and wizards who were known to frequent the fair. She had been waiting, counting her coins. If she could sell a few more baskets, she told herself, she would seek aid that very day. For she had come to Ithkar with two goals.

First, she would find someone to cure the affliction that forced her to scratch her small chin until it was raw. Minor though it seemed to others, this condition had caused her much suffering. She had been taunted for it since childhood; in recent years, she blamed her diseased appearance for keeping away all suitors. For though she was not unattractive, what young man would express aloud an interest in Flarrin Red-chin?

Her parents were dead, and her peers knew her only by that horrid name. Why, she asked herself, should she remain in the mountains? Once she found the suitable salve or spell, her plan was to make her way downriver through the Ith Valley and settle in a town that needed a basket-weaver. In the absence of her affliction, or anyone who knew of it, she hoped to find a new life for herself.

Flarrin saw a young couple in the crowd, each carrying small household items. She touched her amulet for luck and cried out to them. The laden girl turned and smiled; her man nodded assent. Flarrin grinned as she made another sale. Again she felt the weight of her purse. Soon, she told herself.

By late afternoon, she had sold six more baskets; at last she felt ready to seek out her healer. Leaving the rest of her wares in Jejnon's care, she hurried to join the fairgoers. The first days here she had been so tied to her stall that she had seen little beyond her baskets. Now she wandered past rows of weavers with their clacking looms, heard hammering cobblers, breathed the sawdust smell from cabinetmakers. Her village possessed simple artisans, but no craftsmen like these.

She passed stalls where men and women discussed goods she had never before seen. Of what use, she puzzled, was such elaborate cutlery? And why would one need so many kinds of drinking glasses? She shook her head and considered again her plans to settle in the lowlands. She had much to learn of town ways.

All the while she walked, she was heading away from the temple and toward the outskirts of the fair; she knew that the practitioners she sought were not welcomed by the fairwards. Nonetheless, many potion-makers carried on a surreptitious business at Ithkar. She hoped that at least one of them knew more than the healer in her village.

Once more, her fingers found the amulet that hung from a thong about her neck. She lifted it out and gazed at the piece she had carried since childhood. Her father had been a fine carver; this birchwood swan with its outstretched wings seemed almost to have life. Flarrin touched the bird once to her lips, then let it slip back between her small breasts. Bring me the luck of the Three, she thought.

Skirting the displays of glassware and lamps, the basketmaker realized that she had reached the last of the booths. Behind them she came on a row where battered wagons stood in disorderly array. Here the ground was slimy with spilled slops and stank of men and animals. Tentcloth stretched on hoops concealed the wagons' contents; she heard muffled voices from within speaking a tongue she could not comprehend. Was this the place Jejnon had told her about?

With her chin itching furiously and her arms covered with gooseflesh, she dared walk past the weathered wagons. What should she look for? There would not be a signboard. She peered into one opening and glimpsed a kneeling woman whose gray hair streamed down over her face. At once there was a shout, and someone raised a blanket to conceal whatever the woman was doing. Flarrin shuddered and hastened her steps. Perhaps she had misunderstood Jejnon's directions.

"Come here, young lady. I have just what you need," sounded a voice from within the hollows of the final wagon in the row. The lampmakers' stalls, with their comfortingly familiar displays, were not far off. She could hurry back to them before the man spoke again.

"I can see your trouble from here," said the deep voice. "Why don't you let me help you?"

Flarrin hesitated. A hand emerged from the gloom, and then she saw a squat figure beckoning. Now the sun had fallen below the tips of the palings that bordered the fairground. The wagon was in shadow, and the young woman could discern only the speaker's heavy brows and broad, thick lips. Overcome by curiosity, she stepped closer, until she could smell the heady odors of the dried herbs that hung within the wagon.

"Your problem . . ." the small man said with an accent she couldn't place. "Tell Pino. The trouble, it is in your face, but I can't tell you more."

"It's my cursed chin!" she shouted suddenly, unable to contain herself. "The itch won't let me sleep, and the soreness gives me the look of someone afflicted."

"Chin! Chin!" said Pino with surprising glee. "I am the specialist in chins here."

Eager as she was, Flarrin did not believe her luck could be that good. She considered fleeing at once, but the man's voice made her feel oddly safe.

"I am no horseleech," Pino insisted, "but a serious student of the maladies that afflict us. Come. I charge nothing for a consultation. If my cure fails, you do not pay me."

Flarrin nodded weakly and waited beside the wagon while the little man rummaged within. One part of her wanted nothing to do with this sordid place. And yet she had come so far to seek her cure. . . . If Pino could not help, then she did not know where else she might turn.

"A moment longer and I'll be ready," the man called. She heard a clattering, and then he emerged carrying a small carved wooden box. Though she had spent many hours in her father's shop when she was young, she had never before seen such peculiar, twisting patterns as decorated this piece. "I will take a little time," Pino said, "but you can be sure I'll get to the answer this way. Now you tell me if your problem gets worse.'' Pino brought the box closer to her chin. The itching had ceased for now, and she wondered if he had already found a solution. What if he offered a cure, yet asked a price beyond her means?

He took the box away, made more noises within the wagon, and then returned to repeat his earlier actions. Only on the fifth try was there a difference. As soon as the box neared her chin, she felt a furious itch. Pino clapped his hands but insisted on additional experiments. At last, when her patience was nearly gone, he pronounced himself satisfied.

''Then you have my cure?''

''Soon,'' he answered. ''But please . . .'' He slapped his hand against the wagon's hard bench. ''You wait here while I go see a friend.''

Reluctantly, Flarrin climbed up and sat in the uncomfortable place while Pino hurried off along the row of wagons. The little man looked back several times, as if afraid she might vanish in his absence. And he had reason to be concerned, she thought. Dusk was approaching, and the basket-weaver did not fancy remaining in this dark place much longer.

Pino returned quickly, accompanied by a pair of tall and dangerous-looking men. When she saw them, Flarrin was doubly eager to hurry back to the safety of Jejnon's cookstand.

''We'll go for a walk, young miss,'' said Pino. ''In order to know for sure what your malady is. I want you to be careful to tell me exactly when the itch gets very bad.'' Then one of the toughs offered clumsy assistance as she stepped down from the wagon. His breath reeked of cheap wine and garlic, and his clothes stank of manure.

She felt slightly more at ease when she realized that they were heading back into the main part of the fairground. Here torches and lamps were already being lit for evening. Yet there remained many shadowed places where a person might vanish. Her pulse raced with fear, though she still half believed that Pino meant to cure her.

"Remember," said the short man. "Only when the itch is strong." With the toughs flanking them, they toured the potters' stalls and lingered in the area where the most expensive wares were displayed. Flarrin felt a mild tickle but said nothing. Then they reached the perfume sellers, whose tiny vials commanded substantial prices. "Look around," Pino suggested.

The basketmaker found the perfumers' stalls uninteresting to look at. The smells fascinated her, but she could not think of wasting coppers on such luxury. Coppers? They probably wanted silver! Then an odd-looking fellow in a disheveled gown strode past. By his clothing he did not look prosperous, but he walked with a certain haughtiness that suggested a noble upbringing. Suddenly her fingernails were clawing at her chin.

Pino whispered loudly enough for his companions to hear. "The grimy one with the short beard!" At once, the toughs took off after the man who had started her itching. Pino remained with Flarrin while his friends followed the unwary stranger.

There was a gap between the stalls up ahead; then the three were in shadow. A cry rang out of "Thief! Thief!" Pino stood his ground for a moment, then took the young woman's arm firmly and began to run in the opposite direction. The basket-weaver's only thought was to flee with him. But a fair-ward was coming, his bronze-shod staff held ready to smash anyone who disobeyed. Pino released her and dodged to his right, but another ward blocked his way. Then Flarrin felt a harsh hand on her shoulder.

Several dark-garbed women were being held in the ante-chamber where Flarrin was taken. A fair-ward stood at the doorway while the women huddled together in a corner away from the single lamp. "So," said one on seeing the basket-weaver pushed into the room. "A palm reader by the looks of her. She chose the wrong place for that flam."

"Palm reader, my bony feet. She's a pickpocket. I can tell every time."

"They *hang* pickpockets," observed the first. "She's better off a witch even than a dip. Is that it, lass? Got caught casting a tiny spell?" The two began to laugh.

Flarrin wiped away a tear and said nothing. Her thoughts were in a scramble; she must prepare herself to face the judge. But even if she could tell her story exactly as it had happened, why should he believe her? Pino and his rogues were already having their say. If they could blame the whole incident on a friendless basket-weaver, they would surely do so.

Ithkar's justice was moving quickly that night, Flarrin discovered. The women in the corner were still discussing her fate when she was summoned before the fair magistrate. On the writing desk to his left stood a candelabrum, its three smoky candles dripping wax onto the scribe's ledger. Behind the magistrate stood a tall man wearing flowing yellow robes and a peaked silvery cap.

"State your name and origins," said the magistrate in a bored tone.

For a moment she could not find her voice. Her fingers trembled, and she sought the amulet for assurance. But when the fair-ward shook her, she answered quietly. The scribe leaned forward to catch her words, then dipped his quill and began to write.

"You are Pino's woman," the magistrate said, more in statement than question. The scribe continued writing.

"I am not," protested Flarrin in a strengthening voice. "I never saw the man before tonight. He promised to cure my . . . ailment."

"And what sort of ailment might that be?" The magistrate's expression suddenly turned to one of lecherous curiosity. The scribe held his quill in readiness, and the tall man took a step forward.

"I'm cursed by my chin," she said with a sob. "And because of it, I've been ruined by three scoundrels." She lifted her face, thinking he might see the chafed skin and take some pity on her. Or perhaps she would only provoke disgust. . . .

"Chin?" The magistrate's leer vanished, and for a moment he seemed unable to form his next question. Suddenly the yellow-robed man leaned forward to whisper in his ear. After a brief exchange, the magistrate looked up and barked an order to the ward. "Take her to be examined and bring her back when he's done with her." He pointed to a side room. A moment later, Flarrin found herself closeted with the man in the peaked hat.

"You . . . you're a mage," she dared say.

He smiled in an ugly manner. His pale beard, though neatly cut, smelled of cloyingly sweet perfume. One of his eyes studied her coldly, but the other was a featureless orb that shone like silver. "From your point of view, a most important mage," he said. "I have to advise the court whether you're guilty."

"And will you hear my story?"

"I've heard enough from your . . . companions. Let me see if I can come up with the answer my own way." On a table sat a polished wooden casket. He opened the lid and removed a small silk handkerchief that glowed redly in the lamplight. "Study this carefully," he said. Then he took the square away and turned from her briefly. When he turned back, he showed her two closed fists.

"I want you to tell me which holds the silk. Now to do this properly, you must have the image fixed clearly in your mind." Flarrin noticed that one fist was larger than the other, its fingers arrayed unevenly. "Think of the handkerchief," he ordered as he moved the uneven fist close to her chin and held it for several breaths. Then his fists traded places.

If her itch was to condemn her, then she would not give in to it. But she could not help squirming. He held his position, and at last she was obliged to scratch. "Good," he said. He opened the hand she had thought empty, the one close to her chin, and the balled silk fell out.

"Now let's try another," the mage said, showing her a mother-of-pearl button. This time she knew how to fool him. She would disregard his instructions and *not* think of the button. But how do you *not* think of something without, in fact, thinking of it? She bit her lip to keep from scratching but lost again. Her itch found the mother-of-pearl.

"No reason to prolong this," he said with another unpleasant smile. "Dowsers aren't common around here. And it so happens I have need of your talent tonight."

"Dowsers?"

He slapped her smartly across the face. "Vixen! Would you like me to charge you with use of unauthorized magic?"

"But . . ." The blow had caused more surprise than pain. She vowed not to let him see her tears.

"Maybe you are such a fool that you don't know what you've got. Where you come from, they probably think dowsing means finding water with a forked twig."

Flarrin shook her head. There was some kind of sense in his words. He had just proved to her that by thinking of something, the itch would tell her when she was close to it. Earlier, she had been concerned about money. Pino found that much out through his tests and tried to use her to find a heavy purse. Now this dishonest court mage had another purpose for her affliction. "All right," she said with a sigh. "What do you want of me?"

A leer crossed the mage's face for a moment, but then his expression darkened. "That, too, maybe. But later. What I want now is this." He took from the casket a large brooch on which a craftsman had portrayed the features of a woman. Flarrin could not say how this wonder had been achieved, but the face appeared like living flesh. The woman possessed a broad, pleasant mouth, high cheekbones, peaked eyebrows, and eyes with a curious, impish tilt. "Can you remember that face?" he asked.

To Flarrin, the features were so distinctive that she could still see them when he closed his hand. She nodded.

"Then find her for me. She is here, at Ithkar." He raised one hand and splayed his fingers. "I can sense that much. But I've had men looking to no avail. And I myself searched several times. . . ." His voice trailed off in a tone of despair that suddenly aroused Flarrin's sympathy.

"Your daughter?" she asked.

"Daughter? She's my wife." He put the brooch away. "Are you ready to go find her?"

"And if I succeed? Suppose she won't come with me?"

He gave a self-satisfied smile. "I have an arrangement with the fair-wards. When my servants need help, they merely call out my phrase. If you shout 'Silver-eye,' then someone will come to your aid at once."

"And what of my charges before the court?"

"They'll be dropped. Come. I must tell the magistrate now that I find you innocent. But before I let them release you, I need some assurance . . . that you'll do as you promised rather than run back home to the mountains. You'll leave me a bond."

"Bond?" Her hand moved to her purse. "All the money I have is here."

"A few coppers?" he said with a sneer. He pulled the purse from her hands and put it aside with a dull chinking of metal. "You must have something that means more than this to you."

Flarrin said nothing.

"Do you know the penalty I can ask for? You'll be stripped naked and whipped out of the gates. You'll lose whatever it is anyway." He held out his palm.

Still she said nothing.

"Then I have no choice. The court awaits my decision." He pushed her roughly toward the door.

"No." She reached for the amulet. "My father carved this. I've worn it all my life. . . . And I don't know if my dowsing really works."

"It will have to work now," he said with a final laugh as he continued to push her ahead of him. Then he took her arm and propelled her toward the scribe's desk. "And just in case you decide to run off anyway," he whispered, "I'll have the wards watching for you at every gate."

*   *   *

Flarrin was escorted roughly out of the court and back to the fairgrounds. The court's fair-ward gave her a last shove with his staff and laughed as she nearly stepped in a pile of dung. She was just outside the temple enclosure now and heard the clink of coins in a money-changer's box. Her chin felt numb.

Where ought she to search for the lost lady? Might she be here, right under her husband's nose? Flarrin had never seen this part of Ithkar. Past the money-changers sat vendors of rare objects and strange substances. On one table, illuminated by a pair of bright lamps, lay shards of twisted metal. At another stall, withered sacs hung from a transverse rod. These Flarrin guessed to be desiccated organs of small beasts. She shuddered and looked away. Still her chin felt nothing.

She closed her eyes and brought back the face from the brooch. Then she turned her head slowly, but not the smallest tickle arose. Perhaps the idea about her dowsing talent was a mistake after all. Her itching had always come and gone with seemingly no explanation. The mage might have been misled by an eagerness to find his wife.

Without thinking, her hand went to touch her amulet. When she recalled why it was absent, she nearly wept. Now she was a captive within the palings of Ithkar, held by the mage's invisible cord. Scarcely noticing her direction, she began to push through the crowds.

The face. Remember it, she kept telling herself. But her stomach was empty, and her chin itched as she passed a cookstand. How could she find her quarry if she was hungry? Her chin would merely lead her to the nearest foodstall.

With a sigh, she leaned down as if to fix her shoe. The mage had taken her purse, but she was not totally without funds. Unraveling a bit of her skirt's hem, she extracted one of her hidden coppers. At once she bought bread and cheese and began to eat while she walked.

A tickle came again. Had she been picturing the woman? she wondered. Flarrin stopped where she was and tried to ignore the jostling by passersby. Turning one way and then another, she felt the itch once more. But the direction her chin pointed ran straight toward the weavers' tents, and she saw no way through their closely packed row.

The crowds thickened as she tried to reach another footpath. Where she had hoped to turn, a wagon blocked the way. The fairgoers cursed the merchant who was unloading his goods at this hour; they surged about the wagon like stream water swirling about a boulder. Flarrin was pushed along with them, crushed by the packing of bodies. Then she realized that she was going under the belly of the wagon, for there was no other way to pass. She ducked her head and tried to keep her balance. One misstep, she knew, and she would be trampled here. And suddenly she was on the far side, spat out into a thinning and receding throng. She had missed her turning and could not go back.

She hurried forward, at last finding another path to lead where her chin had pointed. Here the traffic was lighter, and she could stop to seek her bearings again. But this time she found nothing. Had the lost wife moved, she wondered, or was she too far away now for the talent to work?

The basket-weaver pressed on, turning back to reach the area behind the weavers' tents. A stout man staggered toward her, and she smelled the reek of ale. "Join me for some 'freshment?" he said, trying to grab her arm. She dodged him and began to run. But when a fair-ward gave her a suspicious glance she slowed to a hurried walk.

"Some trouble?" said a hoarse voice as a hand grasped her arm painfully. She looked up into the ward's scowling face. "You'd better show me what you're hiding."

Flarrin was nearly out of breath. What had the mage told her about fair-wards?

"Now!" demanded the ward. He began to feel for hidden pockets in her clothing.

The young woman found her tongue. "Silver-eye," she said softly, and then repeated it louder. "I'm on his business."

The ward's expression suddenly changed from one of hostility to respect. "My mistake," he said quickly. He raised his staff in salute, nodded once, then turned away.

At last she reached her destination and paused to try her peculiar talent again. Nothing. In despair, feeling not a feather's tickle, she turned about slowly once more.

What if she failed in this foolish quest? The mage could do what he wished with her. Not only was her hope for a cure gone, but she would never reach the towns of Ith Valley. Perhaps, she thought bitterly, she should have endured the miseries of home.

She slapped her fickle chin. If it had once possessed powers, it was serving her no longer. She began to wander without thinking of where she was going. "Make way. Make way!" voices called. There was a rush of people as a horseman came past. Flarrin was pushed into the side of a tent and then knocked to the ground.

The horseman rode by, and the crowds moved off. Flarrin picked herself up and guiltily brushed her grimy hands on the cloth of the tent. A lantern seemed to be shining directly in her face. Then someone shouted a curse and shoved her out into the midst of the path. She hurried off, her cheeks burning with shame. And all because of a straying wife. . . .

At that moment, the itching returned. Which way? Quickly checking her directions, Flarrin found where the sensation was strongest. This time she did her best to run.

By the number of amorous sailors she passed, Flarrin knew she was near the docks. She was forced to dodge more than a few embraces. Fortunately, most of the men were too drunk to pursue her. One beardless youth persisted, however, and she raced around a corner before she was halted by a troupe of performers whose audience clogged the path.

She could lose herself in the crowd, she thought as she glanced nervously back. The youth was no longer in sight. The basketmaker threaded her way through the onlookers, aware only vaguely of the acrobats who leapt and tumbled in the clearing. All this time she had been trying to keep the face before her. Now, as she reached the far side of the crowd, her fingers suddenly flew to her chin.

Flarrin halted at once. She was breathing heavily and her heart was pounding. Here? she wondered. In front of her, a gaily checkered harlequin collecting offerings from the throng. The harlequin approached, and Flarrin's itch grew fiercer. The masked woman stepped right up to the basket-weaver, and yet Flarrin could not say by sight if this was the woman she sought. Hurriedly, she found another bit of copper in her hem and dropped it in the offered hat.

Now the basket-weaver could not decide what to do. Should she shout "Silver-eye" at the first fair-ward who passed and ask that he strip the woman of her mask? And what if she were mistaken? The prospect of seeing the harlequin suffer at Flarrin's orders was far from appealing. She remained watching as the costumed woman circulated through the crowd.

When Flarrin turned away, the itching ceased. When she faced the woman, and pictured the brooch, the sensation was maddening. How could she doubt the connection? Yet she hesitated to act.

The performers continued their show, but Flarrin took little interest. The acrobats used an unfamiliar trained beast in some acts. The small, crouching form would spring up onto one trouper's shoulders, stand, and leap over to another's. The manlike creature would then clap its floppy hands, eliciting cheers and shouts from the audience. But Flarrin's attention kept returning to the harlequin, whose only task seemed to be collecting offerings.

Again she held out her bit of copper. This time the masked woman paused. "Why have you been watching me?" she demanded in a loud whisper.

Flarrin stepped back in surprise.

"What is it you want?" the woman asked again, her voice and manner more refined than her dress and station would indicate.

"Do you . . ." the basket-weaver managed. "Do you have a husband with a silver eye?"

Suddenly the harlequin grasped Flarrin's wrist and pulled her aside from the crowd. The basket-weaver was ready to shout for the fair-wards. But it would hurt nothing to hear what her quarry had to say.

"He's no more my husband than you are," the masked one protested when they could speak in private. "He was married to another when he made his false vows to me. And now he wishes to hold me to his lies."

"Then you . . . don't want to go back to him," Flarrin said in a voice of misery.

"I'm not the whipped dog that crawls back to her master's bed. . . . No. And I shouldn't have dared to come anywhere near him. But my profession is healing, and I need ingredients that only can be purchased at Ithkar.''

''Healing?'' Flarrin's mouth fell open as she looked again at the costume.

''My supplier was delayed,'' the woman explained. ''I had to disguise myself while I waited for him; I was lucky to meet some friends who could help. But tonight, if the Lordly Ones bless me, I'll find my tardy herb-dealer and be finished here.''

Flarrin shook her head. ''Your husb—'' She corrected herself. ''The mage told me I have a dowser's talent. I promised to call the fair-wards if I found you.''

''How so?''

''By shouting 'Silver-eye,' they would know I was on his business.''

The harlequin pressed for more details. Flarrin hastily related the story of her plans and subsequent ill fortune.

''Then betray me if you must,'' said the masked woman throatily. ''Or earn a friend who can never repay you.''

''But I'm a prisoner here. Even if I give up the amulet— the one gift I have from my father—I won't get through the gate. He's got his wards watching for me.''

The harlequin smiled. ''I think you have other gifts from your father, though you may not be able to hold them in your hand. For one thing, I daresay he was a man of honor.''

Flarrin nodded and hung her head.

''I can put you in a costume that will get you past the gate,'' said the woman. ''I can do more than that. You told me you planned to go downriver. I'll send a bravo to escort you to Bear River Canal. Wait for me there and I'll join you at dawn.''

The basket-weaver stared at the mask and wondered why

she trusted this woman. She had trusted Pino, and where had that gotten her? But if she was planning to raise a shout, why were her lips pressed together?

"Come meet my companions," said the harlequin with a smile. "My name is Moravid."

Jejnon was just closing up his cookstand when she returned. He stared at her curiously but showed no sign of recognition until she spoke. If the acrobat's costume could fool her friend, then indeed it might get her by the wards.

"Flarrin, why are you dressed like that?"

"Better not to ask," she said. "If the fair-wards question you, just say I ran off and left all my things."

"Your baskets . . ."

"Sell them if you can. As for my belongings . . ." She shook her head sadly. He had a small trunk in his wagon that held her mother's cooking pots and a few pieces of clothing. "Give them to some poor woman of the village. I can carry nothing." She embraced the old man quickly, then hurried away before she could say more.

Moravid's bravo caught up with her, and they made directly for the main gate. "I'll collect my sword, miss," said the rangy warrior. "And a lit torch as well. Then we'll be off to the canal."

Re-armed, and with his brand held high, the bravo strutted toward the fair-wards who flanked the gates. Flarrin attempted to stroll casually behind him.

"Business must be slow this year," commented one ward as she approached. "You folks usually stay longer."

Flarrin had gone over her story with Moravid but wondered how badly her lips would tremble as she spoke it. "A lord hired me," she answered softly. "For a private performance."

"Private indeed!" the ward said with a leer. "Show us a handspring before you go." He stepped forward with a grin and blocked her path.

"Shall I tell Lord Gabensty why I was late?" she countered.

The ward shrugged and spat in the dirt. "Who needs a skinny doe like you, anyway? Your lord has peculiar tastes to my thinking." He glowered at her, then stepped aside. She felt all of Ithkar's eyes burning at her back.

But there was no challenge as they walked the moonlit path. Flarrin and the bravo reached the canalside dock and resigned themselves to a long night's wait. "It will help to pass the time," the warrior said, "if I sing a ballad or two."

Just as the sun cast its earliest light on the water, a pair of riders appeared on the path from Ithkar. Still arrayed as a harlequin, Moravid was flanked by a mounted bravo. And while the two approached, as if the moment had been prearranged, a raft slipped silently up to the quay.

The horses were taken aboard, and the two women followed. While the bravos walked back to the fair, the bargemen began to pole the craft along the narrow channel. A mist was rising from the water.

"I did well last night," said the healer as soon as they were under way. "I collected all the supplies I needed." She patted her bulging saddlebags. "My patients will be grateful that I took the risk."

Flarrin nodded, yet she did not share her companion's joy. Though she was heading at last for a new life, a tie with her past had been left behind; she could never retrieve it.

"Now tell me this," asked Moravid. "Do you still seek a cure?"

"My chin has caused me more trouble than you can know."

"Do you relish your work with reeds? There's always need for a basket-weaver, I suppose."

Flarrin looked sadly down at her hands. "These are not the nimblest of fingers. But I've no other way to live."

"Ah, but you do. Join with me. What better partnership than a healer and a dowser?"

"Do you know what you're saying?"

"You'll have more business than you can handle. Think of all the strayed animals, dropped rings, wandering children . . ."

"But dowsing almost ruined me, and nearly sent you back to Silver-eye."

Moravid peeled off her mask and stared at Flarrin from beneath the peaked eyebrows of her portrait. "Will you remain a basket-weaver after all?"

Flarrin frowned. All her life, her chin had tormented her. Now that she understood its purpose, could she learn to accept it? "I've a rare talent," she admitted in a low voice, "but one that can harm as well as help. You should be the first to agree that I mustn't misuse my gift."

"Then what will you do?"

The basketmaker thought again of her village, and of the day she had watched her father carving the birchwood swan. That morning, rough mountain men had approached him with handfuls of coppers. They had asked him to carve a demon's image to be used in an outlawed rite, and he had refused. And though the swan would bring no food to his family, he had labored over the amulet for an entire afternoon.

Now the amulet was gone, but her father's deeds could not be taken from her memory. "I have an answer," said the former basket-weaver suddenly. "I won't set myself up as a

143

finder of *anything*. I'll use my talent, but only when I'm satisfied the quest is an honest one."

"A good principle." Moravid began to smile.

Words came unexpectedly to Flarrin's lips. "Let this be my motto:

> "My name's Flarrin Red-chin.
> I'll find anything
> That's not better off staying hidden."

"Well spoken," said Moravid with a laugh as she clapped her friend on the shoulder. "Then partners we are—healer and dowser. I'm sure we'll do well together." Turning, she shouted, "Pole faster, bargemen! An extra five coppers if we reach the road by noon."

COVENANT

P. M. Griffin

The day was gloriously bright with just enough of a breeze that the temperature could not oppress busy people, and Roma rejoiced in its perfection, taking it as a fine omen of good fortune.

The wagons were halted before the gateway to the great Ithkar Fair while Jespar Mac Jespar, her father, gave over Clan Lorekin's weapons into the guardians' care and made the required but in their case unnecessary declarations as to their purpose, the nature of their goods, and the fact that they neither possessed nor had employed any magic to enhance their wares.

She smiled to herself. That was perfectly true. The birthright was but another sense, an adjunct to eyes and ears, albeit a most uncommon one and one best left unmentioned for the peace of mind of some of their more insecure patrons.

As usual, they were not held long with these formalities

and proceeded to their usual place, a prime site in the out-skirts of the temple precinct amongst those others dealing in small ornamentals and works of art.

Roma swung to the ground from the high wagon as lightly as if she were a cat.

"Everything seems in order," she said to her father, who had not bothered to climb back up beside her after leaving the gate.

"Aye, lass, though it would be hard for an empty space to be otherwise. See to the animals and start setting up while I take our thank offering up to the temple. It promises to be a good fair," he added. "Three days before the opening, and look at this crowd already."

The woman nodded and turned to obey, but her eyes were like twin spears of ice when she again faced the temple a few minutes later.

Thank offering! her thought crackled. "Not my portion, Sky Lords. I give no thanks and no offerings to any lying god, not ever again. That is another tax exacted by human greed, nothing more, and most unwillingly do I pay it."

The spleen soon left her. The Three Lordly Ones sparked little real feeling within her, although she had turned to them the previous year in her despair. They had always seemed more gods of the intellect to her, if divinities could be so described, than gods of the heart and had never penetrated very deeply into her inner core of believing. She had not even been too keenly disappointed when their promise had proven as false as the Mother's.

There was too much work to be done and too much need of haste for the clanhead's daughter to squander her energies on esoteric ponderings. Ithkar Fair might not officially open for another three days, but many of the merchants were here, and so, too, were many of their patrons. That was particularly the case in this section with its one-of-a-kind items and the play upon human vanity inherent in exclusive ownership.

The clan worked as a unit to set up their roomy stalls, a task thus soon accomplished, then each member went to his or his family's assigned place to unpack his own stock.

Roma's wares were figures, mostly human, but some animals and mythical beings, too, none larger than a man's hand. Each was utterly perfect in every detail. Each could truly be called magic, although not in the sense those at the gate used the term. She herself was charmed by them, and her fingers caressed every one lovingly as she set it in its place.

All of Clan Lorekin's displays were unique, but hers was exceptional even amongst them. None of the other stalls had anything like so many human representations, just as no one else received nearly as many requests for portrait dolls. All her kin possessed the birthright in full measure, but whereas they, as she, could read the memory for knowledge and detail that their varied arts might reproduce, Roma Ní Jespar alone could delve the heart for its dreams.

She hummed a snatch of a tune as she carefully lifted out her latest and currently her favorite piece from its packing.

It was a bard, a young man whose lute rested against his knee while he gazed into a half-filled wineglass, the strangest of smiles playing upon his lips, as if he contemplated some biting satire on the follies of mankind or a softer verse about some one of her sex who sparked his own. Perhaps his song was a mixture of both.

She touched the lute her uncle had wrought, a tiny marvel whose strings gave off the shadow of a sound if gently brushed, as if music itself could be miniaturized. . . .

"That is beautiful."

She looked up with a start to find one of the fair-wards standing before her. He was not one of those she knew from previous years, but then, some new men were hired for each fair.

This one certainly wore the uniform well. He had the body and stance of a warrior and the sternness of feature that was usually the mark of a man long accustomed to tightly ruling himself and, perhaps, others.

She frowned briefly. There was that in his carriage, too, which suggested that he might not only be able to wield a sword but also to command others who did. Why would such a one choose to put on the brass helm at Ithkar Fair?

She smiled, however.

"Which draws you?"

"All, lady artist, but I was speaking of the tune you were humming. I have not heard its like before."

"It's one of my own making."

Pleasure and anger both rose within her, but she was quick to quell the latter. He was not responsible. . . .

Their eyes met then, and she felt suddenly sick in her heart. She had hoped never to find another who knew this depth of desperation. Experience had taught her well that only pain could fire it, and she knew even as she recognized the surge of empathy rising within her that she could no more relieve it than she could her own.

It was an effort, but she made herself address him naturally once more.

"Can I help you, or perhaps one of my kin may?"

"You. Roma Ní Jespar of Clan Lorekin is famed throughout the fair for her portrait dolls. I would have one of these from you."

She looked at him in surprise and with some discomfort. Folk at Ithkar generally knew what lay within their reach. He had a strange accent, however, soft and easy on the ear but one she could not identify. Perhaps he truly did not know. Directness would be her most considerate approach, she decided.

"You do realize what's involved?"

He gave her a smile that was echoed in the stormy eyes. "I have never witnessed the making of the like, but, aye, master crafter, I do read your meaning. I can pay your fee, or believe I can. I did make inquiries before coming to you."

"What precisely is it that you want?"

"A young man, one month less twenty years, gold of hair, eyes blue like to your own, dressed in hunter's garb and armed with longbow and knife."

Roma named a sum.

He nodded. "Agreed, though from what I see before me, no amount of coin is truly a worthy exchange for your work."

His eyes fell, then rose but looked into some demon hole rather than at her.

"This is a grief gift for my mother, and if I fail in my errand, it will be the last thing she will receive from me and must thus serve as a remembrance of us both. See that you wrought well, lady artist."

By force of will, he caused the dark mood to clear from him. "When can we begin? You will need a description. . . ."

"Not now. My waxes aren't prepared. You're right that I shall require your presence, though. Can your duties be so arranged as to give you the morning free?"

"Aye."

She smiled. "Come at the first true light, then. I shall be ready for you."

Roma watched the fair-ward go. ''Mother, lift his grief,'' she whispered.

Nay! Never that again! Never would she make less of herself, beg, plead, implore fulfillment of a promise of aid from that one or from any other of her ilk.

This anger went deep, and she stood still while it flooded her, spirit and heart, mind and body.

No talent was made for a vacuum, but rather to enrich life, its possessor's and those of all around her, as the birthright enriched Clan Lorekin and everyone whose lives they touched. She would have been content with that, more than content, but, nay, another gift had been given her as well, a minor one, perhaps, but as much a part of her, as much a need, as this greater power of her hands and mind.

Songs sprang from her, not from her lips, for her voice was less even than mediocre, or from any instrument, but from herself. They were good, very good, but strange, and no bard to whom she had tried to convey them, the few who would give her any hearing at all, would accept them. She asked no payment, nothing but that they should be granted life and that her name should be put to them.

A mother seeks weal for the babes of her body, and so did she ache for the acceptance of these offspring of her soul. The longing for that fulfillment, that justification, was terrible in its strength and had been on her since before she had begun to change from child to woman. She had begged, crawled, for that boon, to meet with a singer who would accept even part, the smallest part, of what she hungered to give, until her heart was empty of hope and of all trust and respect for those upon whom she had been raised to rely in spirit.

Why this torture? Why bestow that which must ever lie maimed, stillborn?

The master crafter brought herself firmly under control. Very well. Devotion supposedly brought aid in need, and need of heart equaled that of body, but long years of pointless hope had taught her the lie of that claim.

Her face had become a hard mask.

She had not yielded to the ultimate cowardice of disbelief despite that. The Mother was real, right enough. She existed, but not as the benevolent power she chose to seem for some unfathomable reason of her own. She was crueler, more callous, than the vilest force she was supposed to oppose, monstrous in the falsehood she foisted upon those who truly loved and tried to serve her.

Roma would not feed that warped vanity again. She would not in word or deed attempt to lead anyone else into her awareness or her resolution even if she had to play the hypocrite to avoid doing so, for she would not force such pain on another sentient being, but she herself would no longer live by a covenant whose precepts she alone kept.

Roma Ní Jespar could no more do battle against her than could any other mortal thing, but compliance, willing cooperation, that she could and had vowed to refuse utterly, even to denying three good men already because she would not play the role assigned to woman in that one's plan for the continuation of life. If her womb were filled by some act of force, so be it, but it would be a tyrant's deed. She would give the Mother no conscious help, in this matter or in any other.

Her eyes were like wizard's fire, cold and dangerous.

There was more she could do, a way in which she might at last achieve her desire whether these supposedly beneficent divinities chose to help her or nay.

The priests of more than one belief came to Ithkar Fair,

and at least one of the alien gods they served was reputed to be quick in his response to his worshipers' call.

Thotharn was rumored to oppose both the Mother and the Three Lordly Ones, but that was no longer her concern. If they valued her worship or cared for her at all, they should have kept faith with her. When a merchant could not or would not supply what was required, one sought out the next stall whether the proprietor be an unfriend to the first or nay. So would she do now.

The price for going to this new god was reputed to be very high, but she knew that and consented to pay it. She had come to Ithkar this year with the firm intention of seeking out Thotharn's priest, and seek him she would, as soon as her duties here gave her the leisure to do so.

Night had fallen before Roma was able to leave her kin, ostensibly to walk the fair a little after this very busy day. Her heart was hammering wildly, and there was an almost hectic flush on her cheeks, but she held her head high, and her step was resolute.

She made her way as directly as she could without drawing attention to herself to the outer section of the fair, where a priest of Thotharn had set his dark, rich pavilion.

She did not pause even when she came within sight of it but walked straight to its entrance.

There, the woman stopped and gazed at that which was emblazoned upon it, a mask of exquisite beauty and workmanship, yet loathsome all the same to everything within her.

She steeled herself. She had known it would be thus. This was no light move that she contemplated.

She felt it then, or her birthright did and clamored warning of the influence, a drawing, a commanding to enter at once, before her purpose weakened.

Roma Ní Jespar stiffened and stepped back several paces in anger.

That was a mistake, a very bad mistake. Compulsion, attempted compulsion, was not the way to gain aught from her.

She straightened again. Thotharn's priest had erred, but it was not him with whom she intended to deal.

The master crafter reeled, almost went to her knees.

The blow did not come from the pavilion but from within her own self, a blinding flash of foreknowledge so sharp and stark and so absolute in its certainty as to well nigh numb her merely finite human mind.

If she went into that place, aye, she would succeed with her tunes, find fame for herself the like of which she had never even dreamed, but there would be no new songs. Never again would her soul stir with new life or glory with the strange rapture of creation.

Never again would her hands give form to tiny bards or to images that could draw a bereaved mother's tears at first and later give comfort to her heart. The birthright would still delve, her hands still mold and paint, but only darkness, corruption, would come from her, bribery and ill to others.

Roma stood poised but a breath's space; then she fled, or would have fled had pride and the will that still ruled her not held her pace to just under a run. Her soul she could risk or give, but not this other.

She slowed a little once she had left the outer section and again found herself within the main body of the fair, in the busy, lively middle section. She turned her face toward the temple and the place near it allotted to her clan.

The great building stood darkly against the starlit sky, and she glared balefully at it and at the heavens towering above it.

"Ye won this time," she muttered, savagely because of the fear and the sense of relief still on her.

The realization of what she had escaped came full upon her again, and with it the need for flight. The ground was much littered in this place, and she gave too little heed to her going. She stumbled, nearly went down, and would have gone down had a strong arm not caught and steadied her.

The master crafter murmured quick thanks and looked up to see the fair-ward who had hired her skills.

His hold loosened but did not entirely release.

"That was a wise choice, lady artist," he said gravely.

Had Roma been a woman like to faint, she would have done so then, but she merely drew one sharp breath and then answered him evenly since it was apparent that she had been seen.

"It was a fool's choice, perhaps, but it is mine, and I stand by it."

For all her firmness of voice, her legs felt unsteady under her, and she did not trust herself to draw away from his hold.

The man sensed her need. He deftly guided her toward one of the wineshops and commandeered a relatively quiet table on the outer ring of those set around it, his glare being sufficient to drive off two others who had been making for it. In another minute, a goblet wench had set a bottle and two glasses before them.

Roma emptied two goblets in quick succession before she felt enough herself to face her companion in something of her old manner.

"I don't even know your name," she began.

"Ruraí. It is a common enough one where I come from."

"And that is?"

"An island in the Western Sea. You would not know its name." He smiled. "You would probably call me a barbarian, although, of course, my people do not consider ourselves such."

"Your manner declares that you are not."

The woman did not want to discuss either what had happened or what might have happened, but neither was she eager to begin the walk back to her kinfolk.

That could not be helped.

"I keep you from your duties. . . ."

"My duty requires that I guard the treasures of this fair, its great artists."

She recalled how very nearly she had betrayed all that gave her claim to that title, and a sob she could not check broke from her.

His hand closed over hers, warm and firm. "Nay, lady. You were sore troubled, and your soul was pressed in hard war, but it conquered most completely. Rejoice in that, and do not think to weep. Come. I shall see you safely to your own place."

He smiled. "You must have rest, you know, if we are to work together tomorrow."

Perhaps the wine emboldened her, for her eyes raised and locked with his. "Ruraí, how come you to be a fair-ward?"

"I would not consent to walk without arms," he answered, "and this was the only way to retain them here."

Morning found Ruraí at Roma's stall.

"Are you still willing to work with me?" he asked.

"Of course. Sit you here in this chair by my workbench and describe your brother as closely as you can for me."

He obeyed, and the woman shut her eyes, listening intently.

When she thought the moment was ripe, she sought his mind, found and entered it.

She gasped. He was there, and consciously aware of her. He started in surprise, then laughed and bade her welcome.

So that is how you work so well! his thought exclaimed. *I imagined I felt something of power in you but could not identify it because it is somewhat different from that of my own clan.*

I do no hurt. . . .

None. Proceed, lady artist. I am as curious now to watch how you do this as to see your finished portrait.

The master crafter worked very swiftly, for with the birthright to guide her hands, there was no hesitancy or need for even momentary pause upon her. The wax almost magically assumed the likeness of a young man, and the paint whose mixing was as much a secret of Clan Lorekin as the birthright itself imparted fullness and seeming life to it.

Ruraí gazed into the still wet face when she held it up to him for his inspection, and he was forced to turn from her.

"Lady, such talent . . ."

He took hold of himself.

"This confirms both the strength of your power and your control of it. Will you give me your aid?"

"How?" the woman asked in amazement. "For what purpose?"

He looked at her in surprise. "You were within my mind."

"Not to read it, certainly not without your consent. That— that would be a violation worse even than the rape of a woman's body!"

"But you do read. . . ."

"I listen! My patrons struggle to convey their meaning through the very limited medium of words, aided, perhaps, by some poor miniature. I can hear the mind and the heart directly, but it is only to that which they wish to impart that I attune my listening."

He looked into her flashing eyes, and fire sparked in his own in response. "What a woman! With you to help me, I almost think I have a hope of winning!"

"You'll not have that aid without giving me more information," she pointed out.

"My story is brief. Better than two years ago, I returned to my parents' house with my newly made bride. It was a festive occasion, the more so because it was also my natal day, but all joy soured when a slate broke loose from the roof, striking and instantly slaying my young wife. The following year, last year, on that same date, a fire began in my brother's chamber which consumed him before it could be quenched.

"The magus of my clan is both strongly gifted and learned, and she was not long in determining that I did indeed lie under a black curse, as all were by then claiming.

"She could not free me of it. Her power was not sufficient and perhaps not her courage, either, though I, for one, cannot fault her if that last be true. No paltry wizard put it on me, but one older and stronger and more terrible than any mere human, one out of the dim past before even our legends took full form.

"She learned enough before being forced to break her search to tell me that a now nameless lord, whose line seed I am, defeated and chained that dark thing, which has at long last wakened again and has discovered its ancient foeman's line still lives. It has determined to annihilate every last drop of that blood, of which I am, apparently, the chiefmost representative, lest a second defeat be dealt unto it.''

''Why not strike you down first, then?''

There was no humor in the smile he bent upon her. ''I represent that long dead man to it. I must suffer the loss of all I love first, before going into doom myself.''

''Your own sword . . .''

He nodded. ''Before my next natal day if I fail here, but then the curse may merely settle on some other. Even were that not so, I prefer to front my foe, defeat it if I can, or at least perish trying if hope be only vanity.''

''That is why you needs must go armed?''

''Aye, though it is but a concession to my own fear. I well know that no sword or knife, much less a staff, will help me against this foe.''

''Your enemy's name?''

He shook his head. ''I know not, nor even its nature, save that it is far beyond ours or our ken.''

Roma was silent a long time. ''What would you have me do, Ruraí?'' she said at last. ''I am no wizard, no magus, no priestess, just a craftswoman with a gift that allows me to please my patrons more completely than most can.''

''Accompany me in mind. Not into battle,'' he hastened to assure her, ''just to the border of its stronghold. I have been able to trace it so far myself but have failed to locate any gate. Another's power linked to mine should enable me to do so or strengthen me enough to force an entrance.''

''Then?''

''This is my enemy, my fight, very probably my death or more than death. I bring no other into that. Only wait for me.

If I do return, it may well be that I shall lack the strength to come back into this waking realm on my own.''

He waited a few seconds, but when she did not speak, he started to rise. At least she had not refused him outright.

''It's no minor asking. Weigh it carefully and also the price. . . .''

''No price!'' the woman said sharply. ''I know not why I feel so, but I think it could be deadly to both of us if I went with you against such a thing for gain.''

She drew a deep breath. ''Aye, I will help you in so far as I can.''

''Gramercy, lady.''

''When?''

''My tour ends at midnight. I shall send my mind for you as soon as I can after that. Be in your cot, as if sleeping.''

''I'll be waiting.''

The new day was scarcely five minutes old before Ruraí came for her as he had promised.

''What now?'' she asked him.

''Just travel with me. I shall tell you when we reach the barrier, though doubtless you will realize that yourself once you see it. Gently now, and try not to fear. The paths we must tread are passing strange.''

That journey was eerie, and she did fear, but Roma Ní Jespar would not give terror any rein whatsoever as she forced herself to concentrate on that eldritch route; it might too easily prove that she would have to return upon it alone, or else bearing a burden incapable of giving her any guidance.

At first, it seemed that they but moved through the fair,

albeit with astonishing speed, but once they reached the outer section, they left it.

They left not only Ithkar but every other known place. It was as if they had leaped from her familiar, solid world into another realm entirely, and the master crafter trembled in her heart because she sensed that this was truly so.

All around them was light or mist or some impossible combination of both, so that nothing of the country, if country it were, was perceptible to her.

They traveled a long while thus before Roma became aware of a change, subtle at first but rapidly growing, a chilling, a darkening, a faint, noxious stench.

Ruraí stopped abruptly, and she with him. A vast patch, an infinity, of muddy blackness blocked all the way before them.

"Therein lies my enemy," the fair-ward said grimly.

The life pulse throbbed painfully within her. She understood. By all she once revered, she knew. . . .

"Ruraí," she whispered, "that is the lair of no elemental thing. It's a god that waits within, a god totally of the dark path."

He reeled as if struck. He had not guessed before but now knew that she must be right, all too terribly right. Scant wonder he had failed to pierce its—his—guards!

"It is hopeless, then. I am lost, and all mine with me."

The woman's head lifted. A god, and a vile one, but they were all that in one sense or another.

To her surprise, she found that she feared this unknown being less than she would have dreaded a confrontation with the Mother. There was no betrayal here, no pretense of benevolence, no lie, nothing but the avowed intention of destruction, the corruption, the warping inevitable to and inherent in all true evil.

"We can front him, at the least, brand him with the knowledge that his stronghold is not inviolable, mayhap put our mark on him. Your ancestor did more than that, after all."

"Not we, but I alone. . . ."

"Nay. I'll not stand here, shaking in terror at what might come ravening out to claim me. I, too, shall face my fate down."

So saying, she swept past him so that he must follow after her, and the barrier that had held the man back gave way before her, for her hate and bitterness were founded upon the violation of what had been deep trust, while that opposing her was without true cause, merely the hatred of life and of all things free and clean.

All inside was filth, spiritual muck. The air was foul, a palpable mist more than half slime. It soiled their souls and would of a certainty have slain their bodies had they ventured here in physical nature.

They halted, waiting. Both knew they were not alone within the canker.

Another was coming. They could feel him draw nigh, an immense, awesome presence of destruction only, desolation given volition, and despite themselves, each clung to the other. They had come for this, but now that the moment was nigh upon them, both knew they could not succeed.

Then Roma saw their foe and recognized him. His face was so beautiful in its reality as to wake her every longing, so corrupt as to wrench the stomach within her, so tragic in the twisting of the potential of what might have been had this entity given his will to the light that she could nigh unto have wept for grief.

Thotharn laughed. They felt that, although his expression did not change.

Without word or sign or forewarning of any sort, he reaised his hand, and a scarlet stream of liquid flame roared toward them.

Ruraí's will rose up, met and scattered it into a shower of sparks.

The next thrust he likewise parried, and the next.

He missed that following in his concentration upon screening his companion, but Roma had seen how he fought, and, although she was no more a warrior in spirit than in body, she interposed her own schooled will as their defense until he should recover himself.

Thotharn was growing angry. He disliked that his power should be resisted by two contemptible mortals. She read that and gloried in it but knew their defense could not hold forever, nay, nor hold very much longer. His strength was as near to infinite as mattered, and theirs must all too soon fail. She hoped that when it did, they would fall together, for she found she did not want to see Ruraí brought down.

At least the woman could be certain their defeat would be into death only. Their souls were their own, and those could not be taken from them. So much of the victory, they would denty Thotharn.

If only they could have a little more! She wished that they might at least score him, but they had no strength even to break through the guards he had set about himself.

I hope you are watching, Mother, her mind hissed. Two of your creatures are fighting here in a battle beyond our strength, a battle that should by rights be yours, because no shielding was given when your kinsman persecuted this good and innocent human being.

She laughed aloud, and such was the contempt revealed in it that the battle for an instant halted between god and man.

Aye, your kinsman I name him, and your liege lord, perhaps, since he pulls down what you claim to build and love, yet you do naught even when it is impossible for lesser things to resist him, though they fight your war for you!

Something filled her, thought, knowledge, as she had been given knowledge before the pavilion of Thotharn's priest.

This being was not death. His canker stronghold was not death. They were something far less. Death was part of life, and life was so infinitely stronger than their mere negation that it would rend and cleanse this place utterly were it ever to gain entrance here.

They were life! She and Ruraí were life and the storehouse of life! They—they were the focus, the channel, for life's power in the realm into which they and their kind had been set!

The dark god caught her thought and literally flung himself at her.

He could not reach her. A wall, a burning light, seemed to have risen up around her.

It was about Ruraí as well. His mind was feeding hers.

They were life's channel, aye, but they were not life itself, not wholly. All their realm had claim to that.

The sea was life, and her waves could cleanse. The wind was life, wind that swept mists away. The soil was life, supporting and feeding. The sun was life, with its light that cheered and warmed and quickened every living thing beneath its care.

She named them, and Ruraí echoed the naming, and as she

163

spoke, it seemed that each force came to them, and other forces subservient to these greater ones with them, and a vast, vast wailing filled their minds and then their very souls until they fell numb with the depth of its terror, and a merciful and caressing darkness came around them to give them release.

Roma awakened with an aching head and a body as sore as if it had been beaten.

Her night clothing was clammy with sweat, and she was glad to strip it off and wash, wash the last remnants of the horror from her.

She dressed, then suddenly her knees threatened to give beneath her, and she staggered to a stool fortunately near to hand.

Full memory was hers again. Ruraí? How was he? Where was he? She recalled how he had stood, pitting his man's strength against that of the dark god, striving as much to shield her as to cover himself. If he had not returned, or had returned blasted . . .

She heard him, not his mind-call, but his voice. He was waiting outside the stall.

"Roma! Will you sleep the day away?"

The woman darted from the resting area.

He was clad in his fair-ward's uniform and, except for a pallor and strain still on him, seemed none the worse for their dire night.

He looked better than ever before. The clouds were gone from his eyes now. They laughed and were glad, as she knew they were meant to be.

"I am pleased to find you well, lady artist," he said

gravely. "There was apparently some great upheaval last night while we slept."

"Sit. Tell me what's happened here while you examine the portrait doll. I finished the outfitting of it yesterday after the paint dried."

He obeyed, lowering his voice when he spoke again. "The temple is like to a hive. Vast amounts of power exploded suddenly over the whole fair area. The priests cannot find the source of it but are blaming Thotharn's followers since the whole of it seemed to settle upon them. The chief priest is dead. His two foremost assistants would be better so, for no remnant at all of a mind remains to either of them. The lesser followers have all fled."

He nodded when her eyes closed. "They were evil and espoused an evil cause, but aye, it was hard seeing what they have become."

"Does anyone suspect us?"

"No one. All the fair-wards are conducting searches and asking questions, but no one saw or sensed anything, not even your kin, whom you may be sure I have read. Their rest was not troubled."

"What—what of—him?"

"Thotharn is hardly dead, but rest assured that we shall be free from his attentions from now on, and I think he will walk far more carefully in his efforts against humankind from this time forth."

He stopped speaking for a moment, then looked at her steadily. "We wrought well together, you and I."

The woman's eyes turned downward. "We did," she agreed softly.

"Could you leave your kin to dwell with me amongst mine? Your arts would be thrice welcome, this of your hands and the other. You will find our bards are more open of mind than are those of the mainland.''

She flushed, but there had been much unavoidable sharing between their minds last night. . . .

Roma loved the people of Clan Lorekin, loved the place she held amongst them, the place her talent had earned. Her eyes met his, however, and she knew her heart's answer.

If it were truly possible and not only a dream of no hope.

He caught her hands as his mind read her doubt.

"I am no lord or lord's son. My mother-brother is indeed chieftain, but I am nothing more than captain of his forces. My bride will of a certainty be well served, but if she chooses to follow her art as a profession and no mere whim and to bring her work to Ithkar Fair each year, it will be no mark on my house but a blessing to it. I have said that my folk value the gods' great gifts and those bearing them.''

She came into his arms then, although strangers were nigh and her kin looked on.

Aye, she would go with him, and she would be his wife in all the fullness of that state.

Her eyes flew skyward for a moment, as they had always done when she had formally addressed the great Lady.

The Mother had fulfilled her pledge in the end, in the opening of the knowledge Roma had needed and used, even in the fostering of the bitterness that had given her the strength to wield it, to act as she had during all her grim adventure. There was, in truth, a covenant between them, and she would hold to her part of it while life and the power to do so were in her.

WHAT LITTLE GIRLS ARE MADE OF

T. S. Huff

The two oxen stopped in front of the gates of Ithkar Fair wearing what could almost be termed relieved expressions. The brightly colored wagon they pulled was not that large, but the old woman who held the reins was immense. Great swooping curves of flesh wrapped her about. From the thick gray braid around her head to the red sandals on her feet, there wasn't an angle of any kind left on the woman's body. The yards of red-and-yellow cloth she wore did nothing to minimize her size.

She looked down at the fair-ward approaching the wagon and chuckled, a sound that involved her whole body. "So, Font, once again you manage to be at the gate when I come to the fair. How do you do it?"

Font, a giant in his own right, although his size owed nothing to fat, returned her smile with a slow one of his own. "Morron owed me a favor, Aunt Arra. I used it." She was not his aunt, but for years the children of Ithkar Fair had used the title, and Font had grown up at the fair. "Hello, Elaina." This to the girl who had peered around her grandmother's bulk to see what was going on.

"Good morning, Font." Violet eyes looked down at him through long, dark lashes. "You look very nice in your uniform."

The fair-ward stammered something unintelligible, and a red flush rose from his collar to the edge of his brass helm.

"Tease," her grandmother admonished, and tugged gently on a golden braid.

"She reminds me," called a voice from the table beside the gate, "of someone I knew, oh, many, many years ago."

"Cortaynous?" Gray eyes widened within the folds of fat. "Cortaynous, you old coot, I thought you shriveled up and blew away years ago."

The old wizard laughed. He was so thin and wrinkled it did indeed look as though a good blast of wind would be the end of him. "And I thought you had decided to end your days in some backwater village. You'd better search her, fair-ward. It looks to me like there's smuggling being done under that tent she's wearing."

"Oh, no, sir," Font protested, "that's all Aunt Arra."

Elaina muffled a shriek of laughter, and Arra buried her head in her hands and shook. Which was something to see.

Font turned from the two women to the wizard, his pleasant features drawn in puzzlement. "What did I say? Did I say something wrong?"

Arra wiped her streaming eyes and patted the young man comfortingly on the shoulder. Font was one of the best fighters and most good-hearted people she'd ever met, but

168

even his own mother admitted he wasn't very bright. "Never mind, lad, we all know what you meant."

"It seems to me," Cortaynous pointed out, getting his own mirth under control, "that he meant what he said."

"I'd come down there and deal with you, you ancient fake, but we're holding up the line as it is." She handed Font a small box, which he carried to the table, and a cloth bag, which he slipped into a pocket of his leather coat. "Anyone can tell you where I am, so I'll expect to see you before the end of the fair."

The old wizard nodded. "I'll be there, if only to further my acquaintance with the lovely young lady at your side."

"If he comes by, Elaina, you are not to sit on his knee."

"Oh, Grandmother!"

"And," Cortaynous continued, ignoring the interruption, "to see how one such as you could leave the path."

"Me leave the path? Pah! You're confusing removal with a change of direction." Arra winked at him and slapped the reins against the oxen's backs. "If you don't believe me, just ask the children."

The wagon moved slowly forward, the beasts pulling with a will, for they knew the end of the journey was near. With a creaking, and swaying, and fluttering of red-and-yellow cloth, Arra and Elaina passed through the gate and into Ithkar Fair.

"The candymaker is here!" The call rang out over the fairgrounds, for the children had placed a watch on the gate to let them know when Arra's wagon arrived. Faster than should have been possible, the wagon was surrounded by what could only be termed a horde of screaming children.

"Aunt Arra! Aunt Arra! What took you so long?"

"We've guarded your booth for you, Aunt Arra!"

"Do you have the red ones again, Aunt Arra?"

"I've grown two inches, Aunt Arra. Can you tell?"

"Aunt Arra, Mother wants you to come to supper tonight."

"Kurtis got married, Aunt Arra, and Papa says it's a good thing he's fond of dogs 'cause his wife looks like one."

"Christa!"

"Well, he did!"

"Uncle Alvin has the berries you wanted, Aunt Arra, but he says you'd better hurry or they'll be past it."

"Can I help pull the taffy this year, Aunt Arra? I'm big enough now, truly I am. Truly."

Arra answered questions, admired growth and lost teeth, and passed out handfuls of barley sugars in hopes of dulling the din. Elaina greeted old friends and made plans to meet and compare notes on the year that had passed since the last fair.

Adults, parents and the childless, smiled indulgently as the noisy cavalcade made its way to the large and permanent booths near the temple. For as long as any of them could remember, the candymaker had been at Ithkar Fair, and more than one of them had grown up knowing both her candy and her kindness. To the casual visitor, she was a fat old lady who held a certain skill with sugar. To the merchants and traders who came back year after year, she was Aunt Arra.

With a deft hand the old woman backed her wagon into the space beside her booth and heaved herself down off the box. Elaina leapt lightly to the ground and began to unhitch the oxen. A boy, Elaina's age or a little older, came forward, took the heavy harness from her, and finished the job. He'd been leaning on the booth when they arrived, trying not to look like he was waiting.

"Shall I take them to the usual place, Aunt Arra?" he asked, looking everywhere but at Elaina.

"Thank you, Tap," Arra replied just as seriously. "I'd appreciate that."

170

The young man, for he could not really be called a boy any longer, nodded and began to lead the oxen away. He took three steps, looked back, and finally met Elaina's eyes. She tossed her head and looked away. He shrugged and walked on.

"He's grown some over the last year," Arra observed in a neutral tone. "Got good-looking, too."

"I hadn't noticed."

Arra snorted. "Not the sort I'd have turned down in my day."

"Oh, Grandmother!"

"He's walking slowly enough; you could probably catch up."

"You need me here."

"Doing what?" The wagon seethed with children, the older, more experienced ones instructing the others in the proper unloading of the candymaker's equipment and supplies.

Elaina hesitated a moment, then with a graceful flash of shapely legs darted down the lane.

"Have to lengthen her skirts again," Arra observed. With astonishing speed in one so large, she dove forward to save one of her favorite molds from an overly enthusiastic youngster.

Arra was not a deeply religious woman. She worshiped the Three Lordly Ones with the same matter-of-fact practicality that she brought to everything else. She would no more have denied them their yearly offering of her best than she would have denied the children who ran her errands their sweets.

She entered the gates of the temple followed by two of the older children, who carried a wooden box between them. They placed it on the tribute table, bowed—with their mothers' warning to be polite showing on their well-scrubbed faces—turned, and tried not to run as they left.

"So, Sefon," Arra greeted the middle-aged priest with a nod and a smile, "how has life and the temple treated you this last year?"

"Life and the temple have treated me well," the priest replied solemnly. "I am truly blessed to serve the Three Lordly Ones."

Arra suppressed a snort. Even as a child Sefon had taken himself too seriously. His religion was one of pomp and ceremony and little joy. She spotted a priest and a priestess heading toward the table and waited until they arrived before twisting the brass clasp on the top of the box. She didn't consider herself to be a vain woman, but she was especially pleased with her offering this year and wanted a more appreciative audience than Sefon.

As the sides of the box folded away, the gasps of delight were all she could have hoped for. Even Sefon forgot his self-importance long enough to stand and sigh with the rest.

In the box was the Shrine of the Three Lordly Ones in perfect miniaturization. No more than two feet high, each layer was an exact replica right down to the sculptured heads and dancing asparas. The colors used made the shrine appear to be bathed in sunlight, and so marvelous was the illusion that, for an instant, the prayers of the priests and priestesses could almost be heard coming up through the hollow pinnacle.

"Magic," breathed the priestess.

"Skill," corrected Arra gently, well pleased with the sensation her offering had caused.

"But what is it made of?" asked the junior priest, not quite putting out his hand to touch.

"Candy," Sefon told him with wonder in his voice. "It's made of candy."

Dragging her gaze from the sculpture, the priestess turned to Arra, recognition in her eyes. "You're the candymaker."

Arra regally inclined her head.

"Last year you brought the floral wreath. I thought at the

time that you could do nothing better or more beautiful." She turned back to the replica. "I was wrong."

"One does what one can." Arra beamed like a benevolent mountain on the three servants of the temple and pulled a small cloth bag from her voluminous robes. "I must be getting back but would be honored if you would accept this small offering as well." She winked at the astounded priestess. "Don't let Sefon eat all the green ones."

"Aunt Arra!" Sefon so far forgot himself to exclaim in protest.

It was the second ten-day of the fair before the man in black approached the candymaker's booth. Arra had expected the visit. She'd been watching him watching Elaina since the day the fair opened, hovering about the child like a storm cloud dodging the sun. When Elaina was helping in the booth, he leaned against the wall of the tavern across the way. When she ran an errand or ran off with her friends, he followed. When she went to see one of the many traveling acts that played the fair, he was also in the crowd. When she went to check on the oxen, he was there.

"As long as he only watches," Arra told herself, "I will wait and see."

And now the waiting was over as the watcher threaded his way through the crowd and stopped at the candymaker's counter.

Arra continued serving her other customers, bantering and teasing as she always did, but took the opportunity to get a closer look at this potential threat. Attractive, in a petulant sort of way, she decided. Thick brown, almost black hair, clipped shorter than was usual, dark eyes with long lashes, and good cheekbones; but he had a weak chin and a sneer that said he was used to getting his own way. The pale skin and the way the flesh was beginning to sag indicated his most strenuous exercise took place in taverns and wineshops. He was younger than he looked from a distance, and Arra tsked over a paunch on one of that age. His clothes were expensive and well made, and he wore a tiny gold mask in his left ear.

"Well?" she asked him at last.

Black brows rose. "I always thought the correct greeting was, 'How may I serve you?'" His voice was cultured, well educated.

"I'm fat and I'm old," Arra snapped, "but I'm not stupid. You're no customer. What do you want?"

"Perhaps we should discuss that privately." His teeth were small and straight. A slight smell of rot tainted his breath.

Arra's eyes narrowed as she followed his gaze to where Elaina was directing an enthusiastic group of children in a taffy pull. *The last time I saw that expression,* she thought, *it was looking up at me from underneath a rock.* But all she said aloud was, "Maybe we should. Elaina!"

The girl turned, saw who was with her grandmother, and began to twist her apron up into a sticky knot. Arra had not been the only one to notice the man in black.

"That lot can manage on their own; only Josie has never pulled before. I need you to serve for me."

Elaina came forward slowly, her eyes smoldering, her gaze trying to roast the stranger where he stood. "Where are you going?" she demanded.

"Just across the way. I have business to discuss with this . . . person." Arra patted her granddaughter on a stiff shoulder. "Try to remember the strawberry creams are for sale."

The shoulder relaxed a little. "Oh, Grandmother!"

Arra grinned, chucked the girl under her chin—which brought a disdainful toss of the golden head—and maneuvered her bulk out of the booth. A black-clad arm waved her on ahead, and she moved across the road like a ship under full sail. Given the option of getting out of the way or being run down, the crowd parted in a bow wave before her.

This early in the day, the tavern was nearly empty. A few serious drinkers, some of them obviously left over from the night before, were scattered about the tables, but Arra and her companion had their pick of the booths along one wall.

Arra squeezed herself between the table and the bench and sat gingerly, relaxing only when she knew the furniture would bear her weight. Granted it always had before, but Arra knew that a person of her size couldn't be too careful. The stranger slid in across the table and waved away the approaching proprietor.

Harrat stopped, in surprise more than anything, and his huge mustache waggled and twisted under the force of his emotions. This was a tavern. If you sat down, you drank; if you had no intention of drinking, you sat somewhere else. Arra caught his eye before he could give voice, and her expression stopped him in his tracks. That was different. A friend in trouble was welcome to the space. Until the lunch crowd came in. He bowed and went back behind the bar.

"Well?" Arra asked.

"I want your granddaughter."

"You can't have her." Arra began to pull herself from the booth, but the stranger waved her back onto the bench.

"You don't understand." He smiled unpleasantly. "I want the girl, and I always get what I want."

Arra returned a smile just as unpleasant. "Not this time."

He fingered the gold mask in his ear. "You still don't understand."

Arra sighed. She understood only too well. She knew the type that Thotharn often attracted. Along with the truly evil—and only a fool would deny that the truly evil found a home with the dark god—came the petty and the bored. This young man obviously belonged to the latter group, with self-indulgence his driving force.

"We've already determined I'm not stupid," Arra said dryly. "I'm not blind, either. I saw your jewelry days ago, and I'm well aware of what it means. But you're acting for yourself here, not for the god, and while the priests of Thotharn may approve of what you do—evil for its own sake is not discouraged among the acolytes—they will not help." She folded her arms over her chest and glared across the table. "I can protect myself and my own from you."

"I don't doubt that you can." He conceded her the point. "But can you protect all the children of Ithkar Fair?"

As one they turned and looked out the front of the tavern. Across the lane, two children were struggling to the candy-maker's with a basket of peaches. They were met at the booth by a tiny girl, her mouth stretched wide over a sweet, and all three disappeared inside.

"The children run your errands, do you deliveries. . . . They could begin to have fatal accidents."

"I could report you to the temple."

"The temple can do nothing until I do something, and I will very obviously do nothing. But the children will still die. And the children will continue to die until you give me your granddaughter."

Arra weighed her granddaughter against all the children of Ithkar Fair. She studied the man, making an inventory of all the strengths and weaknesses of his face. "Drop dead," she said at last.

"I swear by the Three Lordly Ones I didn't even see her. One minute the way was clear, the next she was under my wheels. I didn't have time to stop. I swear it."

Arra pushed past the nearly hysterical wagoner and dropped awkwardly to her knees beside the bloody bundle in the middle of the lane. Someone had draped a cloak over the body. Arra lifted a corner, already damp with blood, and peered beneath. It was the tiny girl they had seen from the tavern.

"Are you all right, Arra?" Cortaynous touched her gently on the shoulder. "Is it someone you knew?"

"I know all the children of the fair. And no, I'm not all right." With the old wizard's help, she heaved herself to her feet. "I've made a terrible misjudgment. This is my fault."

"This?" Cortaynous waved a hand at the tragedy. The wagoner was still trying desperately to explain to the gathered crowd that he hadn't seen the child. The tiny corpse was buried under the wailing body of its mother. Fair-wards stood awkwardly, staves in hand, unsure of what to do until the priest arrived. "How could this be your fault?"

Arra's voice was stone. "I forgot that for some tasks weakness can be strength."

"Someone did this?"

"Yes."

"Then tell the temple!"

"No. I have no proof. They will watch him. He will watch me. More children will die." She ground the words out. "I will take care of this myself."

Cortaynous stared at the candymaker. What he saw in her

eyes made him step back and sketch a sign in the air between them. "What will you do?"

Arra's lips drew back in what was not quite a smile. "I'm going to give him what he wants."

"Elaina will stay with me until the last day of the fair."

"Agreed." He could afford to be generous; he had won. "But I will continue to watch, and if I see anything that says you are trying to get out of our agreement—"

"I have a business to run," Arra cut him off. "I won't have you interfere with that."

He spread his hands. "By all means, business as usual."

Arra snorted and turned away.

He watched the fat woman waddle back to her booth, and the corners of his mouth turned up.

On the day the candymaker's booth shut down and her wagon was loaded and ready to leave, the man in black came forward to claim his prize. He had watched and seen nothing that said the bargain had been broken. Children had streamed in and out as usual, but none went near the section of the fair given over to magicians and sorcerers. The old fool of a wizard who was the candymaker's friend had not come near the booth. Deliveries had grown more numerous, but business had been brisk. Even the boy who tended the oxen had arrived bowed under the weight of a bag that dusted his clothing with white powder. Elaina had taken over the serving of customers. He assumed this was so he would know she had not been spirited away, and he applauded the candymaker's good sense.

The oxen regarded him blandly as he approached, but the look Arra gave him should have felled him on the spot. He didn't even notice. All he saw was the slight figure half-hidden behind the bulk of the old woman, golden hair glimmering under a veil, violet eyes demurely lowered. He caught his lower lip between his teeth and rode the wave of pleasure that rushed up from his loins. He reached out to take what was his, but Arra's hand, a band of steel around his wrist, stopped him.

"Gently," she snarled, feeling contaminated by the touch. "I've given her something to calm her, but I can't guarantee that a public mauling won't overcome it and you'll be treated to a hysterical scene like you've never imagined."

He freed his arm and stepped back, bowing slightly to acknowledge the advice. Once he had the girl alone, hysterics wouldn't matter. And when he'd finished with her, hysterics wouldn't be possible.

Arra moved aside and drew Elaina forward. She bent and planted a kiss on the golden hair. "The children of the fair are safe? Now and always?"

"You have my word on it." And he led Elaina away, an arm about her shoulders, the fingers toying with a silken braid.

"His word, hah!" Arra spat and hoisted herself up onto the wagon seat. There were deep shadows under her eyes, and her face, for all its roundness, looked peaked and tired. She slapped the reins against the oxen's backs and headed out of Ithkar Fair.

Just past the gate a familiar voice called out, and she reined in.

"Arra! Arra!" Cortaynous ran up, black robes flapping about skinny legs. "Did you truly do it?"

"A number of times, and I've grandchildren for proof," Arra answered, dimples digging wells of amusement in her face. "Did I truly do what?"

Cortaynous leaned against the painted wood of the wagon, sucking air into ancient lungs. "A rumor says you traded Elaina for the lives of the children of the fair," he gasped.

"A man your age should know better than to listen to rumors," Arra rebuked, and parted the curtains that separated the wagon seat from the storage area. "Come here, child."

Elaina poked her head through the space and smiled down at the old wizard.

"But I saw . . . and others saw . . ." Cortaynous sputtered. "If you didn't give him . . ." Understanding dawned. "You didn't give him . . . ?"

"I gave him exactly what he asked for," Arra said calmly. "Something sweet for his bed."

Cortaynous shook his head. "He won't be pleased when he finds out, and even your skill won't stand a . . . uh . . ." He looked up at Elaina and blushed. "Uh, physical activity. You've only postponed the problem."

"Oh, I don't think so. You see, that much sugar would have been extraordinarily expensive, so I made a small substitution."

"Substitution?"

"Sugar and lime look very much alike from a distance."

"Lime?" Cortaynous repeated weakly. He winced.

"I have a certain skill with duplication," Arra added, not at all modestly. "He'll find the sugar coating covers a somewhat caustic interior." She rubbed her hand over Elaina's shorn head. "Much like the original."

"Oh, Grandmother!"

EYES OF THE SEER

Caralyn Inks and Georgia Miller

Dark clouds towered in the sky, and the sound of distant thunder came to Tamm's ears. By the feel of the wind on his face, he knew the storm would reach him before day's end. He eased the heavy pack off his back and massaged the stiffness from his muscles. No choice; he must stop. He took the packs off Haddis and, with the ease of long practice, set up camp.

To the best of his reckoning he was still two days out from Ithkar Fair. He'd been born there. His parents belonged to the merchant class who lived permanently near the temple from fair to fair. Tamm learned the family trade, making household utensils, and was a skilled worker even before his voice deepened. Though he loved his family and working with his hands, there was a hunger deep within him nothing had yet satisfied. In his bones Tamm knew he was a magician.

His parents made a modest living, but it did not stretch far enough to adequately grease the grasping palms of the cleric priests who guarded access to the true priests of the Three Lordly Ones. Kept from receiving the teachings he yearned for, Tamm refused to be swayed from his dream. He left. And he hadn't been back in years.

The life of a tinker was not for him, but it would serve, for now, to mask his real purpose, to search for a master who would agree to teach him the magecraft.

But in the meantime, a man had to eat.

Since the Northern War and the coming of the priests of Thotharn, there were a few households that welcomed a tinker at their back doors. Fancy ribbons or mended pots might bear the touch of alien sorcery. His customers often turned him away, all but the desperate. And even they had few copper bits or hearthcraft they'd willingly part with for mending a pot or sharpening kitchen knives.

But Tamm was industrious and persistent. His pack was bulging with wares, many of his own making. In his need to create and fill the hours around a night's fire, he took to making fanciful creatures out of tin. Carving drinking cups from wood, he combined the two, metal and wood, into a pleasing whole. But he grew lonely, hungry for conversation and food not of his own making. And, he admitted to himself, the hope that the master he searched for all these years might be at the fair.

Tent raised and stores covered, he slipped a nosebag over the mule's head.

"Supper, Haddis," he said. Tamm patted her on the flank, then set about seeing to his own meal.

Two days later he could smell the aroma that always surrounded Ithkar Fair even before he could see the campgrounds. His mouth watered as he thought about the cookstalls and the spice merchants. Even the sour-sweet smell of penned animals, lying beneath the other odors, smelled like home. But that was an illusion, he thought as he approached the fair gate. There was no home here for Tamm the tinker. He had put all that behind him when he gave his heir-rights to his sister—for to remain heir, he couldn't leave Ithkar. His dream would not allow him to be hearthbound.

"Weapons must be turned in at the gate, master tinker," said the fair-ward at the entrance.

"I've no weapons but a staff. A craftsman I am, and no fighter."

The fair-ward sighed and smiled tiredly. "You'd be surprised at how many 'humble craftsmen' find it convenient to carry a bow, or even a sword."

"Well, I've neither. You can look if you want."

"Oh, don't worry, I shall. And don't think we won't keep an eye on you. You could make a blade as easily as you can mend a kettle."

"Could, maybe. But won't."

"See to it." Looking to the wizard standing beside him, the fair-ward asked, "Is he magic clean?" At the woman's nod, he waved them through.

Presently, after leaving the requisite "thank offering" at the temple, Tamm went in search of the spot he'd been assigned to set up his tent. He found the small strip between two more pretentious traders' pavilions. To his left was the potter, Valdorf, and to the right of him was Drisko, dealing in leather and furs. They agreed among themselves to watch each other's stalls, so each could sample the entertainment the fair offered.

Grateful that his neighbors appeared to be congenial, Tamm

set up his tent and took Haddis to the boarding pens. On his way back, he gathered stones to line a firepit. Soon, he had a small charcoal fire going and his wares displayed.

A woman came, holding a dented cookpot with a hole in it. Giving thanks to the Three Lordly Ones, Tamm began working on it. Soon he handed the mended pot back to her and said, "No charge."

"Truly?" she asked with a suspicious glare. Her dark good looks proclaimed her eastern heritage.

"It's a superstition of mine," he said, smiling. "No charge to the first customer of the day. Or the last," he added, seeing the lift of her eyebrow and the calculating gleam in her eye.

There was a steady stream of customers throughout the day, not just for the pot mending, but to purchase his other wares as well. And there were several more waiting to be served as the shadows began to lengthen in the street.

"Three jobs, and that's the end for the day," he announced loudly. "I've got to rest."

There was an immediate hubbub as women began to argue among themselves as to who was next in line. Tamm left them to work out who would receive the free mending job as he applied himself to the task of putting a loose handle back on a skillet.

Satisfied with the results of his first day at Ithkar Fair, he banked his fire and asked Solette, the potter's daughter, to keep an eye out for his belongings. Then he went in search of something to eat.

A copper bit bought him a savory meat pie, and another bought him a mug of ale to go with it. He sat down on a bench beside the Blue Lily cookstall to enjoy his supper. Sipping ale, he watched the passing crowds of fairgoers. An old man seated on the other end of the bench caught his attention. He'd seen him before, sitting in front of the door to the temple with an alms bowl in his lap. Tamm recognized him by the bandage he had wrapped over his eyes. Now the old one sat comfortably, enjoying his supper. He emptied his bowl of whatever coins he had gathered during the day and now drank soup from it, alternately taking bits from a large slab of bread.

With a prickling at the back of his neck, he saw that a scorpion had crawled up on the blind man's ragged garments and was perched on his shoulder.

Tamm got up, moving cautiously. He drew back his hand—

"Don't do it," the old man said.

"W-what?" Tam asked, so startled he nearly lost his balance and fell.

"Thank you for your kind thoughts, but I am in no danger. The scorpion is my friend, at least for now." As he spoke, he turned his head toward Tamm.

Tamm made a guess. "You can see me?"

"Several of you, in fact," said the old man. "Scorpion's eyes are very interesting to look through. Sit down, sit down. Bring your food and talk with me for a while."

"I noticed you this afternoon," Tamm said, getting the fragments of pie and mug of ale. "Your begging place is just across the path from mine."

"Yes, I know."

The tinker put the last bite of pie into his mouth and licked the crumbs from his fingers. He watched, fascinated, while the old man broke off a small piece of bread and offered it to the scorpion.

"Small friend, thank you for your help," he told it. "Now,

go in peace. I have someone else who can guide me to my home.''

The scorpion took the bread in one of its front claws and climbed onto the old man's outstretched palm. Tamm could have sworn he heard it purr. When the old man lowered it to the ground, the scorpion scuttled onto the packed earth and disappeared under the bench they were sitting on.

"I didn't know they ate bread," Tamm said. He shifted on the bench, drawing his feet out from the shadows. It wasn't just the scorpion that troubled him. There was a strange, unsettling presence about this man.

"They don't, no more than their cousins the spiders do," the old man replied. "But bread will draw insects, which my friend will enjoy for his supper."

Tamm shook his head. "That's quite a trick."

"No trick, tinker, for one who can commune with all the faces of nature."

"Do you mind my asking . . ." Tamm whispered, looking around to see if anyone was nearby. "Are you a mage?"

"No, not a mage. I am, or at least I was, a seer."

"There have been hard times everywhere," Tamm said.

The old man laughed. "But not for me. At least, not until recently. Can you imagine it? Once I was more powerful than any of these psalm-chanting fools who walk up and down in their velvet and gold, and wear those badges that give off sweet-smelling scents of oblivion. So much more powerful that the priests have no way of detecting it. You see, mine comes from the very forces of nature itself, and not from spells, potions, or twiddling fingers."

"If you are so powerful," Tamm said skeptically, "why are you now a beggar?"

The old power shaper sat without moving for a while.

Sighing, he said, "I think you may be the one I've been waiting for for a long time."

Tamm stiffened, hope suddenly alive in him. "What's your name?" he asked.

"Mordecai."

Tamm stared unseeing at the constant stream of passersby. "Mordecai, you have waited and I have searched, and long has been my seeking," he said. The seer drew breath to speak, but Tamm rushed on. "I've been looking for a person such as you. Will you be my master?" He turned to the old man when he felt the seer's hand fall onto his shoulder with a hard grip.

Mordecai stood. "You can begin by guiding me to my home. On the way I will tell you how I arrived at this state." He took a deep breath. "Two fairings ago, I came to purchase some near-virgin gold," Mordecai began in the tone of a storyteller.

"What—?"

"Gold that has been purified in the fire, yet not worked into any form. Now as I was saying, there was this goblet wench named Renilda . . ."

Renilda worked as a goblet wench. Her days were taken up with the drudgery of carrying heavy trays full of ale flagons and joints of mutton and avoiding the pinching fingers of the patrons; her nights were taken up with whatever she chose to do with her free hours. Sometimes those same patrons who had been slapped for their familiarity in the light of day found her much more agreeable once night had fallen. She preferred a softer bed than a tavern bench.

There was a certain patron she'd been watching. He was blind, but that didn't bother her. He was clean and his clothes

free from patches. Mordecai claimed to be a visiting seer.
She didn't believe him even though the fair-wards had inves-
tigated him, then let him alone when they discovered he never
took money for seeing. They tolerated this activity as a
harmless game and treated him as someone who was slightly
soft in the head.

Renilda, however, noticed the old man always seemed to
have plenty of coins with which to pay for his meals. She
began to use the tricks of not-so-subtle seduction on him. She
knew full well it was more than a warm bed he'd be sharing
with her; she would have his coins as well. Renilda started by
brushing past him so he could feel the outlines of her body.
Sometimes she sat on the same bench with him, pretending to
help him with his food, sitting so close he couldn't move his
arm without jostling her breasts. She made conversation and
laughed with him, and occasionally she let him touch her
hair. Finally she maneuvered him into asking her to accompany him to his tent.

"I'll see for you," he promised.

"Oh, aye," she responded, laughing. "Some future I've
got! Still, if it would please you to do it, I'll agree."

"Your presence pleases me," he said.

She went with him when her work day ended. His tent was
nondescript on the outside. Inside, however, it was separated
into two areas by a fine drape of lemon-colored silk. Thick
furs and multihued pillows covered the hard-packed earth.

He bade her sit, then struck a flint, lighting a small lamp.
The perfumed oil gave off a sharp, pleasing scent.

"I seldom use this, as you might imagine," he said,
smiling, "but you might enjoy some light."

"Thank you," she said. By lamplight Renilda examined
the tent, her eyes picking out what might be good to steal.

She'd learned through the years just what was safe to take and thus kept the fair-wards from her. She watched Mordecai pass through the curtain to the inner room. When he returned, he was carrying a beautifully carved chest.

Renilda sucked in her breath, trying to stifle her gasp of amazement. Not only was the box deeply and richly carved, but it was heavy with expensive brass inlays. Small jewels winked from the boss plate on the top. The box itself was worth a fortune; too bad she didn't dare steal it. She fairly squirmed in her seat; she was on fire to see what it contained. Eagerly, she watched him open the box and take out two rather crudely molded raw clay goblets.

"What are those?" she asked. Anyone who would store raw clay in such a chest must be cloudy-headed.

"Tools of my trade. I am a seer, my dear, as I told you. These are my eyes, eyes by which I not only see the future, but which allow me to feel it as well," he said, placing the empty goblets on a small folding table.

"Oh, yes," she said, not truly paying attention.

Renilda wondered how much longer she'd have to wait until she could search through the chest and find the treasure he surely had hidden within. Treasure there must be, since the fool had adorned the clay.

There was a silver-and-gold chain connecting the vessels. The small gems, set on interlocking links, caught points of light from the glowing lamp. The chain fitted snugly around each stem and looked to be welded in place. She put a hand over her mouth to muffle her laugh. Welded or not, it wasn't much protection; one hard pull and the raw clay would tear like bread dough. Oddly, the goblets were taking on a ruddy hue. The clay was slowly drying!

She blinked in surprise. The goblets now brimmed with

water. Puzzled, Renilda looked for the pitcher or waterskin he must have used to pour from, but she saw nothing. He was bent over the vessels, and it seemed as if he were gazing into them. But, of course, that was impossible. Mordecai was blind.

"Now, Renilda, I will foresee for you."

A cold chill ran through her, raising the fine hairs on her body. Maybe the old man wasn't lying. "No!" she gasped, putting her hands out and backing away. Renilda knew only too well what the future held for her sort. She had no illusions about that! But she couldn't bear to hear it voiced.

"Why, you're afraid," said Mordecai. "If you do not wish a seeing, I'll put my eyes away."

She shuddered. "No! It's not for the likes of me." She did notice when he put the goblets into the chest that the liquid had disappeared and the clay once more was raw. Well, she'd seen stranger happenings during fair time. Now that they were out of sight, she felt relief, and, laughing seductively, she approached him.

After Mordecai was truly asleep, Renilda crept from the bed and searched through the outer room until she located the treasure box. It was hidden in a far corner of the curtained alcove.

She laughed softly as she fumbled at the clasp of the box, barely able to make it out in the gloom. The old fool had been so grateful for the attention she had shown him! How he had prattled of her nonexistent beauty. She knew what she looked like—too thick in the waist, pockmarked, sallow-skinned. But her hips were wide and welcoming. She seldom had any complaints on that score.

Renilda felt no pangs of conscience about robbing him. No doubt this chest held his entire hoard of wealth in rubies, diamonds, or, perhaps, sapphires. It wasn't heavy enough for gold.

She felt frustrated enough to scream by the time the catch finally gave. In the dim light, she could make out the contents only vaguely. Trusting more to her fingers than her eyes, she felt around inside. A rich fabric lined the box. It felt like samite, perhaps, or damask. She touched a smooth, rounded surface. It was so closely molded by the chest she had to work it loose. It was one of the goblets.

Curious, Renilda rubbed it and felt the cool, sensuous texture of raw clay. The chain connecting it to its mate rattled against the wood. Frightened, she grabbed it, silencing the small sound. Hardly breathing, she listened closely, but no sound came from the old man other than snores. Link by link, she traced the chain to the other vessel and lifted it out from its matching niche. Holding both in one hand, she rummaged through the chest. Nothing.

Nearly frantic, she rapidly searched the hollows the vessels had rested in. There must be a false compartment. Again, nothing. Not even a Lords-rotted copper piece for all her trouble.

Well, by the Three, she'd get something out of this! She took a goblet in each hand; she pulled, ripping the chain free from the soft clay. Warm water flowed over her fingers. At that instant the old man screamed, sounding as if his soul were being ripped from his living flesh.

"By the high priest's left tit!" she exclaimed, dropping the ruined goblets and the chain. Renilda fell to her knees. Her hands shook, but she forced herself to seek the chain. The cold links tangled in her fingers, and she fumbled in the dark until she found the edge of the tent and crawled out. Behind her she heard the old man sobbing. What nighmares troubled the old fool, she neither knew nor cared. Barely she could make out a few words he was mumbling. Something about a curse, and flesh hanging from bones.

Long before dawn, Renilda had pawned the gold-and-silver chain, receiving more coins that she thought she would get. Wisely she kept the gems for a later time of need.

"And so, you see, without knowing what mischief she had done, Renilda made me truly blind."

Following the old man's directions, Tamm led him through the district where the "permanent" residents of Ithkar lived from one fair to the next. It was a place of twisted alleys, lined with shacks that were tossed together from the debris each fair inevitably left behind.

Tamm didn't quite know what to make of Mordecai's tale. He felt sure many things had not been explained. "Why," asked Tamm, "if you are a mage, were you reduced to this state? It makes no sense if you have the power you say you have."

The old man sighed heavily and said, "I am powerful, yes, but the eyes were not only the source of my seeing, through them I could also call on the forces of nature. Until they can be made whole and the water of seeing replaced, I am a doomed beggar. I knew, though, that someone would come and restore my sight sooner or later."

"But I didn't know myself until a few weeks ago that I would be at this year's fair," Tamm said.

Mordecai shrugged. "I asked for you. Or, if not for you specifically, then for someone like you." The seer stopped. "This is my abode. Come and share a cup of ale with me, before you return to your pot mending."

Pushing aside the old blanket that served as a door, the

seer shook off Tamm's hand. Striking flint, he lit an oil-soaked rag, then handed the tinker a small chest. "This is where I kept my eyes," he said.

"But how am I to help you?" Tamm asked. "I came to you to learn, and you act as if I should know everything beforehand."

Mordecai shrugged. "If you're meant to be my apprentice, and I your master, then you will find the way. One thing only will I tell you, and that because of your ignorance. The clay must be reworked only with the tears of the one who ruined the cups."

"But master—"

"That is all I will tell you," Mordecai said firmly. "If you are truly intended to learn from me, then that is all you need to know. Now, return quickly to your tent before somebody steals your tools and materials."

For the next handspan of days, Tamm worked as he had the first day, when he had met Mordecai. Each day, also, the old beggar took up his post outside the temple, receiving alms from the pilgrims and nodding pleasantly to Tamm when he spoke to him. He never asked how Tamm's assigned task was progressing.

Fortunately for Tamm, he could mend pots and pans in his sleep, because he wasn't far from that state. His mind was entirely preoccupied with the puzzle of how to prove his worth to his master.

"I'm no potter!" he told himself a dozen times a day. And yet—

He began to watch Valdorf at his work, hoping to learn some secret he could use. But the potter's craft remained a mystery to him. He would have to draw from his own store of knowledge, inadequate though he felt it to be.

As he worried over the problem, slowly he began to see a possible way to solve it.

But nothing could be accomplished without Renilda. He searched for her in what free time he had, but without success. And then he had an idea. He started to chuckle. "Why not?" he said to himself. "Get the priests to do the seeking for me!"

Putting aside the knife he'd been sharpening, he went to the temple. Mordecai was sitting in his usual spot on the temple steps, and as Tamm passed him, he dropped a copper into his master's bowl.

"Good day to you, sir," Tamm said, and smiled at the seer, knowing full well the old man would be using the eyes of the small mouse he glimpsed half-hidden in the long gray hair.

"And to you," Mordecai replied, nodding in his direction.

Tamm nearly stumbled when a man grabbed his arm.

"Halt!" said the man. Tamm looked up and saw a temple guard. "You, tinker, can go no farther unless you've an appointment with a temple priest."

Tamm reached into his pouch and took out a copper coin. Unobtrusively he slipped it into the guard's hand. "I would like an appointment."

"State your business," the man said.

"I'm looking for my cousin, Renilda, a goblet wench. She was working here three fair turns ago. I've had no luck locating her."

"What do you want with her?" The man looked at him skeptically. "You say she's your cousin?"

"Actually, my mother's kinswoman. My mother is ill and

needs help. She thought Renilda might return home with me." Tamm felt guilty for the lies, then resolutely cast the feeling out.

The temple guard cleared his throat. Tamm saw the man glance at his pouch and raise an eyebrow. Tamm sighed, knowing what was expected. He dropped coppers, one by one, into the man's outstretched hand. When the eyebrow lowered, six coppers had disappeared into the palm. Tamm closed his pouch.

"You'll not be needin' the priests for this," the man said. "I'll set fair-wards to the seekin', and even if she's dead, we'll bring you word."

It hadn't occurred to him Renilda might be dead until the man he had spoken to suggested it. He'd been worried the two days it took them to find the goblet wench. Tamm followed the fair-ward who had come for him, wiping the sweat from his brow. They walked a narrow path through a trash-ridden alley. The farther they went, the higher the stench. Tamm thought there had to be more decaying here than mere refuse. It smelled like death rot.

"Watch your step," said the fair-ward, stepping over a pile of timber and rags. Tamm noticed he now held his staff in two hands instead of slung over his back. "This is where the wench lives, if you can call it that," he said, pointing to a hovel that was nothing more than a few boards leaning up against what had to be the back wall of the temple. "This is not a place to be walking alone and unprotected. For a couple of coppers, I'll wait for you."

Tamm thought a moment, then nodded. "Here's one. I'll give you the other when I'm finished." He hesitated, then pushed aside the rags serving as a doorway and stepped in.

He nearly gagged. The place reeked of old vomit, ale, and a body that had repeatedly soiled itself. A woman huddled against the far wall. Tamm didn't know what he had expected, but it wasn't this. Her skin hung from her body in great folds, masking and yet revealing the shape of her bones. Never had he seen such a desolate human being. Mordecai lived like a prince in comparison. Pity moved him, and he knelt beside her.

"Renilda?"

"They told me I had a cousin seeking me. I have none." Her voice was no louder than the rustle of paper being rolled up on its scroll, and he had to lean close to hear her.

"I know," Tamm said, picking up one of her clawlike hands. "But I will help you nonetheless." Her greed had brought her to this state, but even so, he couldn't walk away from her.

"What do you want from me?"

"Your tears."

Carefully, Tamm stoppered the glass vial. The goblet wench had wept enough to fill several vials while she told him her tale. He lifted the rag curtain. Surprisingly, the guard was still there.

"Here are three coppers," Tamm said. "Would you fetch me a litter and bearers? I want my—my mother's cousin taken to the healer's tent."

There wasn't much he could do for Renilda, pity her though he might. He knew she wouldn't live long, but at least he could try to make her dying as comfortable as possible.

Later when he inquired after her, the healer told him that

when she had been washed and fed and cared for, she had smiled and died.

"It happens that way sometimes," the healer said. "They need only a kind word or deed to release them."

Tamm offered to pay the man, but he waved the coppers aside.

"No need. I performed no service, so I merit no pay."

"Then you have my thanks," Tamm said.

"That will suffice."

Tamm closed his tent to customers. Using all his skill, he made two tin cups, one slightly smaller than the other. He worked hard, smoothing them until they were perfectly shaped.

When he finished, he put the cups into his doublet and went in search of Mordecai. He found him at his usual place in front of the Blue Lily, drinking his evening bowl of soup.

"I see you still have your mouse companion," Tamm said as he sat down on the bench. "How do you get it to stay with you?"

"It is very simple. I merely ask, politely, if I may borrow their sight for a while. Usually, they agree. If not, then I wait for another. This small mouse and I have had a delightful few days together."

Tamm placed his hand on Mordecai's arm. He cleared his throat. "Master, I have Renilda's tears. And—and I think I know a way to repair your sight," he said.

The old man nodded his head. "I never doubted. Come, let's go to my home." Unhurriedly he set the mouse on the ground, gave it a morsel of bread, and stood up. "Tell me of Renilda as we walk. How does she fare these days?"

*　　*　　*

As before, Mordecai lit his lamp and got the carved box. He opened it and offered it to Tamm.

"I need something to work on, master. A slab of stone, perhaps, or a piece of oiled paper."

"Ah, yes. Of course." The old man got up and returned in a few minutes with a piece of slate. "Will this do? I got it from a stonemason who said it was spoiled for his use. I find it useful on a chunk of wood, beside my pallet."

"It is perfect," Tamm said.

"Could you use a mortar and pestle?"

Tamm caught his breath. Mordecai had told him he felt, as well as saw, through the cups. "Can you bear the pain, master?" he asked, knowing as he reworked the clay a corresponding echo would resonate to the seer.

"I've felt dead; the zest for life has dimmed without my spirit eyes. I'll welcome the pain for what will come after." Mordecai got up again and fetched the utensils, carefully wiping away any traces of what had been pulverized there previously. Tamm sniffed; it smelled faintly of herbs, a pleasant scent.

Carefully, Tamm emptied the bits of clay from the box, making sure to shake out even the smallest particles. It seemed the clay was even drier and deader than it had been when he first saw it. He began pressing them in the mortar as gently as he could. Mordecai winced occasionally, and his face grew pale, but he made no outcry or protest even when Tamm had to crush the larger shards.

"I've finished with this part," he said. "Now for the tears."

Tamm unstoppered the small vial and poured the contents into the mortar, mixing clay and tears. He was surprised how quickly the mixture became soft and workable. He turned the clay out onto the slate piece. He looked at his master; Mordecai was smiling.

"It's cool," he said. He slid his fingertips under the rag veil he always wore covering his eyes.

Tamm smiled. He continued working, with more confidence now that he was not causing his master such great pain.

He kneaded the clay briefly, then divided it into two equal lumps. Taking the two tin cups from his doublet, he set them on the table. He began to press one lump of clay into the larger tin, smoothing it carefully over the entire interior of the mold. When it was spread to his satisfaction, he put the smaller tin into the clay-lined mold and pressed them firmly together.

He could feel the small irregularities in the earthy substance smoothing out under the pressure he was applying. Cautiously, he jiggled the smaller tin, fearful of tearing the clay if he tried to remove it. But it came away cleanly. He turned over the larger half of the mold, and the newly formed cup dropped out into his hand.

Trembling a little, he molded the other half the same way and dropped the second cup out of the mold.

"I—I feared it wouldn't work this well," Tamm said.

"This is no ordinary clay," replied Mordecai. "Now, let us try my new eyes, and see how well you have done."

Tamm carefully scored the cups and fastened them together with a piece of deerhide rope. They accepted the linkage eagerly, it seemed to him. He handed the precious cups to Mordecai, and the old man placed his eyes on the slate in front of him. The seer caressed them, running his fingers over their smooth perfection. He adjusted the deerskin cord until the cups were placed precisely to his liking. Then he bent his head and began concentrating.

Tamm watched, and the hairs on the back of his neck stirred. The raw clay dried as the water of sight seeped from the cups to fill the hollows. A drop or two of liquid spilled over the brims of each.

"Forgive me," the old man said in a broken voice. "I can't help weeping just a little. Oh, young Tamm, I can see better than I ever did before! The old cups were not made as carefully as these, and they distorted my sight. But now, if I choose, I feel that I could see clear until the world's ending! How can I ever thank you?"

"By accepting me as your apprentice."

"Oh, that." The old man shrugged. He looked up from the cups, and, very slowly, the tears that had filled them began to reabsorb into the clay. "That is up to you."

"What do you mean? I thought—"

"Yes, yes, I know what you thought. But my power, as I told you, isn't the same as that of ordinary wizards. Perhaps you should go and seek one of them instead. I can arrange it for you, you know."

"No. I want to serve you!"

"Are you sure?"

Tamm's heart was beating rapidly, and he drew a deep breath. His heart's desire lay before him. Without hesitating, he replied, "Yes."

"There is a price. There always is." The old man sighed. Putting the cups into the box, he closed the lid and latched it carefully.

"I am prepared," Tamm ventured.

"Are you? I wonder." The old man bowed his head, then looked up. "Very well. I will set you the hardest task, give you the biggest secret. Then we shall see." He reached inside his tunic and brought out a small cloth sack that hung on a leather thong around his neck. Carefully, he opened the sack and slipped the contents out into his hand. "Do you see this?"

"Yes."

"What is it?"

Tamm stared, wondering what the trick was. "It's just a pebble, master. A common pebble, such as you can pick up nearly anywhere."

"Very good. That's it exactly." Mordecai returned the stone to the sack and slipped it back inside his clothing. "It is also the most powerful talisman you could ever imagine. It is so powerful, and yet so simple, that not a one of the fools who imagine themselves versed in magic here in Ithkar would ever recognize it for what it is."

"What, master?" Tamm questioned.

"The truth is often simple. And now, I am going to tell you how to get a talisman of your own. Go down to the river's edge, or anywhere else that you fancy, and pick your own pebble, one that pleases you for one reason or another. Leave me for a year. Wherever you go, when you prepare for the night, put the pebble in a relatively inaccessible place. Each night for a year you must rouse yourself before you waken normally, and do this one ridiculous thing: You must find the pebble where you have put it, and turn it over."

"But master, that is not magic—"

"Oh, is it not? You think it is so simple that it cannot possibly be effective? Let me assure you, unless you are truly gifted, it will take well over a year to accomplish this one task. I know of would-be apprentices who are still trying to do it. Once you have mastered it, however long it takes you, return to me. Only then will we consider what you should ask for, when it comes to your own particular area of power."

Things were moving too swiftly for Tamm. "What I should ask for? Master, I still don't understand!"

"Of course you don't. But you'll have a year—or more—in which to try. You see, when you have created your talisman, imbuing it with your own personal life force, you may have anything you want from that moment forward. You may ask for any power, any amount of material wealth, any woman you desire—in short, the world is open to you. You have only to be willing to sacrifice the full price."

Bewildered, Tamm could only reply once again, "Yes, master." He still didn't understand. But he was willing to do what Mordecai asked. He saw the seer smile.

"Perhaps it would help if you could see an example. As you know by now, I asked for the gift of seeing. And to get it I paid what the power demanded." The old man reached up and began unwinding the rags from his face.

"By the Three," Tamm swore in shock. There was nothing where Mordecai's eyes should have been. No lids, no sockets, no line of lashes. The only indication they had once been there were two gray, wormlike eyebrows.

The seer replaced the bandages, saying, "Do not be concerned, young Tamm, it happened a long, long time ago. So, too, will you pay when the time comes. Now go, if you please. I think I would like to look into my new eyes again."

Once again the only words Tamm could speak were, "Yes, master."

Stunned by all he'd seen and learned, he left, wondering if he would ever have the courage to go and seek a smooth river pebble. And if, having done so, he would be willing to pay the price his lifelong dream demanded.

He didn't see much of Mordecai for the rest of the fair. At fair's end, he got Haddis from the stable. The mule had grown fat and glossy during his stay. Everything went on Haddis's back easily, as he'd sold nearly all the goods he had brought. Tamm passed through the gates without looking back. He was wealthier than he had been on arrival three ten-days ago, but more troubled as well.

He paused at the bank of the river Ith, staring at a bed of yellow-streaked stones for a long, long time.

Taking a deep breath of the autumn air, he said, "Not today, Haddis. Not today."

FIDDLER FAIR

Mercedes Lackey

All the world comes to Ithkar Fair.

That's what they said, anyway—and it certainly seemed that way to Rune as she traveled the Main Trade Road down from her home near Galzar Pass. She wasn't walking on the dusty, hard-packed road itself; she'd likely have been trampled by the press of beasts, then run over by the carts into the bargain. Instead, she walked with the rest of the foot travelers on the road's verge. It was no less dusty—what grass there had been had long since been trampled into powder by all the pilgrims and fairgoers—but at least a traveler was able to move along without risk of acquiring hoofprints on his anatomy.

Rune was close enough now to see the gates of the fair itself, and the fair-ward beside them. This seemed like a good moment to separate herself from the rest of the throng, rest her tired feet, and plan her next moves before entering the fairgrounds.

She elbowed her way out of the line of people, some of whom complained and elbowed back, and moved away from the road to a place where she had a good view of the fair and a rock to sit on. The sun beat down with enough heat to be felt through her soft leather hat as she plopped herself down on the rock and began massaging her tired feet while she looked the fair over.

It was a bit overwhelming. Certainly it was much bigger than she'd imagined it would be. It was equally certain that there would be nothing dispensed for free behind those log palings, and the few coppers Rune had left would have to serve to feed her through the three days of trials for admission to the Bardic Guild. After that . . .

Well, after that, she should be an apprentice, and food and shelter would be for her master to worry about. If not—

She refused to admit the possibility of failing the trials. She couldn't—the Three surely *wouldn't* let her fail. Not after getting this far.

But for now, she needed to get herself cleaned of the road dust and a place to sleep, both with no price tags attached. Right now, she was the same gray brown from head to toe, the darker brown of her hair completely camouflaged by the dust, or at least it felt that way. Even her eyes felt dusty.

She strolled down to the river, her lute thumping her shoulder softly on one side, her pack doing the same on the other. Close to the docks the water was muddy and roiled; there was too much traffic on the river to make an undisturbed bath a viable possibility, and too many wharf rats about to make leaving one's belongings a wise move. She backtracked upstream a bit, while the noise of the fair faded behind her, crossed over the canal, and went hunting the rapids that the canal bypassed. The bank of the river was wilder here and overgrown, not like the carefully tended area of the canal side. Finally she found a place where the river had cut a tiny cove into the bank. It was secluded; trees overhung the water, their branches making a good thick screen that touched the water, the ground beneath them bare of growth, and hollows between some of the roots just big enough to cradle her sleeping roll. Camp, bath, and water, all together, and within climbing distance on one of the trees was a hollow large enough to hide her bedroll and those belongings she didn't want to carry into the fair.

She waited until dusk fell before venturing into the river and kept her eyes and ears open while she scrubbed herself down. Once clean, she debated whether or not to change into the special clothing she'd brought; it might be better to save it. . . . Then the thought of donning the sweat-soaked, dusty traveling gear became too distasteful, and she rejected it out of hand.

She felt strange and altogether different once she'd put on the new costume. Part of that was due to the materials—except for when she'd tried the clothing on for fit, this was the first time she'd ever worn silk and velvet. Granted, the materials were all old; bought from a secondhand vendor and cut down from much larger garments. The velvet of the breeches wasn't *too* rubbed; the ribbons on the sleeves of the shirt and the embroidery should cover the faded places, and the vest should cover the stain on the back panel completely. Her hat, once the dust was beaten out of it and the plumes she'd snatched from the tails of several disgruntled roosters were tucked into the band, looked brave enough. Her boots, at least, were new and, when the dust was brushed from them, looked quite well. She tucked her remaining changes of clothing and her bedroll into her pack, hid the lot in the tree hollow, and felt ready to face the fair.

The fair-ward at the gate eyed her carefully. "Minstrel?" he asked suspiciously, looking at the lute and fiddle she carried in their cases, slung from her shoulders.

She shook her head. "Here for the trials, m'lord."

"Ah." He appeared satisfied. "You come in good time, boy. The trials begin tomorrow. The guild has its tent pitched hard by the main gate of the temple; you should have no trouble finding it."

The wizard-of-the-gate ignored her, looking bored. Rune did not correct the fair-ward's assumption that she was a boy; it was her intent to pass as male until she'd safely passed the trials. She'd never heard of the Bardic Guild admitting a girl, but as far as she'd been able to determine, there was nothing in the rules and charter of the guild against it. So once she'd been accepted, once the trials were safely passed, she'd reveal her sex, but until then she'd play the safe course.

She thanked him, but he had already turned his attention to the next traveler in line. She passed inside the log walls and entered the fair itself.

The first impressions she had were of noise and light; torches burned all along the aisle she traversed; the booths to either side were lit by lanterns, candles, or other, more arcane methods. The crowd was noisy; so were the merchants. Even by torchlight it was plain that these booths featured shoddier goods: secondhand finery, brass jewelry, flash and tinsel. The entertainers here were . . . surprising. She averted her eyes from a set of dancers. It wasn't so much that they wore little but imagination, but the *way* they were dancing embarrassed even her; and a tavern-bred child has seen a great deal in its life.

She kept a tight grip on her pouch and instruments, tried to ignore the crush, and let the flow of fairgoers carry her along.

Eventually the crowd thinned out a bit (though not before she'd felt a ghostly hand or two try for her pouch and give it up as a bad cause). She followed her nose then, looking for the row that held the cookshop tents and the ale-sellers. She hadn't eaten since morning, and her stomach was lying in uncomfortably close proximity to her spine.

She learned that the merchants of tavern row were shrewd judges of clothing; hers wasn't fine enough to be offered a free taste but wasn't poor enough to be shooed away. Sternly admonishing her stomach to be less impatient, she strolled the length of the row twice, carefully comparing prices and quantities before settling on a humble tent that offered meat pasties (best not ask what beast the meat came from, not at these prices) and fruit juice or milk as well as ale and wine. Best of all, it offered seating at rough trestle tables. Rune took her flaky pastry and her mug of juice (no wine or ale for her, not even had she the coppers to spare for it—she dared not be the least muddle-headed, not with a secret to keep and a competition on the morn) and found herself a spot at an empty table where she could eat and watch the crowd passing by. The pie was more crust than meat, but it was filling and well made and fresh; that counted for a great deal. She noted with amusement that there were two sorts of the clumsy, crude clay mugs. One sort, the kind in which they served the milk and juice, was ugly and shapeless (too ugly to be worth stealing) but was just as capacious as the exterior promised. The other, for wine and ale, was just the same ugly shape and size on the *outside* (though a different shade of toad-back green) but had a far thicker bottom, effectively reducing the interior capacity by at least a third.

"Come for the trials, lad?" asked a quiet voice in her ear.

Rune jumped, nearly knocking her mug over and snatching at it just in time to save the contents from drenching her shopworn finery. (And however would she have gotten it clean again in time for the morrow's competition?) There hadn't been a sound or a hint of movement or even the shifting of the bench to warn her, but now there was a man sitting beside her.

He was of middle years, red hair going to gray, smile wrinkles around his mouth and gray-green eyes, with a candid, triangular face. Well, that said nothing. Rune had known highwaymen with equally friendly and open faces. His dress was similar to her own: leather breeches instead of velvet, good linen instead of worn silk, a vest and a leather hat that could have been twin to hers, knots of ribbon on the sleeves of his shirt—and the neck of a lute peeking over his shoulder. A minstrel!

Of the guild? Rune rechecked the ribbons on his sleeves and was disappointed. Blue and scarlet and green, not the purple and silver of a guild minstrel, nor the purple and gold of a guild bard. This was only a common songster, a mere street player. Still, he'd bespoken her kindly enough, and the Three knew not everyone with the music passion had the skill or the talent to pass the trials. . . .

"Aye, sir," she replied politely. "I've hopes to pass; I think I've the talent, and others have said as much."

His eyes measured her keenly, and she had the disquieting feeling that her boy ruse was fooling *him* not at all. "Ah, well," he said, "there's a-many before you have thought the same, and failed."

210

"That may be"—she answered the challenge in his eyes—
"but I'd bet fair coin that none of *them* fiddled for a murdering ghost, and not only came out by the grace of their skill but were rewarded by that same spirit for amusing him!"

"Oh, so?" A lifted eyebrow was all the indication he gave of being impressed, but somehow that lifted brow conveyed volumes. "You've made a song of it, surely?"

"Have I not! It's to be my entry for the third day of testing."

"Well then . . ." He said no more than that, but his wordless attitude of waiting compelled Rune to unsling her fiddle case, extract her instrument, and tune it without further prompting.

"It's the fiddle that's my first instrument," she said apologetically, "and since 'twas the fiddle that made the tale—"

"Never apologize for a song, child," he admonished, interrupting her. "Let it speak out for itself. Now let's hear this ghost tale."

It wasn't easy to sing while fiddling, but Rune had managed the trick of it some time ago. She closed her eyes a half moment, fixing in her mind the necessary changes she'd made to the lyrics—for unchanged, the song would have given her sex away—and began.

> "I sit here on a rock, and curse my stupid, bragging
>   tongue,
>   And curse the pride that would not let me back down
>   from a boast
>   And wonder where my wits went, when took that
>   challenge up
>   And swore that I would go and fiddle for the Skull
>   Hill Ghost!"

Oh, aye, that had been a damn fool move—to let those idiots who patronized the tavern where her mother worked goad her into boasting that there wasn't anyone, living or dead, she couldn't cozen with her fiddling. Too much ale, Rune, and too little sense. And too tender a pride, as well, to let them rub salt in the wound of being the tavern wench's bastard.

> "It's midnight, and there's not a sound up here upon
>   Skull Hill
> Then comes a wind that chills my blood and makes
>   the leaves blow wild."

Not a good word choice, but a change that had to be made—that was one of the giveaway verses.

> "And rising up in front of me, a thing like shrouded
>   Death.
> A voice says, 'Give me reason why I shouldn't kill
>   you, child.'"

Holy Three, that thing had been ghastly: cold and old and totally heartless. It had smelled of death and the grave, and had shaken her right down to her toenails. She made the fiddle sing about what words alone could never convey and saw her audience of one actually shiver.

The next verse described Rune's answer to the spirit, and the fiddle wailed of fear and determination and things that didn't rightly belong on earth. Then came the description of that nightlong, lightless ordeal she'd passed through, and the fiddle shook with the weariness she'd felt, playing the whole night long; and the tune rose with dawning triumph when the thing not only didn't kill her outright, but began to warm to the music she'd made. Now she had an audience of more than one, though she was only half-aware of the fact.

> "At last the dawn light strikes my eyes; I stop, and
>   see the sun.
> The light begins to chase away the dark and midnight
>   cold—
> And then the light strikes something more—I stare
>   in dumb surprise—
> For where the ghost had stood there is a heap of
>   shining gold!"

The fiddle laughed at death cheated, thumbed its nose at spirits, and chortled over the revelation that even the dead could be impressed and forced to reward courage and talent.

Rune stopped and shook back brown locks dark with sweat, looking about her in astonishment at the applauding patrons of the cookshop. She was even more astonished when they began to toss coppers in her open fiddle case, and the cookshop's owner brought her over a full pitcher of juice and a second pie.

"I'd'a brought ye wine, laddie, but Master Talaysen there says ye go to trials and must'na be amuddled," she whispered, and hurried back to her counter.

"I hadn't meant—"

"Surely this isn't the first time you've played for your supper, child?" The minstrel's eyes were full of amused irony.

"Well, no, but—"

"So take your well-earned reward and don't go arguing

with folk who have a bit of copper to fling at you, and who recognize the gift when they hear it. No mistake, youngling, you *have* the gift. And sit and eat; you've more bones than flesh. A good tale, that.''

''Well''—Rune blushed—''I did exaggerate a bit at the end. 'Twasn't gold, it was silver. But silver won't rhyme. And it was that silver that got me here—bought me my second instrument, paid for lessoning, kept me fed while I was learning. I'd be just another tavern musician, otherwise. . . .''

''Like me, you are too polite to say?'' The minstrel smiled, then the smile faded. ''There are worse things, child, than to be a free musician. I don't think there's much doubt your gift will get you past the trials—but you might not find the guild to be all you think it to be.''

Rune shook her head stubbornly, wondering briefly why she'd told this stranger so much and why she so badly wanted his good opinion. ''Only a guild minstrel would be able to earn a place in a noble's train. Only a guild bard would have the chance to sing for royalty. I'm sorry to contradict you, sir, but I've had my taste of wandering, singing my songs out only to know they'll be forgotten in the next drink, wondering where my next meal is coming from. I'll never get a secure life except through the guild, and I'll never see my songs live beyond me without their patronage.''

He signed. ''I hope you never regret your decision, child. But if you should—or if you need help, ever . . . well, just ask for Talaysen. I'll stand your friend.''

With those surprising words, he rose soundlessly, as gracefully as a bird in flight, and slipped out of the tent. Just before he passed out of sight among the press of people, Rune saw him pull his lute around and begin to strum it. She managed to hear the first few notes of a love song, the words rising golden and glorious from his throat, before the crowd hid him from view and the babble of voices obscured the music.

Rune was waiting impatiently outside the guild tent the next morning, long before there was anyone there to take her name for the trials. It was, as the fair-ward had said, hard to miss: purple in the main, with pennons and edgings of silver and gilt. Almost . . . *too* much; almost gaudy. She was joined shortly by three more striplings, one well dressed and confident, two sweating and nervous. More trickled in as the sun rose higher, until there was a line of twenty or thirty waiting when the guild registrar, an old and sour-looking scribe, raised the tent-flap to let them file inside. He wasn't wearing guild colors, but rather a robe of dusty brown velvet: a hireling therefore.

He took his time, sharpening his quill until Rune was ready to scream with impatience, before looking her up and down and asking her name.

"Rune, child of Lista Jesaril, tavern-keeper." That sounded a trifle better than her mother's *real* position, serving wench.

"From whence?"

"Karthar, east and north—below Galzar Pass."

"Primary instrument?"

"Fiddle."

"Secondary?"

"Lute."

He raised an eyebrow. The usual order was lute, primary; fiddle, secondary. For that matter, fiddle wasn't all that common even as a secondary instrument.

"And you will perform . . . ?"

"First day, primary, 'Lament of the Maiden Esme.' Second day, secondary, 'The Unkind Lover.' Third day, original, 'The Skull Hill Ghost.' " An awful title, but she could hardly use "Fiddler Girl," its real name. "Accompanied on primary, fiddle."

"Take your place."

She sat on the backless wooden bench trying to keep herself calm. Before her was the raised wooden platform on which they would all perform; to either side of it were the backless benches like the one she warmed, for the aspirants to the guild. The back of the tent made the third side, and the fourth faced the row of well-padded chairs for the guild judges. Although she was first here, it was inevitable that others would have the preferred first few slots: those with fathers already in the guild or those who had coins for bribes. Still, she shouldn't have to wait too long—rising with the dawn had given her that much of an edge, at least.

She got to play by midmorning. "Lament" was perfect for fiddle, the words were simple and few, and the wailing melody gave her lots of scope for improvisation. The row of guild judges, solemn in tunics or robes of purple, white silk shirts trimmed with gold or silver ribbon depending on whether they were minstrels or bards, was a formidable audience. Their faces were much alike, well fed and very conscious of their own importance; you could see it in their eyes. As they sat below the platform and took unobtrusive notes, they seemed at least mildly impressed. Even more heartening, several of the boys yet to perform looked satisfyingly worried when she'd finished.

She packed up her fiddle and betook herself briskly out—to find herself a corner of temple wall to lean against as her knees sagged when the excitement that had sustained her wore off. It was several long moments before she could get her legs to bear her weight and her hands to stop shaking. It was then she realized that she hadn't eaten since the night before—and that she was suddenly ravenous. Before she'd played, the very thought of food had been revolting.

The same cookshop tent as before seemed like a reasonable proposition. She paid for her breakfast with some of the windfall coppers of the night before. This morning the tent was crowded and she was lucky to get a scant corner of a bench to herself. She ate hurriedly and joined the strollers through the fair.

Once or twice she thought she glimpsed the red hair of Talaysen, but if it was he, he was gone by the time she reached the spot where she had thought he'd been. There were plenty of other street singers, though. She thought wistfully of the harvest of coin she'd garnered the night before as she noted that none of them seemed to be lacking for patronage. But now that she was a duly registered entrant in the trials, it would be going against custom, if not the rules, to set herself up among them.

So instead she strolled, and listened, and made mental notes for further songs. There was many a tale she overheard that would have worked well in song form; many a glimpse of silk-bedecked lady, strangely sad or hectically gay, or velvet-clad lord, sly and foxlike or bold and pompous, that brought snatches of rhyme to mind. By early evening her head was crammed full—and it was time to see how the guild had ranked the aspirants of the morning.

The list was posted outside the closed tent-flaps, and Rune wasn't the only one interested in the outcome of the first day's trials. It took a bit of time to work her way in to look, but when she did—

By the Three! There she was, "Rune of Karthar"—listed *third*.

She all but floated back to her riverside tree roost.

The second day of the trials was worse than the first; the aspirants performed in order, lowest ranking to highest. That meant Rune had to spend most of the day sitting on the hard wooden bench, clutching the neck of her lute in nervous fingers, listening to contestant after contestant and sure that each one was *much* better on his secondary instrument than she was. She'd only had a year of training on it, after all. Still, the song she'd chosen was picked deliberately to play up her voice and deemphasize her lute strumming. It was going to be pretty difficult for any of these others to match her high contralto (a truly cunning imitation of a boy's soprano), since most of them had passed puberty.

At long last her turn came. She swallowed her nervousness as best she could, took the platform, and began.

Privately she thought it was a pretty silly song. Why on earth any man would put up with the things that lady did to him, and all for the sake of a "kiss on her cold, quiet hand," was beyond her. Still, she put all the acting ability she had into it and was rewarded by a murmur of approval when she'd finished.

"That voice—I've seldom heard one so pure at that late an age!" she overheard as she packed up her instrument. "If he passes the third day—you don't suppose he'd agree to become castrati, do you? I can think of half a dozen courts that would pay red gold to have him."

She smothered a smile—imagine their surprise to discover that it would *not* be necessary to eunuch her to preserve her voice!

She lingered to listen to the last of the entrants, then waited outside for the posting of the results.

She nearly fainted to discover that she'd moved up to second place.

"I told you," said a familiar quiet voice in her ear. "But are you still sure you want to go through with this?"

She whirled to find the minstrel Talaysen standing behind her, the sunset brightening his hair and the soft shadows on his face making him appear scarcely older than she.

"I'm sure," she replied firmly. "One of the judges said today that he could think of half a dozen courts that would pay red gold to have my voice."

"Bought and sold like so much mutton? Where's the living in that? Caged behind high stone walls and never let out of the sight of m'lord's guards, lest you take a notion to sell your services elsewhere? Is *that* the life you want to lead?"

"Trudging down roads in the pouring cold rain, frightened half to death that you'll take sickness and ruin your voice—maybe for good? Singing with your stomach growling so loud it drowns out the song? Watching some idiot with half your talent being clad in silk and velvet and eating at the high table, while you try and please some brutes of guardsmen in the kitchen in hopes of a few scraps and a corner by the fire?" she countered. "No, thank you. I'll take my chances with the guild. Besides, where else would I be able to *learn*? I've got no more silver to spend on instruments or teaching."

"There are those who would teach you for the love of it—welladay, you've made up your mind. As you will, child," he replied, but his eyes were sad as he turned away and vanished into the crowd again.

Once again she sat the hard bench for most of the day

while those of lesser ranking performed. This time it was a little easier to bear; it was obvious from a great many of these performances that few, if any, of the boys had the gift to create. By the time it was Rune's turn to perform, she judged that, counting herself and the first-place holder, there could only be five real contestants for the three open bardic apprentice slots. The rest would be suitable only as minstrels, singing someone else's songs, unable to compose their own.

She took her place before the critical eyes of the judges and began.

She realized with a surge of panic as she finished the first verse that they did *not* approve. While she improvised, she mentally reviewed the verse, trying to determine what it was that had set those slight frowns on the judicial faces.

Then she realized: *boasting*. Guild bards simply did not admit to being boastful. Nor did they demean themselves by reacting to the taunts of lesser beings. Oh, holy Three—

Quickly she improvised a verse on the folly of youth; of how, had she been older and wiser, she'd never have gotten herself into such a predicament. She heaved an invisible sigh of relief as the frowns disappeared.

By the last chorus, they were actually nodding and smiling, and one of them was tapping a finger in time to the tune. She finished with a flourish worthy of a master and waited breathlessly.

And they *applauded*. Dropped their dignity and *applauded*.

The performance of the final contestant was an anticlimax.

None of them had left the tent since this last trial began. Instead of a list, the final results would be announced, and they waited in breathless anticipation to hear what they would be. Several of the boys had already approached Rune, offering smiling congratulations on her presumed first-place slot. A hush fell over them all as the chief of the judges took the platform, a list in his hand.

"First place, and first apprenticeship as bard—Rune, son of Lista Jesaril of Karthar—"

"Pardon, my lord," Rune called out clearly, bubbling over with happiness and unable to hold back the secret any longer, "but it's not son—it's *daughter*."

She had only a split second to take in the rage on their faces before the first staff descended on her head.

They flung her into the dust outside the tent, half-senseless, and her smashed instruments beside her. The passersby avoided even looking at her as she tried to get to her feet and fell three times. Her right arm dangled uselessly; it hurt so badly that she was certain it must be broken, but it hadn't hurt half as badly when they'd cracked it as it had when they'd smashed her fiddle; that had broken her heart. All she wanted to do now was to get to the river and throw herself in. With any luck at all, she'd drown.

But she couldn't even manage to stand.

"Gently, lass." Firm hands took her and supported her on both sides. "Lady be my witness, if ever I thought they'd have gone this far, I'd never have let you go through with this farce."

She turned her head, trying to see through tears of pain, both of heart and body, with eyes that had sparks dancing before them. The man supporting her on her left she didn't recognize, but the one on the right—

"T-Talaysen?" she faltered.

"I told you I'd help if you needed it, did I not? I think you have more than a little need at the moment—"

221

"Th-they broke my fiddle, Talaysen, And my lute. They broke them, and they broke my arm—"

"Oh, Rune, lass . . ." There were tears in *his* eyes, and yet he almost seemed to be laughing as well. "If *ever* I doubted you'd the makings of a bard, you just dispelled those doubts. *First* the fiddle, *then* the lute—and only *then* do you think of your own hurts. Ah, come away, lass, come where people can care for such a treasure as you—"

Stumbling through darkness, wrenched with pain, carefully supported and guided on either side, Rune was in no position to judge where or how far they went. After some unknown interval, however, she found herself in a many colored tent, lit with dozens of lanterns, partitioned off with curtains hung on wires that crisscrossed the entire dwelling. Just now most of these were pushed back, and a mixed crowd of men and women greeted their entrance with cries of welcome that turned to dismay at the sight of her condition.

She was pushed down into an improvised bed of soft wool blankets and huge, fat pillows, while a thin, dark girl dressed like a gypsy bathed her cuts and bruises with something that stung, then numbed them, and a gray-bearded man tsked over her arm, prodded it once or twice, then, without warning, pulled it into alignment. When he did that, the pain was so incredible that Rune nearly fainted.

By the time the multicolored fire flashing cleared from her eyes, he was binding her arm up tightly with thin strips of wood, while the girl was urging her to drink something that smelled of herbs and wine.

Before she had a chance to panic, Talaysen reappeared as if conjured at her side.

"Where—"

"You're with the free bards—the *real* bards, not those

pompous pufftoads with the guild," he said. "Dear child, I thought all that would happen to you was that those inflated bladders of self-importance would give you a tongue-lashing and throw you out on your backside. If I'd had the slightest notion they'd do *this* to you, I'd have kidnapped you and had you drunk insensible till the trials were over. I may never forgive myself. Now, drink your medicine."

"But how—why—who *are* you?" Rune managed between gulps.

" 'What are you?' might be the better place to start, I think. Tell her, will you, Erdric?"

"We're the free bards," said the gray-bearded man, "as Master Talaysen told you—he's the one who banded us together, when he found that there were those who, like himself, had the gift and the talent but were disinclined to put up with the self-aggrandizement and politics and foolish slavishness to form of guild nonsense. We go where we wish and serve—or not serve—who we will, and sing as we damn well please, and no foolishness about who'll be offended. We also keep a sharp eye out for youngsters like you, with the gift, and with the spirit to fight the guild. We've had our eye on you these three years now."

"You—but how?"

"Myself, for one," said a new voice, and a bony fellow with hair that kept falling into his eyes joined the group around her. "You likely don't remember me, but I remember you—I heard you fiddle in your tavern when I was passing through Karthar, and I passed the word."

"And I'm another." This one Rune recognized; he was the man who'd sold her her lute, who had seemed to have been a gypsy peddler selling new and used instruments. Unaccountably, he had also stayed long enough to teach her the rudiments of playing it.

"You see, we keep an eye out for all the likely lads and lasses we've marked, knowing that soon or late, they'd come to the trials. Usually, though, they're not so stubborn as you." Talaysen smiled.

"I should hope to live!" agreed the lanky fellow. "They made the same remark my first day about wanting to have me stay a liltin' soprano the rest of me days. That was enough for me!"

"And they wouldn't even give *me* the same notice they'd have given a flea." The dark girl laughed. "Though I hadn't the wit to think of passing myself off as a boy for the trials."

"But—why are you—together?" Rune asked, bewildered.

"We band together to give each other help; a spot of silver to tide you over an empty month, a place to go when you're hurt or ill, someone to care for you when you're not as young as you used to be," said the gray-haired Erdric. "And to teach, and to learn. And we have more and better patronage than you, or even the guild, suspect; not everyone finds the precious style of the guild songsters to their taste, especially the farther you get from the large cities. Out in the countryside, away from the decadence of courts, they like their songs, like their food, substantial and heartening."

"But why does the guild let you get away with this, if you're taking patronage from them?" Rune's apprehension, given her recent treatment, was real and understandable.

"Bless you, child, they couldn't do without us!" Talaysen laughed. "No matter what you think, there isn't an original, creative master among 'em! Gwena, my heart, sing her 'The Unkind Lover'—your version, I mean, the real and original."

Gwena, the dark girl, flashed dazzling white teeth in a

vulpine grin, plucked a gittern from somewhere behind her, and began.

Well, it was the same melody Rune had sung, and some of the words—the best phrases—were the same as well. But this was no ice-cold princess taunting her poor knightly admirer with what he'd never touch; no, this was a teasing shepherdess seeing how far she could harass her cowherd lover, and the teasing was kindly meant. And what the cowherd claimed at the end was a good deal more than a "kiss on her cold, quiet hand." In fact, you might say with justice that the proceedings got downright heated!

"That 'Lament' you did the first day is another song they've twisted and tormented; most of the popular ballads the guild touts as their own are ours," Talaysen told her with a grin.

"As you should know, seeing as you've written at least half of them!" Gwena snorted.

"But what would you have done if they had accepted me anyway?" Rune wanted to know.

"Oh, you wouldn't have lasted long; can a caged thrush sing? Soon or late, you'd have done what I did—escaped your gilded cage—and we'd have been waiting."

"Then *you* were a guild bard?" Somehow she felt she'd known that all along. "But I never heard of one called Talaysen, and if the 'Lament' is yours—"

"Well, I changed my name when I took my freedom. Likely, though, you wouldn't recognize it—"

"Oh, she wouldn't, you think? Or are you playing mock modest with us again?" Gwena shook back her abundant black hair. "I'll make it known to you that you're having your bruises tended by Master Bard Merridon himself."

"Merridon?" Rune's eyes went wide as she stared at the

man, who coughed deprecatingly. "But—but—I thought Master Merridon was supposed to have gone into seclusion—"

"The guild would hardly want it known that their pride had rejected 'em for a pack of gypsy jongleurs, now would they?" the lanky fellow pointed out.

"So, can I tempt you to join with us, Rune lass?" the man she'd known as Talaysen asked gently.

"I'd like—but I can't," she replied despairingly. "How could I keep myself? It'll take months for my arm to heal. And—my instruments are splinters, anyway." She shook her head, tears in her eyes. "They weren't much, but they were all I had. I'll have to go home; they'll take me in the tavern. I can still turn a spit and fill a glass one-handed."

"Ah, lass, didn't you hear Erdric? We take care of each other—we'll care for you till you're whole again." The old man patted her shoulder, then hastily found her a rag when scanning their faces brought her belief—and tears.

"As for the instruments"—Talaysen vanished and returned again as her sobs quieted—"I'll admit to relief at your words. I was half-afraid you'd a real attachment to your poor, departed friends. 'They're splinters, and I loved them' can't be mended, but 'They're splinters, and they were all I had' is a different tune altogether. What think you of these twain?"

The fiddle and lute he laid in her lap weren't new, nor were they the kind of gilded, carved, and ornamented dainties guild musicians boasted, but they held their own kind of quiet beauty, a beauty of mellow wood and clean lines. Rune plucked a string on each, experimentally, and burst into tears again. The tone was lovely, smooth and golden, and these were the kind of instruments she'd never dreamed of touching, much less owning.

When the tears had been soothed away, the various medicines been applied both internally and externally, and introductions made all around, Rune found herself once again alone with Talaysen—or Merridon, though on reflection, she liked the name she'd first known him by better. The rest had drawn curtains on their wires close in about her little corner, making an alcove of privacy.

"If you'll let me join you . . ." she said shyly.

"Let!" He laughed. "Haven't we made it plain enough we've been trying to lure you like coney catchers? Oh, you're one of us, Rune lass. You'll not escape us now!"

"Then—what am I supposed to do?"

"You heal, that's the first thing. The second . . . well, we don't have formal apprenticeships amongst us. By the Three, there's no few things you could serve as master in, and no question about it! You could teach most of us a bit about fiddling, for one—"

"But"—she looked and felt dismayed—"one of the reasons I wanted to join the guild was to *learn*! I can't read or write music; there's so many instruments I can't play. . . ." Her voice rose to a soft wail. "How am I going to learn if a master won't take me as an apprentice?"

"Enough! Enough! No more weeping and wailing, my heart's oversoft as it is!" he said hastily. "If you're going to insist on being an apprentice, I suppose there's nothing for it. Will I do as a master to you?"

Rune was driven to speechlessness and could only nod.

"Holy Three, lass, you make a liar out of me, who swore never to take an apprentice! Wait a moment." He vanished around the curtain, then returned. "Here—" He set down a tiny harp. "This can be played one-handed, and learning the ways of her will keep you too busy to bedew me with

227

any more tears while your arm mends. Treat her gently—she's my own very first instrument, and she deserves respect."

Rune cradled the harp in her good arm, too awe-stricken to reply.

"We'll send someone in the morning for your things, wherever it is you've cached 'em. Lean back there—oh, it's a proper nursemaid I am." He made her comfortable on her pillows, covering her with blankets and moving her two—no, three—new instruments to a place of safety, but still within sight. He seemed to understand how seeing them made her feel. "We'll find you clothing and the like as well. That sleepy-juice they gave you should have you nodding shortly. Just remember one thing before you doze off. I'm not going to be an easy master to serve. You won't be spending your days lazing about, you know! Come morning, I'll set you your very first task. You'll teach *me*"—his eyes lighted with unfeigned eagerness—"that ghost song!"

THE SILVERLORD

Morgan Llywelyn

The booth was always closed—or so it appeared. A limp and dispirited awning sagged over the boarded-up display window; a lock rusty with disuse clamped the splintery door. Yet from time to time a whiff of sulfurous smoke curled out under that door, and a muted tinkle of chimes could be heard by passersby.

The sign over the booth proclaimed "Fine Leatherwork By a Master" in gilt letters beaten thin by wind and rain, but there were other leatherworkers at the fair who plied their trade much more aggressively. Still, a newcomer to the fair, wandering the far fringes of the area where animal dealers operated, might find himself knocking at the locked door in hopes of getting a bit of harness or having a simple repair done. And occasionally that door opened.

When it did, as it had on this overcast morning, the face that peered out was like a closed fist. Hard red cheeks, hard black eyes, a predatory slash of a mouth—his was a frightening visage, and he knew it. Appreciating the effect of his ugliness, Melger the master saddler enjoyed seeing people cringe from him.

But the girl who stood in the roadway before him did not cringe. "I need a set of bridle reins for a racing bridle," she said in a clear voice.

"We're closed. Go away."

"You opened the door," she pointed out. Her eyes were gray, and though her mouth was soft and gentle, she had the square jaw of one not easily discouraged. "I've been to the other leathershops, and they're all too busy to make a special set of reins until at least tomorrow, which will be too late. I must have what I need now." She spoke in the tones of one accustomed to having orders followed.

Melger raised his bushy eyebrows. "What family are you?"

"My father is a nobleman with land on the Bear River," she said, being careful not to tell the man more of herself than she knew of him. Her father had taught her to be suspicious. "He raises horses as a hobby, and every year we race them at the fair. We have a mare running this afternoon, that's why I need the reins."

Just then she heard the tinkling of the chimes and simultaneously an angry curse, followed by the unmistakable sound of a shod hoof striking wood. The girl's eyes brightened with curiosity. "You have a horse in there? What are you doing to it?" She tried to peer in past him, but Melger shifted to block her view.

"Who gives you the right to question me?" he demanded.

"Who denies me the right?" she countered. He could tell she spoke the truth about being a nobleman's daughter. Con-

idence was bred in her bones. A crafty look stole into his
ard black eyes; the girl would require careful handling.

"A young woman like yourself shouldn't be alone in this
part of the fairgrounds," he said. "There should be servants
with you, and a bodyguard. It gets rough down here." He
wanted her to feel intimidated so she would go away without
asking any more questions.

"I slipped away from my father's servants because I was
tired of being guarded all the time," the girl told him with a
mischievous twinkle in her eyes. "Besides, the mare is mine,
a gift from my father, and she is my responsibility. He
cannot be here this time to see her run, and I am determined
he will win as a tribute to him. Now tell me what's going on
in there." She had distracted him with the talk about her
servants and her horse, but now she darted back to the topic
that really interested her, her mind so agile it caught Melger
briefly off guard.

"It's none of your business," he started to tell her, just as
they both heard the sounds of a scuffle inside and more
cursing. There was the thud of a blow struck to solid flesh.
The girl gave Melger one horrified look and then somehow
ducked under his arm and was through the doorway before he
could stop her.

Once inside the booth, the girl realized it was larger than it
appeared from outside. Leatherworking materials occupied
only the front portion, beyond which a ramshackle wooden
building stretched into gloomy shadows. Felt hangings covered the walls so no spying eye could peer in through the
cracks.

The girl stopped and stared.

In the center of the room a pen had been rigged from rope
and planks, and inside the pen stood a horse. It was quite the

largest horse she had ever seen, and it glimmered like pol
ished silver in the dim light—silver marred only by fresh whip
welts across its back. Hypnochimes hanging from the roo
beams stirred in the breeze from the open doorway, making
sounds calculated to soothe. Fumes emanating from censers
were intended to drug the animal into further submission, for
otherwise no such shabby shed could have held him. He was
a magnificent stallion, rippling fit, and even in his drugged
state he arched his neck and snorted at her.

"Aaahhh," the girl breathed in admiration.

The stallion was possessed of such beauty his perfection
seemed a reproach to lesser creatures. From the sculptured
curve of his ears to the roundness of his mighty haunches he
embodied grace.

"Hello, you," the girl whispered softly, losing her horse-
loving heart to him.

The stallion snorted a response, flaring his nostrils until
she could see the moist, shell-pink flesh high in his nasal
passages.

A human throat was cleared, and human feet shuffled.
Looking beyond the penned horse, the girl saw a little gang
of men standing in the shadows, watching her with angry
faces.

The stallion was aware of them, too. One ear rotated to
listen to the mutter of their voices. But they weren't saying
anything important. They reeked of flesh eating and they
inflicted pain, but they never said anything important. Only
the girl was interesting. Her breath was sweet, she smelled of
the fruit she had eaten that morning. Her voice was low and
kind. The stallion stretched his neck toward her so he could
focus his drugged eyes on her face.

"You leave him alone!" yelled one of the men in the shadows. He had a braided leather whip in his hand.

"What are you doing here?" the girl demanded, turning to Melger.

"This horse is ours, we can do what we want with him," the saddler told her. Her inborn air of authority made him feel defensive. "We bought the mare who bore him for good money, and we've spent a lot more on raising him. He's the fastest horse in the . . ." Too late he caught himself and bit his tongue.

"Shut your mouth, you bragging fool!" hissed one of the other men. "Why did you let her come in here and see him? It could ruin everything if she tells."

"I didn't let her do anything," Melger protested. "She shoved her way in; she's a trespasser."

"A trespasser who will go straight to the stewards!" the other man said.

And then the girl understood. These men had bred and raised and were concealing this horse so they could enter him in the race that afternoon at the last moment, as an unknown whom no one had even seen. He would leave the post at very long odds and make a fortune for the few who knew enough to bet on him . . . if he was as good as they thought.

The stallion and the girl looked at each other. I am better than you can possibly imagine, he said to her silently, fighting the drug.

He always fought. There were too many of them, and they had too many ways of controlling him. But he always fought.

Someday he would beat them, beat the predators, the eaters of flesh, the cruel men with their cruel whips and their smoke that fogged his mind.

"We'll have to keep this girl here until after the Silverlord races," said the man who had been talking to Melger.

At the mention of his name, the stallion raised his head higher and shook his heavy mane.

"How can he run at all when you have drugged him?" the girl could not resist asking.

"We have done a lot of experimenting on this animal," Melger told her. He did not want this highborn woman to take him for a fool. "The censers are almost empty now, and the effects will pass off entirely by the time we take the Silverlord to the paddock to be saddled. We've had numerous rehearsals for this; we've brought the horse here many times to be certain we could keep him concealed and controlled. We've planned for everything."

"Except me," the girl said.

With instincts more sensitive than a human's, the Silverlord felt menace gather around her as she spoke. The horse flattened his ears against his head and pawed the ground.

"Watch out," said one of his captors, suddenly grinning with inspiration. "You are indeed a trespasser, and you could get hurt here. This horse is savage." He came forward, intending to grab the girl and throw her under the stallion. They all knew the horse would trample her; they had fought with the creature too many times to doubt its strength and anger.

The girl glared at them all in cold rage. "I am An Serra, daughter of Lord Gaorlain," she announced. "If any harm of any kind should come to me, my father would spare no effort to find and punish those responsible."

The men in the shed froze, exchanging nervous glances. The name and reputation of Lord Gaorlain were indeed well known, especially among people like themselves. He was judge of the court to which condemned criminals applied in their extremity, and from which no mercy had been granted in twenty years.

The Silverlord sensed a change in the atmosphere. The menace hovering over An Serra lifted slightly. But this was still an unhealthy place for both horse and girl, and the stallion hated it. He had always hated it, since they'd first brought him here hobbled and blindfolded and the doctors had come to inject him with strange compounds to enhance his strength. Experiments. Pain and fear and change, in the filthy shed behind the leathershop.

And after the doctors there were sorcerers who chanted incantations and poured blood and painted signs on the earth. And then other medicine men and different practitioners of magical sciences and others and others . . . altering the cells of body and spirit, prattling of scientific advancement while they tampered with the destiny of a living creature.

But their kinds of magic were unstable at best. Its immediate effects might be apparent, but its long-term potentials were unpredictable. The men who worked over the horse did not care; it was only the near future that interested them.

The superhorse they had sought to create was complete now. He had become whatever they had made him in their greed and ignorance. The chemicals were part of his flesh, and the magic was part of his soul—no known test would reveal either.

But the Silverlord knew.

One of the men from the shadows was moving again, quietly circling around the pen toward An Serra. He liked her looks. He ran his tongue over his chapped lips. A soft, silken woman like that might be worth risking the wrath of Lord Gaorlain—and if they were careful, no one would ever know what happened to her. Men who could conceal a huge horse could conceal many other things.

But as Melger had said, the effects of the drug were wearing off. The stallion was no longer immobilized by it. He flexed his muscles and found he had control of them all. His hearing was acute. His vision was clearing—he saw the man sneaking up on An Serra.

I will protect you, the Silverlord said, unheard, to the girl.

The man leaped forward and grabbed her, spreading one callused hand across her face to stifle breath and scream together. And the Silverlord rose onto his hind legs, towering over them, sounding his own scream of defiance. One flinty hoof struck out and sliced the top of the skull from the man holding An Serra almost as cleanly as if a surgeon's scalpel had done it.

Blood poured. Yes! thought the Silverlord, remembering.

He reared even higher, focusing his untested strength. Whatever he had become was gathered and ready. He loomed like a white giant over the men who crouched in fear and the girl who had been thrown to the floor, stunned and startled. The stallion dropped back to earth and nudged her gently, urging her to her feet. He looked past her, and the wall on the far side of the shed . . . shimmered. For a moment he could actually see through it before it solidified again, but now he knew the power he possessed. He concentrated harder, and the wall was nothing more than mist. Beyond lay the roadway and a weed-choked alley running between the nearest booths.

The air reeked with the coppery smell of blood. The horse hated it. His ancestors had been gentle creatures who did not kill, who did not torture and abuse. Gentle . . . like the girl.

The Silverlord commanded An Serra to grab his mane and

swing onto his back, but she did not seem to hear him. Melger the master saddler was squatting on the floor, cradling his head with his arms in case the stallion tried to shatter his skull, too. The other conspirators were scrabbling like ants in a disturbed nest, running over each other in their desperation to escape the enraged animal.

The girl looked up, staring at the horse.

One smash of his forelegs was sufficient to destroy the flimsy pen that held him, and then the Silverlord was bending over An Serra, seizing her shoulder with his teeth. He tried not to break the skin, but she gasped and slapped at his muzzle. He shifted his grip slightly without letting go, then pulled her after him as he plunged forward, through the vanished wall to freedom.

He entered the unknown environment like a newborn bursting into an unfamiliar world. For the first time in his life the choices were his to make, and his brain stalled. Where to go? What to do? And the girl was squirming in his grasp, badly shocked by the sensation of having been pulled through what had been a solid wall.

She had no way of knowing about atoms of matter that could dissolve, change shape. . . .

Some of the experiments done on the Silverlord had been magic in its truest sense, the manipulation of matter. Like pebbles thrown into a pond, they set up ripples; they taught the horse's body techniques no horse had learned before. In his freedom, in his brief disorientation, he too experimented.

Hard-packed earth could be made yielding, enabling him to gallop more effortlessly. The clamp of his teeth on the girl's flesh could be softened without losing its holding ability, so they fastened on bone yet did not tear flesh. Many things were possible once the matrix of the mind and the cells it controlled were altered.

The stallion galloped away, away from the brutal men who had thought to dominate and use him.

He was faster than fast; he could diminish the resistance the air offered and slip through it so his passing was no more than a blur to human vision. The girl felt a terrible burning throughout her body as the friction of their flight overheated her flesh. She thought she was dying and tried to murmur a prayer.

Then the hoofbeats slowed, and stopped. They were standing beneath a tree on a high hill, looking down at the patchwork colors of the fairgrounds far below. The only sound was the wind in the leaves and the girl's gasping for breath.

The stallion released her, and she sagged against his shoulder. We are safe now, he told her. For now, though they will surely look for me when they get over their fright. But all of this is new to me. You must help me decide what to do next.

She rubbed her shoulder, astonished to find it was not bleeding. Looking up at the massive animal beside her, she saw that his eye was brown and benevolent, free at last of the drugs.

"What am I going to do with you?" she asked in wonder. "There is no such horse in the world. . . . Have I stolen you? Will Melger dare to send someone after us and reveal their own activities? And if they don't . . ."

She thought of her father's breeding farm and the mares who could be mated to this horse. The foals he could sire! The idea dazzled her.

The stallion, hearing her thoughts, nickered and rubbed his nose against her.

But An Serra had been raised by a judge to whom the law was a religion and any tampering with it anathema. She could not take something that did not belong to her.

I do not belong to anyone but myself, the Silverlord told her. I can go with you if I choose.

Did she understand? Was she hearing him at all? He spoke with his mind as horses had always spoken to one another, because intuition told him this gentle girl should be responsive to subvocal communication. Her empathy with the animal kingdom radiated from her like light. Yet she was not responding. Was something wrong with her, with the way she was made?

He studied her intently. Those little round, pink ears—how well could they hear? They were not shaped to detect faint sounds from a far distance. And her nostrils were too tiny to take in much air, so how far could she run? He sent a probing thought directly into the girl's body and discovered the stiffnesses and limitations of an upright spine. And only two legs! She had hands, of course, those wonderful multifingered hands with their opposed thumbs—but were hands a sufficient asset to outweigh the liabilities of her human form?

An Serra had a beautiful mind, however; he noticed that much. It lay in her skull like eiderdown, shot through with colors and music and tenderness and the possibility of passion.

As he examined her, An Serra was shaking off the effects of her shock and trying to decide what to do next. Even if he was not hers, she could not make herself surrender the stallion to men who wanted to exploit him. She would have to take him to her father's estate and work out the legalities of ownership later.

The priests of Ithkar may have something to say about that, the Silverlord interjected.

"What?" An Serra glanced around, thinking someone had spoken. But she was alone except for the horse. Yet the seed lay in her mind. The priests—did they and their avaricious magic have anything to do with this? The stallion was surely a creation exceeding natural law; in him, science and something beyond science had melded to produce a demigod. If his existence and capabilities were made public, the priests of Ithkar would doubtless claim him for their rituals. The authority of Lord Gaorlain might be sufficient for dealing with Melger and his pack, but the strength of the priestly hierarchy existed outside the courts. She might save the Silverlord from Melger only to lose him to an uglier fate.

An Serra sighed. She was young and suddenly faced with a responsibility she did not know how to meet. One step at a time, then. She stooped and began plucking the long grass that crowned the hill. She wove it into a halter, a flimsy grass halter to control a horse who could disembody solid walls.

When she held the halter toward the Silverlord, she could have sworn she heard a sound of laughter in her own mind. But he lowered his great head and let her put the halter on him. When she tugged at it he followed willingly, making no effort to break away.

His docility surprised her, reminding her of something . . . of her own father, and the way she surrendered to his will, staying with him when she could have married some likely lad and been away in a home of her own, leading her own life. That was what she wanted most in the world, yet she had always surrendered to the will of Lord Gaorlain, subduing her own proud spirit and obeying him as the stallion now obeyed her.

An Serra shook her head to clear it of the thoughts that buzzed around it like flies. "I will take you home now," she said aloud to the horse. She took a deep breath and caught hold of his mane. With one lithe leap she swung onto his back. She expected him to rear and buck, but the stallion only trembled slightly beneath her, then stood still. When her legs squeezed him he moved forward willingly.

Her legs were warm, and their embrace was pleasant to him. Uncertain what to do himself, he gladly allowed her to guide him, though with every step he took he was aware of his strength and his power. The obedience he gave her was a gift, easily taken back if necessary.

They rode in harmony for a long time, until the steel-and-crystal towers of Gaorlain's fortress caught the sun on the horizon and hurled it toward them in blinding spears. On the back of the Silverlord, An Serra had reached her home sooner than she expected. The valley of the Bear River spread before her, lush and green, and her heart warmed at the familiar sight of brood mares grazing in its pastures.

The stallion saw the mares, too, and caught their scent on the wind. He lifted his proud head and whinnied to them.

In his office in the tallest tower of his castle, Lord Gaorlain heard that commanding whinny.

For the first time in years, the judge had been unable to go with his racing stable to the fair due to the demands of his profession. He was frustrated and angry at being denied the one pleasure he allowed himself, aside from the company of his daughter. His daughter, his only daughter. His, his.

Slamming shut the law book on his desk, Gaorlain hurried to the window and saw An Serra riding down the road toward the castle astride a huge white horse, a horse not from his stable. She rode alone and unaccompanied upon an animal that was almost free except for a silly grass halter on his head.

Lord Gaorlain whirled and ran down the stairs to meet his daughter.

The judge was a square-bodied man with a broad forehead

and permanent frown lines carved deeply into his skin. His normal expression was a scowl; his normal gesture was a clenched fist. What he held, he held tightly. He was not happy to see his daughter return unaccompanied. It was a cruel world, as he, a cruel man, knew very well. Anything might have happened to her.

He hurried toward her with a sour grimace instead of a welcoming smile, but An Serra knew her father too well to expect a smile. She saw him as a gloomy man made gloomier by his exposure to the meanest side of the law, and her love was mingled with pity. Or perhaps it was pity—she had never tried to sort it out before.

Now she saw him for the first time as the Silverlord was also seeing him: an irritable, grasping man.

The stallion shied backward.

Lord Gaorlain's scowl deepened. "Someone take this animal and put it into the stable," he barked to the nearest servant. "Come inside and explain all this to me," he continued to An Serra in a tone hardly gentler. But there was a spark in his eyes that was only there in her presence. He, who would never show it, was glad to have her home.

Over dinner that night, An Serra told her father of her discovery of the Silverlord. Gaorlain heard the tale with mounting anger. "Horse racing is one of the few things in the world that has been kept relatively clear of a criminal element," he said, "but now that too is being corrupted. Is nothing pure to be left in this world?" He reached across the table and put one heavy hand on his daughter's shoulder. His pure daughter, his only daughter.

She could feel the anger in him. She had little appetite in spite of her adventure. She was nibbling at a salad, but she just pushed her poached fish around on her plate. The main course did not appeal to her. She could not eat it without thinking of the living creature whose life had been sacrificed to make her meal, so she contented herself with vegetables and a goblet of wine.

Lord Gaorlain fussed and fumed over his own meal, growing angrier every time he thought of the abnormal beast that had been created to perpetrate a fraud in his chosen sport.

Abnormal.

He did not want the animal kept in his stables. But neither did he want it to go back to those who had bred it. "The creature should be destroyed," he told An Serra.

The girl jumped to her feet. There were tears in her eyes. "You mustn't do that, Father! Oh, he is splendid! It isn't his fault, he is only what they made him. But he is so beautiful and so good . . . you don't know. He could have hurt me, but he didn't; he saved me from them. I think they would have killed me otherwise, to protect themselves. Now I must protect him, don't you understand?"

Gaorlain did understand, though he did not like it. "We will stable and feed him, then," he decided. "After all, the animal will be evidence against Melger and the others when they are caught and brought to trial for attempted fraud, as I mean them to be. I would see to it myself, but I have to go away for a few weeks on business. When I return, I promise you the matter of that white horse will be my first concern, An Serra. Justice will be served on those men, and . . . and then we will determine what disposition to make of their horse."

He was not totally convinced he wanted the stallion to live. He had seen the way his daughter's hand caressed the horse before it was led away. He did not like to think of An Serra being fond of such an animal, such a perverted animal.

The meal concluded, the judge offered his arm to his daughter when she rose from her chair, but for the first time in her life she shied away from his touch. An Serra noticed, with distaste, that her father's breath smelled of the flesh he had eaten, and she found it disagreeable, as his heavy clutching hand was disagreeable.

Yet he was her father, and she must love him.

In the sleepless night she went to her chamber window and stared out toward the stable, where the Silverlord was.

While Lord Gaorlain was away, An Serra spent all of her free time in the stable and the paddocks with the huge white horse. She was so preoccupied she did not notice that the servants who had accompanied her to the Fair at Ithkar avoided her now and moved with the careful gait of men who had been badly whipped.

Gaorlain's towering anger upon learning that his daughter had slipped away from them and put herself in danger had resulted in a savage whipping for every one of her servants. Before he left, he had assigned new servants to her, giving them strict orders not to let her leave the grounds of the estate.

"The people who owned that stallion may come looking for her," Gaorlain had told his guards. "Kill them on sight. We will have to keep a close watch on her from now on. I do not ever want her going off on her own again like that, it is too dangerous."

In his absence, Gaorlain's net closed around his daughter. But she did not notice; she was too entranced by the beautiful horse who was her constant companion now.

She spent days sitting on his paddock fence, dreaming about the colts he would sire. She was determined to breed him to some mares before her father returned. If the colts produced by such a mating were as exceptional as she knew they would be, surely Gaorlain would soften toward the Silverlord and give him a place of honor in the stables.

As she watched the stallion, so the Silverlord watched her. He came to understand that she was lonely, had always been lonely, raised without a mother in this distant place, dependent upon servants and her father for what little human contact she had. If such a life was unnatural, she did not yet realize it, but she would someday. She would know she was a prisoner as the horse had known himself to be a prisoner.

Meanwhile, Gaorlain concluded his business faster than he wanted anyone to know—especially his daughter, who had a gentle nature and would not approve of his plans. When the routine work was out of the way, he devoted himself, with the relentlessness for which he was notorious, to tracking down everyone who had worked on the secret project to produce a superhorse. He listened with opaque eyes and a stony face as doctors babbled of "incalculable benefits to medical knowledge" and "long-term genetic breakthroughs." They spoke in a language as cryptic as that of the law, and Gaorlain mistrusted them accordingly. Every priesthood had its code to conceal misdeeds. "You are polluters," he accused, "and you will suffer."

After the scientists had trembled and protested and attempted their justifications, Gaorlain found the magicians Melger had hired. He was more careful with them, for magic was as close to a state religion as the land possessed, and the line between charlatan and accredited priest was very thin. But the doctors had already explained to Gaorlain the particularly nasty shape changing they had worked on the white horse, and he knew that sorcerers had played their part. All were guilty; they had forever tarnished something that had been precious to him, the sport of horse racing.

"Execute them," he ordered. "Execute every one, but see that no word of it reaches my daughter. I want nothing evil to touch her or trouble her heart any further."

Melger and his cronies were the first caught and the last executed. Gaorlain allowed them plenty of time in prison, to be tormented by their fear. And only when all were dead did he intend to return to An Serra and decide what to do about the horse itself.

An Serra had, of course, made her own plans. She led the stallion to the breeding shed and had the finest of her father's mares brought to him. But the stallion turned his head away and seemed unwilling to approach them.

"He's a freak all right," the stablemaster commented to An Serra. "What kind of stallion ignores good mares?"

"There's nothing wrong with him!" she flashed back indignantly.

She ordered a second assortment of mares brought for the Silverlord, but he seemed indifferent to them as well. When he looked at them, they did not please him. They seemed such limited beings. Neither his altered spirit nor the body that held it responded to the female horses with their dim animal minds. Yet he longed for mates; longed for a herd of his own and colts to race the wind with him.

An Serra led him in disgrace back to his paddock. She knew the stableboys laughed at him behind their hands. Maybe they laughed at her as well. She was lonely and unmated, as much a freak as the Silverlord.

"When Gaorlain comes back," one of the stableboys commented to another within the stallion's hearing, "he'll have this beast put down. It's obviously no good for breeding, and you know he will never race it; that would be unethical."

The second stableboy shrugged. "I'm glad I don't have to make that decision."

Make a decision, the Silverlord thought. Yes, I must—her father will be back soon. He keeps her here, and I stay because of her, but this is not a good life for either one of us.

He felt her loneliness and understood it; it matched his own. Horror swept over him. Perhaps the two of them would always be so, as isolated as the stars through no fault of their own.

The next morning, An Serra came to the stallion's paddock and brought him the customary lump of sugar. "Hello, you," she greeted him tenderly. She reached up and smoothed his forelock between his eyes; she swatted a fly attempting to bite his neck.

The stallion took the sugar, lipping it delicately off her open palm. She heard the crunching sound of his teeth and wondered again why a being so strong never tried to escape.

Escape to what? the Silverlord asked, rolling an eye at her.

"Who spoke?" An Serra whirled and looked around, but they were alone. Yet she could swear she had heard a deep and resonant voice that seemed to hang, not in the air, but inside her own head.

She looked at the horse and found herself thinking of the forces that had shaped him, creating magnificence from ignoble motives. Could good come from evil, then? And if so, were not the two forces engaged in some symbiotic counterbalance that . . .

She stopped, biting her lip. An Serra did not think in concepts like symbiotic counterbalance. Where had such an idea come from?

The Silverlord was watching her.

I am neither good nor evil, he said. I just am. I have a right to live, to be, to hope for a future. Just as you do.

An Serra shook her head, thinking she was dreaming.

You should not have to stay here and conform to a mold designed by someone else, the Silverlord told her.

I can free you.

An Serra shrank back from the sudden powerful tug she felt inside her mind.

We don't have much time, the Silverlord said. Be brave, just for a heartbeat. I'm sure I know how to do this. . . .

He planted his hooves and gathered himself as if to jump the paddock fence, but the forces he gathered were not muscular. He recalled, or his cells recalled, how matter had been shaped and twisted, and in some secret compartment of his brain a tiny flood was released like scalding acid, inflaming unused pathways and burning them open.

"No!" cried An Serra. But once a process is begun it must continue.

The pain was intense and excruciating. The girl cried out, flinging her hands in the air. Her spine contorted, and she fell from the fence into the paddock. The shadow of the stallion lay across her, cold as death. The animal stood above her with all his energies concentrated. You want this, he told her. You are like me—you are different from the cruel people. I know.

Pain ripped and tore. An Serra shrieked, and the stallion's eyes fogged with sympathy, but he could not stop; he could not spare her. It will only hurt a little more, he told her, willing it to be true.

An Serra could feel her spine lengthen. She gasped in disbelief as the relationships of her leg bones and arm bones were altered. The tips of her fingers strained together and bunched, and she could feel the nails harden into one solid mass.

Like hooves.

Her neck stretched, the muscles swelling as no woman's neck muscles had ever swelled before. She tried to call out, but already her throat was different and the sound she made was no longer human.

I do not want to hurt you, the Silverlord said anxiously, over and over again. But I have a right to live and reproduce my own kind, I have a right to a future. And so do you. So do you.

An Serra's strength was growing, heartbeat by heartbeat. The womb within her unfolded and expanded to provide room for new, larger life. Her cells observed what was happening to them and memorized the process, storing it for future use as the Silverlord had done.

He crowded close to her, encouraging her. The worst of the pain was over now. The pale mare who was not quite a horse felt the almost stallion's teeth close on her withers in the beginning of courtship. She shuddered; her lips were flecked with foam.

I will never leave you, the Silverlord promised her.

When Lord Gaorlain returned he found one paddock splintered and all his servants fled. No one had the courage to remain behind and face him, or to tell him that his daughter had gone with the white horse. Wild with grief, Gaorlain searched the entire area but found no trace other than the two sets of equine hoofprints leading away from his estate.

When other women began to disappear, farther up the valley of the Bear River, a general alarm was raised. But by then it was too late.

SunDark in Ithkar

S. Lee Rouland

Keri did not much like the fog. She had been on the verge of sleep when she had first felt its eerie presence. Long tentacles of bone-chilling mists had crept into her sleeping place beneath a soothsayer's wagon. The tendrils twisted around her ankles as if seeking to ensnare her in their watery grip. Their touch sent shivers down her spine. She shook off the dimly glowing tongues easily enough, but her hidey-hole was fast becoming deep with the invading dampness.

In such a weather one would not choose to be alone. Picking up the small sack that held all of her possessions, Keri set off for the most crowded sector of the fair. As she made her way through the nearly empty lanes, the cold, vaguely sentient mists swirled about her, danced at her feet, and moved on.

There was, strangely, an odor to the fog; a thing she had not encountered in all of her fourteen years. It was the stench of the great eastern swamp, redolent of putrescence and decay. She stopped to watch in amazement as ropes of mist gathered together and rose in unison to slide into the open mouth of a mask of Thotharn. Keri had heard just enough about the strange god to fear him. She moved on hastily.

As she left the fortune-tellers' sector the fog diminished. Thin slivers of mist like tiny vipers darted past her, hurrying to catch up with their comrades. She shuddered. She was glad that there was not more of the stuff. But the long, snakelike appendages that had slithered into the tents, enshrouded sleepers, and invaded their very dreams, had been only a precursor—merely the advance guard of the forces to come.

As Keri watched, a huge wall of fog rolled in from the east. It was neither as icy cold nor as malodorous as the first wispy tendrils had been. It was a far more ordinary fog, yet she felt uneasy with it. She shrugged off her discomfort as being born of weariness and hunger and pushed her way into a crowded beer hall. Threading quietly through the revelers, she slipped, undetected, into a storage room. There, amongst casks of wine and kegs of ale, comforted by the noise of the merrymakers, she settled in for the night.

Morning found her achy and disgruntled—the first because she had slept wrapped around a wooden keg that had been too heavy to move; the second because she was no nearer her goal than when she had entered Ithkar, only now she was penniless.

Today she would have to approach Eldris Fyrl. She was not pleased with the prospect. Fyrl was new to the fair. No one could tell her anything about him. She had caught sight of him only once and instantly had put him at the end of her list. Now she had reached the end of that list. He was her last resort.

Eldris had pitched his multicolored tent in the center of the fortune-tellers' sector. A wide post stood by the tent's flap. "Knock here," it said—in four languages. Keri knocked. A high-pitched, crackling voice answered. She entered.

Keri suppressed a giggle at the figure of Eldris Fyrl. The man wore motley. He had on a high-peaked, wide-brimmed purple hat encrusted with glittering stars. His overrobe was bright pink, made only marginally drab by lack of washing. It and his long-sleeved green shirt were embroidered in gold and crimson with all manner of arcane runes and symbols. Clearly he was an astrologer.

Eldris was seated at one of the two chairs that flanked a small table. He rose and with a sweeping flourish bowed deeply, losing his hat in the process. His attempts to catch it as it fell only knocked it farther across the room.

"Oh, dear, oh, dear. Will I never learn?" He retrieved the headpiece, reached into its crown, and pulled out an elastic band. Replacing the hat, he snapped the band around his chin.

"Do it again," he said, waving her out the doorway.

"Again?"

"Yes. Come in again."

Keri frowned as the astrologer closed the tent-flap behind her. This was ridiculous. The man *was* a fool. But he was her last chance. Her absolute last. She knocked.

The scene repeated, but this time the hat stayed put. Eldris sat in the more comfortable of the two chairs and motioned Keri to take the other.

"You are quite young to be wanting advice," he said.

"I'm not wanting advice, Master Fyrl. Or rather, perhaps I am, but not in the usual way. I'm seeking an apprenticeship."

Eldris was looking at her intently. Keri was acutely aware of her disheveled appearance. The last three days with no warm bed and little food had left their impression. She tried to slip down farther in the chair so that less of her could be seen. Eldris laughed. The ploy had been too obvious. She tried a different tack. Drawing herself to full height, she began to adopt her most regal air. But this was no time for pride. Finally she let all attitude slip from her and relied on simple truth.

"In exchange for your tutelage I can, of course, offer something in return."

"Oh?"

"I have a very special set of magical stones. They show the position of the sun, moons, and planets."

Eldris guffawed. "I have a very special set of magical books. They show me the position of the sun, moons, planets, and the stars. My ephemerides took me a lifetime to develop. What makes you think your stones would interest me?"

Keri shifted in her chair. She had met with this response before. "I cannot say for sure, Master Fyrl. But there is something about the stones that I do not, myself, understand. Perhaps your knowledge will make them more useful."

"And the something is?"

"Let me show you." From a pouch hung around her neck Keri produced ten small, quite ordinary-looking pebbles. She shook them in her hand like dice and threw them on the table.

"Today," she cried. As the stones landed they arranged themselves in a pattern.

"See? This is the pattern of the heavens today." She pointed to each stone in its turn. "Here we are with our two moons close to one another. Both are near the sun. They will cover it tomorrow. Here are Sarn, Junis, and Sagret.''

"What is this pebble here?" Eldris pointed to a small white stone that, of its own volition, had been moving steadily across the table.

"That is the mystery. Now watch again."

She threw the stones once more, this time calling, "Tomorrow," as she threw. The stones formed a similar pattern, but the small white pebble was closer to the moons and was moving faster.

Eldris watched the pebble, which gained speed as it passed above the moons. Keri watched Eldris. He seemed mystified.

The astrologer tugged gently at his beard. "Hmm. Interesting." He looked up at her. "What is your name, child?"

"Keri." She did not say, "Short for Keridwyn." She felt there was something magical about a name so never gave hers away easily.

"You are from?"

"Abearl. In the north."

"Have you no kin?"

"My kin are dead. My father left me the stones. His last wish was that I learn the language of the stars. Ithkar seemed a likely place to find a tutor."

"Well, Keri, there is more to astrology than throwing pebbles at a table." He rose abruptly.

She must not let it end this way. "I know that, good sir, but I thought the use of the stones could pay my way whilst I learned the trade." She had used that reasoning before. None had seemed interested.

Fyrl was pacing. He circled the table, doing a little jig now and again for interest.

"It may well do," he said. "It may well do." He spun

suddenly to glare at her. "You would not be averse to casting your lot with a man as old as I?"

She squinted at him. Was he going to offer her the position? His face was shadowed by the brim of his hat. "You do not seem so old to me. Besides . . ." She caught herself.

"Besides, all others have turned you down," he finished for her. "I'm old enough to be your great-grandfather. I can tell you, my dear, I am at an age where I no longer buy green bananas." He paused, thinking. "You will work for room and board—no payment?"

She squirmed. "Yes."

"Good, then it's settled. You may start tomorrow."

Tomorrow. Keri's joy was tempered. She started to speak but stopped herself. She did not want to seem presumptuous.

"Well?"

"What, sir?"

"You were going to say?"

"Just . . . that I haven't eaten."

"I see." He rummaged in the folds of his cloak but found nothing. "Zangels!" he said. "Wait there a moment." He disappeared through the curtain that divided the tent, reappearing a moment later to throw some coppers on the table.

"Buy yourself some food. I will meet you here at eventide. Now go away. I've patrons coming." He waved his arms like a woman who has found a gaggle of geese loose in her kitchen. His long sleeves whipped through the air, releasing billows of dust that set him coughing. Both annoyed and amused with his method of dismissal, Keri hurried away from the tent.

Keri was one whose feelings ran either hot or cold. But on this occasion she was as lukewarm as the meat pie she purchased. She took some comfort from the pie and from her familiar haunt below the seer's wagon.

She fingered the pouch of stones. "I have sold out," she whispered to them. "But better that then selling you. At least Fyrl accepted me without asking to buy you—as all the others did. I will not part with you. Never."

She took the stones out and, calling, "Tomorrow," cast them on the ground. Again the white pebble moved, slowly at first, then with increasing speed, until it passed perilously near the stone that stood for Ithkar.

So intent was she on watching the pebble, she did not see the four legs that had stopped at the edge of her sanctuary. A head that wore a brass helmet appeared suddenly before her.

"Here you, come out from under there."

Keri gathered her stones, but the fair wizard who had sniffed out her illegal magic snatched them from her. The fair-ward and the wizard took her by either arm. She started to protest that there was no black magic in the stones, but the wizard silenced her.

"Save your explanations for tomorrow. You can tell your tale to the fair-court—at your trial."

By midday the fog had become a sickly green. Against it torches and braziers flamed, sputtering in the damp mist, but their meager light added little cheer to the dreary scene.

The fetchingly bright hues of the hawkers' tents seemed all a dishwater gray. In every section of the fair merchants' wares suffered from the weather. Richly embroidered gowns, designed to lure silver from the pockets of the wealthy, drooped lifelessly from their wooden pegs. Brilliant jewels, covered with mist, lay like mere driplets of water on sodden velvet backgrounds.

It was a day on which only innkeepers and harlots prospered. Even the fortune-tellers' trade fell off, for the hearts of the fairgoers were heavy with the weather. Few were in a mood to have their futures read, lest the fog-dulled senses of the soothsayers cast them an ill fate.

The dampness had its effect, too, on the ancient astrologer who had set his wagon by the outskirts of the temple complex, near the fortune-tellers' sector. The plain oilcloth tent that extended as a canopy from the wagon's back was indeed empty—but that was not the fog's doing. The old man was betwixt patrons, having scheduled two clients every other day as was his wont. For years his patronage had been a constant. Only when one fell ill or died did he accept someone new. Thus his income was unaffected by the weather, but his bones were not.

He sat hunched over the wagon's lone table. With fingers stiff from damp-induced cramp, he updated his ledger. "Ceringh . . . 13 coppers," he wrote. Then, leaving the journal open on the table, he withdrew an almost identical volume from a hidden drawer. "Ceringh . . . 7 gold." He slid the book back in its hiding place. The fee to enter Ithkar Fair was one thing. Taxes in his homeland were quite another.

Seven gold was the least that any patron had ever paid, but the ancient astrologer had taken pity on the boy. "Boy," Aymar called him, although the youth was well into his nineteenth sunturn. Everyone under fifty was a boy to Aymar.

Ceringh was going to lose his mother this year. The stars had predicted it. If Aymar lived to be a hundred—a thing the same stars told him was unlikely—he would never learn to handle the imminent death of a mother. Fathers? Fathers he could take. Mothers, no. Aymar had even been tempted to offer Ceringh an apprenticeship. But in the end, good sense prevailed. He sent the boy off with a warning to be kind to his mother and to have a care for her health. Ceringh, misty-eyed, understood.

Aymar's next client would indeed pay full price; perhaps, if he gave trouble, double price. Menahir Strone was the sort to give trouble—not of the usual kind, of course. Aymar had no patrons who were unbelievers, none who came just to test the old man. Menahir believed; had believed for the six years he had been coming to Ithkar. But the man was an imbecile. What he wanted, what the astrologer knew he wanted but wouldn't give, was to be told what to do.

Aymar sighed. He pulled the top three sheets of parchment from a neat stack on the table—Menahir's chart, his progressed sunturn. A cough sounded from the doorway behind him.

"You are early," the astrologer said without looking up. "You are always early. Have a seat out there and let me look over this work. It's been a ten-day since last I saw it. I tell you this every year, Menahir."

The cough repeated. It wasn't Menahir.

Aymar turned to see the brown cloak of a temple server, a worshiper of the Three Lordly Ones.

As was his custom when in the presence of one who served the gods—any gods, for he was in no way prejudiced—Aymar rose. The newcomer smiled.

"I have heard tales of you, Aymar Dorphus. I see at a glance that many must be true." But it was more than a glance that the acolyte gave the wagon. He peered intently into the gloomy corners. Finding nothing, he continued, "I have been sent by my masters to inquire about a person of whom you may have knowledge. I am not asking, mind you, whether she seeks you as a patron, for I have been made aware that you do not violate a confidence.''

"Correct. But a spy posted outside my tent would tell you soon enough who my patrons are. I have nothing to hide from the servants of the Sky Lords.'' He motioned the man to sit, more for his own bones' peace than the acolyte's.

No sooner had the young man lowered himself sufficiently for a lap to form than a squealing pink weight descended upon it. Cylute, Aymar's pet pig, had been sleeping on a shelf above the cookstove and had taken the opportunity, the stove having gone cold, to avail himself of another warm resting place. It said something for the acolyte that the man did not flinch. Surprised he was, but charmed, too, and charming.

"Ah, piglet, you do me great honor.'' He stroked the animal soothingly. Cylute snorted his pleasure.

It did not seem to Aymar that there was much honor in having a piglet nuzzling one's crotch, but the acolyte's simple act had told the astrologer much about the man. The ice was broken, and the two smiled at each other across the table.

"Wine?'' asked the astrologer.

"I've no oath against it.''

"Qlik! Some wine for my guest and myself.''

In a moment, the woven hanging at the opposite end of the wagon parted, revealing a small creature of uncertain species.

The few glimpses that patrons had had of Qlik produced the rumor that Aymar kept both a piglet and an ape. It was an honest mistake. Qlik was long-armed, bandy-legged, and impossibly hairy. He swung his legs wide when he walked and carried his burden only inches from the floor. Currently he carried two earthenware mugs of steaming apple wine. The acolyte glanced at the hot wine and then at the cold oven.

"I've got a sweet-peat burner in the front," Aymar explained. "We keep mugs on it in weather like this."

"Then this must be your wine, Qlik." He raised his mug. "I thank you greatly for it."

Qlik made the tongue sounds that gave him his name and departed. The stranger had passed yet another test. Not surprisingly, he seemed to know it.

"My name is Harrel-el-Alar." He gazed down at his cup. "Master Dorphus, we grow the finest apples in my homeland. I've not tasted a cider so rich as this since first I came to Ithkar. Lords be exalted! I'm glad it's me was chosen for this mission."

"And your mission?"

Harrel leaned forward. "Know you a lass called Keri?"

"Should I?"

"Not for me to say, sir. She was arrested this morning. She's been going about seeking apprenticeship amongst the astrologers."

"Surely that is not a criminal offense."

"No. She was arrested for illegal use of magic. . . . Perhaps I should start from the beginning."

"A useful point, though somewhat lacking in imagination."

"I'll take the usefulness; events are strange enough as they are. Last night, before the bulk of the fog hit the fairgrounds, long tendrils of mists were seen to enter the tents of those known to serve the god Thotharn. This morning there was a meeting. One of our own acolytes managed to overhear some of what was said. They are planning, it seems, to threaten Ithkar with a SunDark. They will exact tribute in the name of Thotharn."

"I see. But surely that is not a major threat. There is certainly no reason for the people to fear an eclipse. As for the beasts, I have already asked Garner to go amongst them tomorrow—for he seems able to talk with them—and calm them during the event. He and his kin will do their best.''

"Then there will indeed be a SunDark?"

"Yes, a double eclipse. Both moons will cover the sun."

Harrel frowned. "Many of the people would not fear the eclipse alone, although there are plain folk who have never understood a SunDark. But Thotharn will seem to control the weather as well as the skies, for the plan is to announce that the fog will withdraw just before the SunDark. And there is something more, something foretold by Keri's stones. We of the temple cannot decipher it. That is why we have come to you. You have made a lifetime of studying the skies. Will you help us?"

An eyebrow shot up. The temple servers had need of an astrologer? Aymar found the idea strange. He had certain notions as to the identity of the Three Lordly Ones—although to voice his beliefs would be certain death. Among the few things that the Sky Lords had left behind may (must) have been some astronomical lore. Aymar would love to get his hands on it. Perhaps this was to be his chance.

"Does not your own lore predict heavenly events?"

Harrel laughed. "I have been warned that you may want to conduct some . . . shall we say business?" He presented an empty mug.

"Qlik!" Aymar called. Two more mugs appeared, not steaming, but warm enough. They were well into them before Harrel made his proposition.

"I will not have you believe this to be a small matter. If the people are held under sway of Thotharn, there is no telling the result. It is said that the great orator Gaulrue is here. He is reputed to have hypnotic ability—to sway crowds

262

with his speech. Almost certainly the temple will be in danger. You yourself may be in danger. But we need a way to keep the people calm and to nullify Thotharn's threat. If you will but help us with this, you will find your knowledge increased. The Sky Lords know how.''

That was as firm an offer as Aymar could expect. He accepted it.

There was absolutely no trace of fog on the temple grounds. But so dark was the cell in which they had cast her that Keri could not know the time of day or how long she had sat in the dank prison. Once, a man brought food and water. He did not speak to her.

She did know that it was long past time for her appointment with Eldris Fyrl. Would he learn of her fate? Perhaps she should have told the fair-ward that she was an astrologer's apprentice. But no. That would have served only to bring trouble to Eldris. Already he was light three coppers on her behalf.

Keri did not really understand why she had been arrested. She knew well that all magic had to pass inspection at the gate—and indeed she had shown the wizard-of-the-gate her stones. The wizard had only laughed. Nothing magical about them, he had said. It had been a different wizard who had arrested her. At her trial, would they let her name the gate she had entered? Would the wizard admit his mistake? Probably not. Living these past days amongst the soothsayers had not given her an optimistic opinion of human nature.

She was busy imagining the things that might happen to her, all of them unpleasant, when the cell door opened and a temple server entered. He was young, he was handsome, and he was smiling. This was not one of the things she had imagined.

"Keri," he said. "You are wanted in the council chamber. The high priestess awaits. Come along."

"Is it my trial already?" Her eyes widened.

"No. Lords, no. It's only just evening. Don't worry. I think Dorphus has a plan for your freedom."

"Dorphus?"

"You don't know him?"

Keri was hesitant. "Maybe. I've met so many folk these last days. Maybe I've met him."

The two walked through a maze of halls and tunnels. Their destination was a huge, vaulted room supported by enormous pillars. They approached a long table at which three women and a dozen men were seated.

An old man in a dusk-gray robe sat between two of the women and across from the third. On the table before him, spread out in the next day's pattern, were Keri's stones. The white pebble was motionless.

The man spoke. "I am Aymar Dorphus, and these"—he motioned to the rest of the table—"are members of the council of the Three Lordly Ones. We have need of your skills. Would you cast the stones for us? Specify tomorrow, please."

Keri gathered the stones with shaking hands. She wanted to run, but she saw that a guard was posted at each exit.

Aymar had seen her glancing about the room. "Don't worry so, child," he whispered. "Just do as I say."

Keri cast the stones. As the white pebble streaked across the table, a mutter rippled through the council.

"It is as I thought," Aymar said. "I believe we can win this game Thotharn's servants are playing."

"If you can do that, Master Dorphus, the great library

within our walls will be open to you." It was the woman opposite Aymar who spoke.

Even from her position behind Aymar, Keri could feel his
excitement. It must be a great boon indeed, freedom to roam
the library.

"Your offer is very kind. But, if I may, I had something
else in mind—this young woman's freedom."

Keri gasped. He was trading with her very life. Why?

The woman who had spoken before—Keri thought it must be
the high priestess, for only she could have made such an
offer—rose. "I have the power to do many things, Master
Dorphus, but not the power to break the law. Keri has
smuggled unauthorized magic into the fairgrounds. She must
stand trial for her offense. I can ask for leniency because she
has helped us here, but that is all."

"If I may speak, madam?" Keri was amazed at the sound
of her voice. It was that of a child.

"Speak."

"I did present the stones at the gate. The wizard said there
was no magic in them."

"Impossible. Our wizards do not err."

"He did not err, Your Excellency," Aymar broke in.
"There *is* no magic in the stones."

The woman was losing patience. "We saw them move.
We all were witness."

"Yes, that is true. But those are not the stones that Keri
brought to Ithkar. These"—he reached into his robe and
brought out a pouch, dangling it dramatically over the table—
"are her stones."

Keri looked closely at the stones she had thrown. They
were similar to hers, but not the same. In the excitement she
had not noticed the substitution.

Keri looked up at the woman, expecting anger. A thin smile played on the priestess's lips.

"Throw the other stones, child."

Keri did so. They were her stones; they behaved as expected. "But . . . but the false stones moved, too," she objected. "I don't understand."

It was the high priestess who answered. "It is simple, my dear. The magic is not in the stones. The magic is in the user." She looked down at Aymar. "You have ever been one for showmanship, Master Dorphus. But your point is well taken. If the child tried to present the stones at the gate, which seems probable, then no offense has been committed. She is free to go. But her freedom must not be your prize. The offer of the library still stands." Her voice turned grave. "Do not fail us, my friend, or there will likely be no library to visit."

The temple server who had guided Keri to the council chamber cleared his throat. "My lady. It is not wise that Master Dorphus should leave the grounds. Surely if Thotharn's men get wind of his plan, his life is endangered."

Aymar waved the problem aside. "I appreciate your concern, Harrel, but I am in need of my books. My timing tomorrow must be precise. Besides, I am too old to be sleeping in strange beds."

"Then let me go with you. I can offer at least a bit of protection for the night."

"If you do not mind my humble abode, your company would be most welcome."

The high priestess raised her hand in blessing. "I shall have my men posted throughout the grounds tonight and tomorrow—although what help they may be I cannot imagine. May the Lordly Ones be with you all."

The moment they set foot outside the temple gates, the fog enshrouded them. At last Keri found her voice. "I want to thank you, Master Dorphus, for . . . for defending me."

"You can thank me by spending the night in my wagon, Keri. I have further need of your stones, and your advice as well."

She sighed. "I cannot, sir. I am apprenticed to an astrologer named Eldris Fyrl. He is expecting me, or rather was expecting me, at eventide. I am pledged to meet him."

"Not a problem. It was Eldris himself who told me of your abilities. You can meet with him after the eclipse tomorrow. He will understand."

"Shouldn't I at least stop at his tent and tell him where I'll be?"

"He won't be in. He is very old, you know, even older than I. Eldris suffers from an advanced stage of . . . silliness. He will be hiding from the eclipse. He is afraid of it."

They walked on in silence until they reached Aymar's stall by the fortune-tellers' sector. On the tent-flap was embroidered a strange device—an open hand with three spheres in its palm. Keri thought the sigil odd for a fortune-teller, and she voiced her opinion.

"I am not a fortune-teller." He ushered the others into the wagon proper. "I am an astrologer," he concluded.

Keri opened her mouth to speak, but Aymar silenced her. "Questions answered after dinner. Have a seat, and I'll see about some food." He disappeared through a curtain.

Harrel pulled out a chair for Keri, and she began to take her place. Cylute pounced. Keri took an immediate liking to the brazen piglet.

"What's his name?"

"Cylute."

"What will Master Dorphus do with him when he's full grown?"

"He won't get any bigger; he's charmed."

"Will the SunDark tomorrow frighten him, do you think?"

"No, but it may frighten me."

Keri laughed. "You and Eldris Fyrl."

Aymar returned to the table. "What's this about Eldris Fyrl?" he asked, noting the twinkle in Keri's eye. "You don't seem to be taking him too seriously."

"I had better start taking him seriously, Master Dorphus. He is my mentor now." She played with Cylute, avoiding Aymar's eyes. "Master Fyrl was very kind. He gave me money for food and accepted me as apprentice. But you must know all that if you've spoken to him. Was it he who told you of my arrest? I did not think he knew of it."

"No. Harrel brought me the news . . . but here is our food."

Qlik carried a tray of cold meats, cheese, and bread. Keri's eyes widened when first he appeared, but the dwarf gave her a toothy grin which she returned immediately. She forgot her questions as she dove in to the first full meal she'd had in days. Aymar watched her in amusement, Harrel in awe. She ate twice as much as either man but was finished first.

Aymar leaned back in his chair. He motioned to Harrel, who went out to check the grounds. Eavesdropping was easily done at Ithkar Fair, tents and wagons being, as they were, far from soundproof. When Harrel returned, Aymar began his tale. He explained about the fog being under Thotharn's control and about the orator Gaulrue come to Ithkar to sway the faith of the pilgrims. Lastly he told of his need for Keri and her stones. "So you see, my child, we have much work ahead of us this night. And for the beginning, at least, I will need you to practice your magic.''

Qlik and Harrel went to stand guard outside the wagon. Aymar, with his books, and Keri, with her stones, sat elbow to elbow at the table. Keri cast the stones for different times of day. Aymar made notes and calculations—many of which he explained to Keri. She caught on quickly and began to anticipate his next need. At length they had finished. Aymar was satisfied that he had all he needed. He showed Keri a high bunk in the front of the wagon. She rolled herself in a blanket, warm for the night.

"Used to sleep there myself," he said, "before my bones got too old for the climb. Good night, Keri."

"Keridwyn," she mumbled. "My name is Keridwyn."

Keri slept. Aymar went out to speak to the temple acolytes who were scattered throughout the fairgrounds. All had to be in readiness for the morrow.

Morning found a great crowd of pilgrims, cajoled and threatened by Thotharn's men, gathered near the docks. More arrived by the moment. Overnight a makeshift stand had been erected, and on it, high above the crowds, stood Gaulrue. Above him, placed so that it would be just below the eclipsing sun, was a silver-hued mask of Thotharn.

Gaulrue raised his arms in invocation. He did not speak, yet instantly there was a hush over the crowd. Suddenly a great wind swept through the fairgrounds, shaking wagons and loosening tent stakes as it whipped through the lanes, bringing with it all manner of debris. Canopies, torn from their moorings, blew through the crowd and down the piers to the river Ith, and a yowling cacophony issued from the beast-masters' sector.

But over the howl of the winds, the cries of the frightened pilgrims, and the doleful bellowing of the captive dorn beasts; over all of this there rose a great sucking sound, as if all the winds in the world converged and were swallowed by an immense vacuum.

Above the heads of the terrorized fairgoers the fog swirled forward and swept toward the now glowing mask of Thotharn. Great gobbets of mist flowed through its open mouth and disappeared. Within moments the fog was gone. The winds died as quickly as they had risen, and sunlight streamed again from the heavens. It was as though the fog had never been.

Just as a mutter began to rise from the crowd, the priest again raised his arms. "Pilgrims," he said. "Long have you awaited the return of the Three Lordly Ones. Wait no more. The Sky Lords will not return. Thotharn rules Ithkar. The great Thotharn rules the fogs; rules the winds; rules, even, the sun itself. All power lies with Thotharn. Do not doubt. For if only one man doubts the wisdom, the power, the omnipotence of Thotharn; if only one man has doubt, then Thotharn shall cause a great shadow to fall across the sun. Kneel, pilgrims, kneel before the mask of the god of gods. Kneel and be saved lest the light of the sun desert you."

Those nearest the baleful eyes of Gaulrue knelt first, followed by ranks of pilgrims farther back. When about half the people had knelt, Aymar Dorphus began to make his way toward the front of the crowd.

"Unbelievers!" Gaulrue cried. "Thotharn will rule Ithkar. See, even now the shadow begins to eat your sun. Kneel, while there is yet time for the god to revoke his punishment. Kneel and worship Thotharn."

The pilgrims looked up. Through blinking, teary eyes they saw a shadow beginning to form at the edge of the sun. The shadow grew, and with it grew the numbers of those who knelt. Gaulrue droned on and on. His hypnotic, singsong voice swayed the people. Pilgrim after pilgrim dropped to his knees. By the time the moons had nearly obliterated the sun, all were kneeling except Aymar. Even Keri, under orders, knelt. Gaulrue pointed to Aymar.

"There is the man. There is the one man who will not believe what his own eyes tell him. There is the fool for whom we are all being punished. Seize him! Force him to worship Thotharn. Force him to be saved."

Aymar had expected such a trick. The twoscore men nearest him at the platform's base were acolytes, masquerading as fairgoers. In the darkness of the eclipse little could be seen. Even those a dozen strides from Aymar could not see him. He was safe enough, for the moment. He turned to face the crowd.

"Goodmen," he began, "you have seen a great wind blow away the fog."

"Thotharn's wind!" Gaulrue shouted.

"Yes," Aymar continued, "that indeed was the work of Thotharn. But were there none among you who saw the temple grounds? Who saw that there was no fog near the hallowed place?" A few folk muttered. Gaulrue would have interrupted had not Qlik chosen that moment to clap his hand over the priest's mouth. Others who served Thotharn, seeing what they believed to be a hideous animal attack their leader, melted into the darkness.

Aymar went on. "This here"—he raised his arm to indicate the sun—"is but an eclipse. The two moons, Kumeth and Lilith, are crossing the path of the sun. That is all. You have seen eclipses before. Surely a double eclipse is not a magical thing."

"This one is," the disguised voice of Harrel called out. "Thotharn caused the eclipse. Thotharn rules the moons."

The crowd muttered its assent. A few single voices were raised, but Aymar had not the time for hecklers. He continued, louder.

"Not so, goodman. The eclipse is preordained."

"So say you now." Harrel was playing his part well. "It is easy to predict what is already past."

"Then I shall predict the future. Watch the skies. In a moment a great white light with flaming tail will cross above the sun and fall to the west. Like the SunDark, it is a natural thing. But if you wish, take it as a sign—a sign that Thotharn does not rule Ithkar. Watch but a moment. See that I speak truly."

It was a long moment. The crowd grew restless. Aymar had begun to think he had misfigured when a shout rose from the pilgrims. A white ball with a long glowing tail streaked across the sky. The people rose as one. As the comet disappeared in the western sky, the edge of the sun peeked out from behind Lilith.

Within the hour it was over. Fair-wards hustled Gaulrue away from the crowds, who seemed intent on pummeling him to death. The final edge of the sun cleared the moon shadow and shone brightly on the fairgrounds. All was well in Ithkar.

Keri could not bear to speak to Aymar, for to speak was to say good-bye. She watched him accept the congratulations of the acolytes. He was famous now; he would not have time for her. She set off to find her mentor, Eldris Fyrl.

The astrologer was not in his tent. There was nothing to do but wait. She settled down in Eldris's favorite chair and closed her eyes.

A second later she was being rudely shaken. It was Fyrl, his hat askew as always.

"Wake up, girl. What do you mean by sleeping here? Have you no proper bed of your own?"

Keri thought of the warm bunk in Aymar's wagon. "No," she said. "I'm sorry, Master Fyrl. I was waiting for you. I must have dozed off."

Fyrl shook his head sadly, then waved a long finger at Keri's nose.

"You're much too young to be tired at this hour. Probably that scoundrel Dorphus had you up all night with his blasted schemes."

"His schemes just saved Ithkar's temple while you were hiding under some bed somewhere. If you were half the astrologer Aymar is, you would have known . . . What?"

Eldris had begun to laugh. The sound had started deep in his belly and rolled up through his throat. He had lost control. Tears formed in his eyes. He wiped them away with one hand as he pulled off his beard with the other. The hat came off, the mustache, the unruly hair, even the pointed nose.

"Aymar!" Keri cried. "You . . . how . . . why . . . ?"

"Oh, by the Lords, my child, the look on your face while you were defending me. It was worth a thousand disguises."

"You were Eldris Fyrl all the time." Keri was too astounded to be angry with him. Anger would come later, much later.

"Yes. I had need of an apprentice. I never advertise myself as Aymar Dorphus, so I invented Eldris. He was my agent, so to speak. And he did very well, too. Look what an apprentice he brought me."

Keri had buried her head in Aymar's cloak. He could not tell whether she laughed or cried.

"Come along, my child. We have much to learn—and an entire library in which to learn it."

HAIR'S BREATH

Susan Shwartz

"You'll spoil that baby." Lounging on cushions in their quarters within the traders' enclave by the docks of Ithkar, Vassilika held out her arms for her daughter. "Give her to me, Andriu."

"So *you* can spoil her?" Andriu laughed and handed Demetria over to her mother. She was *his* now, he thought. Maybe Thotharn—or his agent, Xuthen, who had died three fairs ago—had sired her, but Vassilika had prayed to the Three Lordly Ones, and Andriu had sung; and they had been answered. Three years ago, Father Demetrios had told him that removing Vassilika from Ithkar during her pregnancy might safeguard mother and child. They had waited three more years to be certain. She is innocent, Andriu thought, and smiled at his daughter, whose plump bare foot took aim, then sent Vassilika's accounts sailing into the air.

Some innocent! he thought, and bent to retrieve them. He

275

glanced at the satisfying totals and smiled at his wife. She grinned back, an expression as hoydenish as it was welcome. There was no trace of Thotharn's shadow upon her or upon the child, the old dream-singer had said. Just let anyone call them demon loving, Andriu thought. Three years among the Rhos had taught him well. If he weren't a master trader or fighter yet, he was no disgrace—and he had a crew to back him up, and the grudging approval of the master traders to call their boat half his.

He reached for his harp, a wedding gift, and smiled at Vassilika. Autumn sun poured in the skylight and danced on her ruddy hair, tumbling loose over her shoulders. Bored with custom, as usual, she had left off the scarf and loose overtunic worn by Rhos matrons. Her elaborately embroidered blouse was tied loosely at the throat; her shoulders and full breasts seemed to glow through the fabric. Three years ago, Andriu had wanted to crawl back to Ithkar Fair and die amid the shattered crates of its back ways. Then he had met Vassilika. Even afraid as she had been, she had restored his will to live and given him a reason for doing so.

He plucked out an experimental run on the harp. Its inlay glistened with faint tints of copper. Demetria laughed and waved her hands. Even some of the crew wandered in. Andriu had started to set Rhos poems to music; it had won their hearts even more than a successful trading voyage or a good fight. Their boat's scrubbed deck had been the battle-field of gods and heroes night after night. Andriu almost wished they were on board right now.

But one crew member hadn't come for music. "Mistress, dream-singer, you remember when the *White Bird* vanished? Well, one of its oarsmen turned up."

"There were no survivors!" Vassilika sat up and plumped her daughter onto a cushion.

"He has part of the logbook," said the steersman. "And he insists on speaking to you."

Andriu laid the harp aside again. "Why us? Surely the master traders could do more in the way of indemnities. . . ."

"They sent him to us," said the steersman. Andriu felt warmed by the "us" before wondering why they bothered. Other junior traders specialized in salvage operations, not they.

He glanced at Vassilika. "Have him come in," she decided. She was more experienced in trade and made such decisions. "You can be captain," he always told her. "Just so long as I'm first—and only—mate."

The crewman who bowed his way in looked hungry enough and ragged enough to be a castaway. And the logbook looked real; Andriu recognized the captain's hand and signature. What drew everyone's attention, however, was the metal plaque he drew from his tattered overtunic. It glittered in the sunlight, and its curves and angles were wrought with more care than any Ithkar smith could manage. On it were etched . . . "Not runes," Andriu told his wife and the steersman. "Those are a very, very old form of the dream tongue."

The language spoken by the Three Lordly Ones, and still preserved in fragmented, barely understood form by men like Father Demetrios! If this plaque were written in that tongue, then it must be . . . "Where did you find this?" asked Vassilika

Andriu opened the boat's log, its leather pages stained and crumbling at the edges. He pointed to a scrawl of blotches and lines that a skilled sailor might be able to follow. "There," he said.

* * *

In the end, leaving the castaway in the custody of their clan, they went: Vassilika for hope of trade and her usual curiosity; Demetria, because the child could not leave her mother; Andriu, in the hope of proving himself—and to find other artifacts for the temple. The crew went, Andriu was convinced, for two reasons besides the chance to make a killing in trade that would let them swagger around the fair as if they owned it, too. The first reason was that they thought he was crazy and needed to be looked after before he scuttled their boat. The second was that Demetria was on board. Andriu had a good idea that if Demetria took a notion to sail off the rim of the world, the crew would take her there.

Besides, even Andriu was tired of land, of the crowded fair, of beds, not bunks, that didn't rock comfortingly beneath one with the rise and fall of the river. So they rowed upriver. Gjellandi and its portages were but three days' journey away when they weighed anchor.

Vassilika glanced from scribbled map to the shores.

"I don't want to pull in closer," she said. "Look at the rocks, well out away from the shore. Could be risky."

"People used to live here," Andriu observed. "That one pile could have been a mill."

"Send out a party?" asked Hjordis, the steersman.

"Aye," said Vassilika.

When the sailors found no one living—or dead—on either shore, Ingvarth, one of the ablest of the younger crew members, came up.

"Do you want me to dive here, mistress?" Vassilika nodded.

Idly, Andriu admired the clean line of his dive, the splashing rainbows of his entrance into the water, the shape of Vassilika's hair on her shoulders. Demetria crooned and

278

kicked; quickly Andriu moved his harp out of the child's way.

"Do you think he'll find anything?" he asked.

"Oh, I hope so," Vassilika said. "If he doesn't, there's those among the masters will say we were too blind to see gems heaped up in front of us for the taking."

It wasn't just the desire to make a killing at the fair, or even to make Father Demetrios smile with wonder. Vassilika and Andriu were half-blood and outsiders, with a daughter (even more suspect) to provide for: among the master traders, some—mostly old unfriends of Vassilika's father—opposed their claim to being true Rhos traders.

He bent over Vassilika in a way that made the crew grin. But what he whispered wasn't love. "You're aware that if Ingvarth finds something that once had life, Father Demetrios might sing it into manifestation?" Vassilika widened her eyes and nodded, storing the fact against future profit.

Ingvarth's red mane splashed through the river's gleaming surface. He waved an arm that dripped with water and weed. Light splintered up like a flare from what he held in his hand; his shipmates glanced away as it spurted over their faces. "Hoist me up, brothers!" he shouted in triumph.

He heaved himself over the rail and laid another piece of metal at Vassilika's feet. "Like the other one." Vassilika touched it. "See, it's lain at the bottom of the river . . . who can say how long? Yet there's no rust, no pitting."

"Bright!" crowed Demetria, and grabbed for the find. Vassilika and Andriu saw her tiny, glowing face reflected in its golden surface. She started to croon to the metal as if it were one of her dolls.

Andriu pried the metal from the child's clutches. No telling what ill she might take of it, he thought. Angered, she twisted her face into a scowl and drew breath.

"With those lungs, the child might make a dream-singer," Andriu observed, wincing. "Little heart, try this!" He drew a deep breath, calling up the special resonances of dream-singing, and sang a song of bubbles, soap bubbles, glistening like rainbows, bobbing up from the river. Demetria laughed and waved her fists at them.

Andriu's song grew more intricate. Now amber and violet and blue animals spun and somersaulted in the bubbles he sang up. Demetria, too, began to sing.

Abruptly, others joined the song. It swelled into an actual presence, a pressure that hurt the ears. Andriu fell silent. His hand dropped from harp to dagger. But still the song rose, and with it, the bubbles rising from the river. They grew larger and brighter.

"By the grace of the Three!" cried Vassilika, one hand clutching a spray of flowers and leaves bound into an amulet. Her other hand drew her child to her.

A giant opalescent bubble bounced onto the deck, engulfed the baby before she could be snatched away, then rose from the deck to plunge deep into the river.

"There, on the shore!" Andriu heard the shouts but didn't pay attention. Demetria! All he'd meant was to give the child pleasure. He flung down his treacherous harp with a crash and dazzle of light and dived into the water.

The song rose to a crow of triumph, then died as if its throat had been cut.

Vassilika was halfway over the rail before Ingvarth could grab her. She screamed and scratched as she fought to plunge over the side after her husband and child. The new silence seemed to mock her as much as the song that had snatched her whole life away. Andriu. Demetria. Gone. She sagged in the crewman's arms, panting.

"There, mistress." The steersman pointed. "Where the master thought a mill might have stood. Do you see them?"

"Vodyanoi," whispered Ingvarth, and made a sign several others imitated.

No wonder no one lived here. No wonder no boats passed them. No wonder the *White Bird* had vanished and the master traders of the Rhos, practical as always, had sent no one to search for it . . . except for a ship and cocaptains whom it would be well rid of. And the cocaptains, of course, were only too happy to trade on rumors they heard, a map they had from the sole survivor. . . .

A killing. She spat over the side and brushed her long hair back in distraction. A killing: the term betrayed what the Rhos might do for a profit. Then a new thought struck, and she blessed the Rhos practicality she had spat at a second earlier. Survived. What if that man had been *released*? The Vodyanoi, mill haunters, river dwellers, boat breakers, capered before her, shifting shape. Now they were delicately female, with a lithe grace Vassilika had never been able to lay claim to. Behind her, the older crewmen restrained their younger brothers and cousins. Captains had lost whole crews to the Vodyanoi in their female aspects.

Then the Vodyanoi shifted again. Now they were triumphantly male, with shoulders and loins the mere glimpse of which might heat a woman's blood—assuming the woman hadn't just lost her family.

Crafty, the Vodyanoi, with their songs and—so the songs claimed—their palace beneath the river's bed, with its eternal, brilliant lamps. She could well believe that they might release a captive, arm him with what she and Andriu—never mind the master traders, whom Vassilika personally was going to tear apart if she made it back to Ithkar alive (no thanks to them)—couldn't resist, and send him out to woo a trader and a dream-singer, intent on making a killing.

That word again. They were traders, not killers of any sort. If Andriu and Demetria were dead, her desire to excel among the Rhos, his desire to prove himself, had killed them. He'd had no need to prove himself, her heart cried out. Least of all to her. Her hands gripped the railing so tight that splinters drew blood from them.

Why *her* ship? She could understand the Rhos. But why had the Vodyanoi wanted her ship and *her* family? The trap had been baited especially for them! She shrugged off offers of ale, or a strong arm back to her cabin, or (the Lordly Ones protect her!) herbal remedies that, at the very least, would leave her as sick of body as she was of heart. There was no time to waste on sickness. She had a question to answer. Of all the traders who plied the rivers, why her?

Obviously, she had something the Vodyanoi wanted—a daughter who had been touched by magic and a husband who could sing flesh into form. Vassilika hadn't wanted the child. She had hated the fact that a demon had sired it upon her, that she hadn't even had the chance to fight. Then she had been terrified, knowing the barbarous laws that might be invoked upon her. Then she had met Andriu. She remembered him crouching outside the Temple of the Three Lordly Ones, spitting up blood into a grimy cloth. Though he'd looked three-quarters dead, he hadn't been too busy dying to offer her hope and a dream-song that had almost gotten him enslaved to Thotharn. Together they had sung a new song. And the jeweled spray turned green and breathing, the gems into dew. . . . Sky Lords help me now! If we did aught for you in crippling Thotharn that day, help us now!

One creature caught her eye and preened himself. Vassilika picked up a hammer and flung it. He arched his long back sinuously, tossing back sleek wet hair. There was no comparison. Andriu, with his diffident smile that widened so easily into a raffish grin, his stooped shoulders, bent from reading in bad light or harping in worse, the gangling frame that had such strong arms to toss a baby up into the air or hold Vassilika close during the midwinter storms. . . .

"What shall we do now?" The steersman looked to her for directions. Clearly his instinct was to steer back to Ithkar as quickly as oar and sail could take them there. *Cut your losses:* it was an article of faith among the Rhos. Just as clearly, he hated to abandon Andriu and the little girl.

"Now what?" Vassilika echoed him. "Now *I'm* going to dive down there and see"—agony clenched at her throat, but she fought the words out—"if there's anything left of them."

A cheer went up from the rocks.

"That's what they want, mistress. Don't do it!"

"I know," said Vassilika. "So if you've got a better plan, tell me."

No one had, of course. Vassilika stripped to her shift and tied her hair back. "Till sunset, Hjordis," she told the steersman. "If I don't return, get back to Ithkar and report. Perhaps the master traders will send a priest to lay the curse hereabouts. Tell them"—the words came with inexpressible bitterness—"to deduct the priest's fee from our estate."

As she turned back to the rail, her eyes fell on Andriu's harp. When he'd flung it from him, trying to snatch Demetria back from the Vodyanoi and their bubble, he had snapped one of its strings. Glints of silver and auburn curled on the deck beside the harp. When it had been made, she had ordered silver strings and wound them herself with her own hair. Andriu had always said the harp had a mellow, loving tone; she was sure he had never noted the hair. More than anything else, the broken string reminded her that he was gone. Andriu would never have let the string go unmended.

She glared at the idiots who were saying that someone (someone else) ought to restrain her and dived before anyone could try it. The water embraced her—head and arms, body and feet.

Vassilika hadn't dived like this for years, not since her father had brought her downriver from the great trading posts of the north to place her in the care of his Ithkar-born wife. The current flowed greenly, coldly, over her eyes, and her hair and shift billowed out behind her. She stretched out her hands, struggling to reach the river bottom, where toppled stones still bore crumbled traces of mortar. Hooking fingers into a spray of slimy weed, she looked around. They were nowhere in sight.

High above her, the river's surface shone like a wet plate of silvery crystal. Faces—now handsome, now leering and twisted—peered down. In an instant the Vodyanoi would dive. . . . Her throat was burning. Her eyes bulged from lack of air, hot against the cool, flowing water. She couldn't see Andriu and Demetria anywhere.

Reluctantly, she released the weed and kicked back to the surface.

Again.

And again.

Somewhere around the fifth dive, Vassilika remembered

the sailors' trick of inflating their lungs. Now her breast felt like a drum, taut from so much air. The drum pounded in her brain. Soon its rhythms would be too much for her, and she would scream, swallowing water, all her loss, all her love, rising up to possess and doom her just as surely as the Vodyanoi possessed and doomed her husband and child. As sunset approached, the river was turning molten, forbidding. Soon it would be too dark to dive anymore.

Vassilika drew in one last breath and plunged downward. This time she vowed not to surface until she found traces of her family. She swam rapidly past the rocks she had observed earlier. There . . . once it might have been a passageway. . . . It would be desperate folly to enter there. A rocky spur might catch her shift and hold her forever, so she ripped it off and plunged into the darkness.

The need to breathe consumed her. Breathe . . . push . . . It was like labor. Andriu had scandalized every woman in the hold by entering her room and playing his harp until her need to push, to see her child draw breath, had overpowered the music. Then, he had grasped her hand and chanted encouragement along with the midwife. Push . . . *this* one was for Andriu . . . *this* was for Demetria. . . . With a gasp she broke through the water. Air pocket, she thought, and blessed the Lordly Ones before she went any farther. Greenish light shone up ahead, strange to her unaccustomed eyes. It grew until it dazzled her. She took another, rash step and found herself floundering in icy water and a current that snatched her feet out from under her and drowned her senses in a rush of frost and sound.

If Andriu had thought that his dream of playing before kings and princes would bring him to a hall under-river, he'd never have dreamt it, he told himself. At least I might have brought my harp! One comfort: across from him, surrounded by women whose gowns shimmered in all the changeful colors of deep water, sat Demetria. She was dressed like a little princess. A gem dangled from her brow and reflected the splendor of the light shining from the great jewel in the firepit.

For an instant, Andriu shuddered at the immense weight of rock and water above this hall.

"Harper," the women crooned to him. "Dream-singer." Long-nailed fingers plucked at his sleeve, pulled him to the center of the hall. Feeling half-drunk from bewilderment, he rose from a crouch and bowed to what had to be the master of the hall. He was even darker than Andriu, and his eyes were strange.

"You are most welcome, dream-singer." The hall lord's voice turned it into a title of nobility. "You and your daughter."

I've been drunk, and I've had raving fevers, Andriu thought, but never, at my craziest, have I come up with a tale like this. And if I did, I would never have been mad enough to sing it.

That meant it had to be real. Well, he'd played to crowds almost as strange. "You do us too much honor, my daughter and I," he said. "We cannot accept your hospitality."

The man smiled and shook his head. "But you must," he said. At his side, a woman rose and walked toward Andriu. Her features and garments altered until it was Corisande Storm-lover herself who sat down and pulled Andriu to sit beside her. Storm-lover. And, judging from her fingers on his thigh, his lover the instant he let his guard down.

Vassilika would use his guts for fish bait if he did anything half that stupid, he reminded himself. Vassilika . . . she'd be frantic. He had to get back.

"Do you worry about your lady?" asked the hall lord. "A loving husband. For certain we cannot keep you apart. And so . . ."

A squat, hunched figure Andriu couldn't quite see a face on shambled out of the hall. The grotesque bore little resemblance to the graceful beings who wooed him. Vodyanoi. They were said to be masters and mistresses of illusion. But it was a thought. This Corisande Storm-lover, whose white body gleamed seductively through the veils of mist and twilight that were her only garments—if he saw her true form, would she, too, be twisted?

"Behold your wife, dream-singer," said the lord.

The servant dropped a body at Andriu's feet. Its pale flesh was bruised. Long strings of weed tangled about the bare feet. But its hair covered bare shoulders and, even dripping wet, that hair was the color of autumn.

Then the soaked head came up. For the moment before the Lady Corisande's hand cupped Andriu's chin and turned his face away, he gazed into Vassilika's amber eyes.

That's my last chance gone, Vassilika thought. How could Andriu ever turn away from the woman who sipped from a jeweled goblet, then insisted he, too, drink, with his lips touching the place her mouth had rested? She was lithe and lovely, more beautiful than the creatures so far overhead, who sat and sang on the rocks. (Lordly Ones, protect my crew!)

It was only in Andriu's songs that a mortal woman could vie with an immortal and come off the winner. Vassilika knew precisely what she was. She freckled in bright sunshine. She had lost only half the weight she'd gained bearing Demetria. The amber girdle she had received as a wedding

287

gift was packed away, part of Demetria's dowry. . . . She won't need it now, part of her brain wailed.

A shadow fell across her face. It was almost a relief from the brilliance of the gem in the firepit. The hall lord knelt over her and laid an elegant, ringed hand on her brow.

"Magic guarded the door," Vassilika reproached him. "Otherwise I'd have made it in here on my own."

"Quite so, my dear," he agreed. "Now, we know from your husband's mind that you are Vassilika. I am Taryn Rhyn Eryn—master here. Can we not make you more comfortable?"

Though the marble on which she lay was wet, it was quite warm. Vassilika remembered that she'd discarded her shift up by the cave. She shrank into a ball, protecting breasts and belly with drawn-up arms and knees.

"My apologies," said Taryn Rhyn Eryn, and gestured. A breath of fragrant air caressed her, and she dared, flushing, to look down. She'd heard of dawnsilk, but now she found she was wearing a gown of it, spangled at hem and sleeves and neckline with gems. What would an ell of it bring at the fair? she thought, forcing herself to practicality. Then Rhyn Eryn's hand brushed back her hair and pulled her face up.

"Beautiful," he murmured, and drew a long finger down her throat. "So warm, so real." While Vassilika wondered how long he would take to kill her if she spit at him (as she had a mind to do), he traced the line of her shoulder. Still, a treacherous part of her purred beneath the caress.

"Demetria!" she gasped suddenly, twisting away from the persuasive, seductive hand. "Where . . . ?"

Taryn Rhyn Eryn pointed. Attended by three women, Demetria sat at a child-size table, richly inlaid with metals and ivory. She ate from a golden bowl. It was her latest grace, to be able to feed herself without spilling . . . or at least without spilling too much. These women praised her with laughter and little cries.

The child had magic in her soul, Vassilika thought. Look how content she seemed. Had Father Demetrios been wrong?

Taryn Rhyn Eryn approached with a goblet. You couldn't eat or drink in places like this, she remembered.

The hall lord's vast, lambent eyes fixed on hers, trying to overpower her. See, they are safe and happy. I worship you. Drink. She shook her head, and he smiled, pleased to be indulgent for now. He led her to share his own high seat, and she dared not draw away.

Vassilika glanced about. The hall was bright not just with gold and silver, but with the strange metal that had sent her on this hunt. Much of the strange metal was worked into shapes that bore as much resemblance to shipboard pumps as Vassilika bore—so she thought—to Corisande Storm-lover. Though they were as shiny as the day when some unimaginable foundry must have delivered them, Vassilika sensed that they were vastly old.

"Yes," murmured her companion. "So many years. . . ."

"Too damned long!" shouted the gnarled creature that had dragged Vassilika into the hall. "Enough of this courtesy. Will they help us, or won't they?"

"I'm trying to ensure their help, idiot!" snarled Rhyn Eryn. He pointed a finger. The creature shrieked, reeled, and collapsed upon itself. The air about it shimmered. And if Vassilika thought its previous form was hideous, its true form was pure horror: tiny head, frog-webbed hands and clubbed feet, and, hanging over the twisted flesh like a fog, a knowledge that the mind and spirit so inadequately housed by

289

deformed flesh were somehow older and angrier than flesh should contain.

Perhaps the hall lord would bargain, Vassilika thought. She glanced over at Andriu. Or perhaps Andriu felt he'd already struck a bargain. She felt a pang of sorrow for him; he was nowhere near the businessman he tried to be for her sake. She folded her hands in her lap and looked attentively at her captor, waiting for the first offer.

"Ah, daughter of traders." He smiled. "You sense trade. So now, I imagine, you will offer me your own presence, or even yours and your husband's, just so your daughter may enjoy the upper air. Is that not so? Look how happy the child is, lady. Your offer is foolish."

Vassilika sat calmly. Let him speak, she warned herself.

"No. I do not offer you your daughter's freedom. The bargain I offer . . . I think," he told the Vodyanoi now assembled in the hall, "that we should not be greedy. We have the dream-singer and his child, and *I* have his wife. Companions of mine, let us allow their ship to pass."

Involuntarily, Vassilika glanced at the table, her hand leaping to her mouth.

"We do not eat flesh," Rhyn Eryn said, his voice thin with fastidious disgust. "Our flesh . . . is like your flesh."

"With all your powers," asked Vassilika, "why do you need us?"

"Because our flesh isn't fit!" Taryn Rhyn Eryn cried sharply.

The light flared. When Vassilika could see more than orange spots with a blue afterglow, she saw Rhyn Eryn's true form: blazing-eyed, erect, but deformed—more deformed, perhaps, than the thing he had punished.

"How long . . ."

"Have we looked this way? Since we of the crew knew how our own ship failed. We stole a *life slip*"—Vassilika heard the words as gibberish—"and abandoned our officers. Some say we also abandoned our souls."

Vassilika had read of a betrayal once, in one of the oldest and least canonical scrolls about the Three Lordly Ones. These creatures must be incredibly old, of an unimaginable heritage, that they claimed kinship with the Lordly Ones.

"Some of us say we cannot die, that we left our souls . . . but oh, our bodies die and die and die. Still, some of us are cursed with the power to sing. Almost to sing true. What you see is the illusion we can sing to comfort ourselves." Once again light exploded, and Taryn Rhyn Eryn stood tall, dusky, and magnificent before her. She shivered at the sight and scent of him. "Whatever else you see is our poor best at dream-singing when our bodies are too old to contain us and we must move to others. Each body is less fit, less beautiful. . . . We weaken.

"And so we tried this. My plan. To find a dream-singer who might help us sing true. We had not dreamed we would find three."

"We are not dream-singers, Demetria and I."

"The power gilds you like a second skin. And while you are here, *he* will cooperate."

Vassilika glanced at Andriu, now nuzzling Corisande's white throat. He appeared to be cooperating indeed.

"Your decision to spare my crew was unpopular," she observed. "Why would your people want them?"

"There are other ways to obtain bodies besides singing them: make them, breed them. Or take them . . . as we took the trader who tempted you with metal from the life slip. Your crew are strong, healthy . . ." Aye, and they'd leap into hell first! Vassilika thought. As would I, before I breed strong bodies for a set of deformed cowards and deserters. Being used once was enough for a lifetime!

"You should not despise me," said Rhyn Eryn.

"Why not?" Vassilika asked.

"Because I don't want you to." He smiled at her with the assurance of a selfish child caught in mischief, yet sure its charm can evade punishment. "I can take your mind, change it for you. I can compel the illusion that you turn to me as your husband now turns to her—" He nodded over at Andriu, now enlaced in the woman's arms. "It could be very, very good. But I would prefer that you turned to me of your own will. I am lonely."

Vassilika shook her head. So Taryn Rhyn Eryn was human to that extent. He wanted love, acceptance, forgetfulness that his treacherous brain was prisoned in deformity her mind and body must be enslaved to overcome. Even if it cost her life, her family, and her crew, she could not consent to help him.

"I am sorry," Rhyn Eryn said. He raised his head. His eyes widened, their pupils glowing, drawing her attention. . . .

"A moment, please. One last time, I should like to hear my husband play with my mind unclouded."

A cup was placed at Andriu's lips, and he drank. He remembered as the fire burned down into his belly. Vassilika had just given him a chance, and he had to make the best of it.

He laid hands on the woman who wore a simulacrum of Corisande Storm-lover's legendary flesh. Her shoulders were too cool to be human; his gift as a dream-singer told him that their shapeliness was a lie. He made himself kiss her in a way she would interpret as a pledge of later passion, then picked up the harp. . . . He thought it hadn't been there an instant earlier. More of *their* work, he supposed.

He clucked his tongue in disapproval. One string was broken. As he bent to repair it, the Corisande-shape left his side. With a hunching gait, it crossed to the tall man (man?) whose hand lay so possessively on his Vassilika's shoulder.

"Giving his mind back like that was madness. Do you know what he might do with a dream-singer's full powers? Do you?"

The hall lord ignored her. His mouth brushed Vassilika's hair as he asked, "Will this content you?"

Andriu saw her nod. He would have given much to hear her voice, but she had done what she could.

He stretched the string to its proper peg, then examined the broken one more closely. Glints of red among the silver of string and inlay . . . why had he never noted those flecks of reddish harvest light before? He teased one free with sensitive, callus-padded fingers and stared at it until he heard how the muttering rose to a snarl in the hall around him.

Vassilika's hair. Strands of Vassilika's hair had been woven around the strings. The hair caressed his fingers as he began his song.

He sang of spring, of birth, of his daughter's first cry, first step, first words. Her babbling ceased as she, too, listened.

A drop of water fell from the ceiling.

Andriu sang of summer, hot and sultry, full of longings and vibrant health, of blue sky, storms lancing down through it.

Rhyn Eryn's hand turned up Vassilika's face. "Ah, I remember," he said.

He sang of hearths and harvest, wind brushing grain into waves in the field; of a line of maidens—each looking like

Vassilika—each bearing a sheaf of wheat, dancing about a fire.

Three more drops of water sprinkled on the fire.

Taryn Rhyn Eryn raised his face and gestured. Around Andriu, the air went thick and drowsy. He felt a surge of longing for the dark woman who wore veils of mist and twilight, who awaited him in the bowers spread beyond this room.

"No!" He could hear outcries rise among the Vodyanoi. They screamed to Taryn Rhyn Eryn to shut up the mad harper, kill him, anything, but he merely stroked Vassilika's hair. Vassilika twisted in his arms. Now Andriu could see her face. Go on, she mouthed. Go on!

The drops of water had become a trickle.

I have killed us all, he thought. The ceiling would cave in, and the water would crush them before anyone had a chance even to try the route Vassilika had discovered. He knew well that she would never abandon him and Demetria.

Andriu felt a tug on his robe. He turned a smile down at his daughter, who hugged his leg. This was the best gift he could make her: she would die free, pawn to no evil creatures.

He struck the harp to sing of winter. Vibrations quivered through table, floor, and the air itself.

Rhyn Eryn turned toward him, his eyes insane, his mouth gaping to sing discords, yelps and howls broken by the cleft in his palate, which was revealed now as his power waned. Andriu struck the harp again.

I can hold him, he thought. I can. It was a stalemate. Their opposed powers struggled in the hall. The floor began to crack, the cracks to gape open. A one-legged servant stumbled, then toppled with a shriek into one of the cracks.

"Not my child!" Vassilika's voice rose in a wail. "Don't let her drown, too . . . I beg you!"

Rhyn Eryn's hands, outstretched for the next attack, trembled. He turned to look at her, and his twisted mouth twisted still further—with regret. Almost negligently, he gestured at the ceiling.

Drowning out her cry and the clash of Andriu's music against Rhyn Eryn's came a rumble, as of stone crashing in on itself, and a sense of engulfing wetness. The hall was breaking up. Andriu had time to stretch out his hand to his wife and feel her take it before water hurled him upward and darkness struck him on the back of the neck.

Rough hands threw Andriu over the rail. His belly crashed into it, and he collapsed onto the deck, trying to heave up what felt like half the river. The sky whirled about him as he hacked and panted. For a second, he wondered if he still had the lung fever—and that Vassilika, his daughter, his fortune, even the Vodyanoi and their doomed, damned hall, were fever dreams and that he now lay in some tavern waiting for delirium and death.

Beside him, Vassilika was coughing, too. Andriu looked up and saw his wife and daughter lying beside him on the deck. Demetria was wailing fretfully, but her hair and clothes were completely dry.

"He couldn't kill her," Vassilika gasped. She coughed up more water. "Taryn. He couldn't let her drown. He diverted . . . I suppose we might as well call it power, to protect her . . . and so the water came down upon them."

Andriu staggered to the rail. Yes, surely, a bite had fallen from the coastline. Strange debris littered the water, wreckage he didn't want to examine too closely lest he see bodies, the grotesque, drowned corpses of the Vodyanoi, floating among it. He didn't want to think of them. He didn't want to think of Father Demetrios trying to make one of them manifest.

Vassilika joined him. Her arm went about his waist, his about her shoulders, as they so often stood. "You couldn't *pay* me to salvage that," she said.

"The crew will be happy." He glanced around the boat. The usually neat rope coils lay strewn over the deck. Two barrels were splintered, contents every place. Even the mast listed to one side. "Must have been quite a whirlpool up here, after the hall collapsed. They'll have enough to do without dragging the river."

He heard the steersman shouting orders and was glad when they started to move. He didn't want to stay here for the night, floating over so many broken bodies. He didn't want to remember what they had looked like when their illusions failed, or the hunger and guilt that drove them. Yet one of them had held the essence of a creature who had sacrificed his own life for Andriu's daughter—and had known what he was doing.

This would make quite a song, he thought. A pity his harp was probably snagged on some rock down there. Vassilika shivered against him. "Someone get her a blanket," he shouted. He remembered with a pang of shame that she had been naked when she'd entered the cave. But she was not naked now, though the dawnsilk that dripped and clung to her body offered little warmth or concealment. She saw the way he looked at her and flushed. He took the blanket from the crewman who brought it and wrapped her in the warm wool and his arms. As he swung her about, she brought up one hand. Starlight glittered off the inlay of his battered harp and off the faint threads of red that clung still to its snapped strings.

"This came with us, too," she told him.

THE SINGING EGGS

Kiel Stuart

The road to Ithkar Fair was almost empty, the day swift, clear, bright. Master portrait painter Maeve drove her wagon lazily in the sun, eyes half-closed. But something was amiss. An irregularity in motion. She opened her eyes fully, and sure enough, Cloudblue was limping.

"This won't do," she said, stopping the wagon, clambering down, and hugging his dappled neck. He had been a gift from her greatest patron, Lord Piellao. (But that was five years gone, when things had been going well and she'd had more work than she could handle.)

Maeve bent to her task, carefully lifting and examining each hoof. Aha! A pebble, lodged in the right front. She drew out her small artist's knife, chatting reassurance to the horse, and expertly pried out the pebble.

"There, my friend," she said. "We'll rest here a minute." One thing about animals, she thought. Their loyalties do not teeter with your latest success. Or failure. Nor even with the doubts you hold about yourself. . . .

Suddenly Maeve let out a yelp. In the back end of her wagon she spied a bright-eyed little beast, its pointed muzzle dripping egg. *Her* eggs! The eggs she needed to bind pigments, her livelihood—

Maeve snatched out her knife again and tensed. The little beast, loudly crunching through eggshell after eggshell, stared at her, direct, unafraid.

It was a pretty thing, with its short glossy fur, explosion of white whiskers, and vermilion eyes like twin jewels in multicolored velvet. Its busy black nose and paws were in constant motion as it gobbled her eggs.

Maeve sighed, put away her knife, and watched it finish its gluttonous feast. It chirped, sneezed, washed itself vigorously, then jumped out of the wagon, where Maeve saw it streak off into the trees. "Shoo," she said halfheartedly, and went to examine the egg basket.

Not a one remained. Ah, well. Eggs could hardly be difficult to come by at the fair. She examined her unharmed panels, brushes, and pigments as she considered using the lost eggs as an excuse to turn back, not go to the fair at all. No. It must be. She had to test herself, had to resist her fears.

She patted Cloudblue and got back in the wagon.

"Walk slowly, friend," she cautioned him, and once more they ambled down the dust-brown road to the fair.

Very soon, Maeve realized that they were being followed. A dirty, ragged, scrawny little figure was walking in their wake, carrying a bundle that bumped against its leg rhythmically. Cloudblue's ears flicked back, catching the sound. Maeve clucked for him to stop, and their little shadow stopped, too. It was a child—a small boy.

She called to him, and the child stood scuffing in the dirt, twisting and turning, then slowly came alongside the wagon. "Why do you follow us, child?"

The boy shrugged, then stood on tiptoe to peer into Maeve's wagon. He turned his dirty face up to Maeve's. "You are a painting master, sir? You are on your way to the fair?"

Maeve laughed, a big bright sound. "Fie! I am indeed a painting master, but no 'sir.' I am called Maeve." She flicked at the buttons on her coat.

"But you are in man's clothing," said the child.

"Something I picked up from a patron, who became my greatest friend and benefactor. He is gone now, but his style remains part of me."

"Let me go into the fair with you?"

Maeve was silent.

"Please?" Suddenly the dirty face brightened. "I know! I see no apprentice with you. Perhaps you could use an apprentice."

Maeve frowned. "I had one. He did not—suit me, and I was forced to release him." She did not say more about her unfortunate association with Gahr, the misbegotten son of that errant, devious, masquerading wizard Gohnd.

"Let me be your apprentice, then! I can do more than care for your horse! Just tell me what to do! Please?"

"Child," said Maeve, "it takes seven full years' study to become a skilled apprentice. And I am a stern master. I demand that my gesso panels be of the finest wood, well and properly aged, and that the gesso comes out smooth as unicorn ivory. My pigments must be ground until they are like liquid gold—and then they must be ground some more. You propose to hop into my wagon and do these things well, if I take you to Ithkar Fair?'' Maeve arched her strong eyebrows at the lad.

The child seemed to melt a little. His head drooped, the grubby hands fell away from the wagon, and he turned to shuffle off.

''Well,'' said Maeve, biting a knuckle. She drew a breath. ''Still,'' she said, then, ''you look to be an able and smart youth.'' She beckoned to him. ''Climb up. Come.''

The child whooped and flung himself into the wagon.

Maeve stifled a smile and clucked to Cloudblue. ''Now, son,'' she said as the wagon creaked into motion, ''you must apply yourself carefully to do all I shall show you. But soon you will— What's amiss?''

The child wiped filthy paws across an equally filthy face. ''I may be an apprentice—but no 'son.' '' The child blinked at Maeve.

''Ah.'' She laughed. ''But you are in boy's attire. So I am caught by my own device! Well met! Let that be our trademark. But,'' she went on, chuckling, ''if you are going to go around in boy's attire, we can surely find some better garments at the fair. As befits the apprentice of a great master. What are you called? Where are your parents?''

''My name is Tuilla. I came down from the north.''

''Ah,'' said Maeve. ''That explains much.''

''My parents are gone. The rest of my people don't need my small help,'' she said a little defiantly, trying to wipe some of the encrustation from her face with her grubby shirt. She only succeeded in smearing it around, rearranging what was already there.

Maeve pulled out a linen square. She passed it over the girl's face, glancing playfully at the dirt. ''Not the *best* red clay. We will not bother to collect it, for I already have a supply of good southern earth in a flask. Here, take the cloth and this skin of water. See what you can do.''

While Tuilla removed the worst of the road from her face, Maeve said, ''I can guess, I think. You wanted a trade, and there were no opportunities with your own people. The fair teems with opportunity, so you took to the road, hoping to find a way in.'' Maeve thought of the sullen, spoiled, overprivileged Gahr and glanced at eager, hopeful Tuilla. ''Yes, well,'' she said briskly. ''I have some bread and dried fruit in that reed basket there. Eat. A great master's apprentice should look well fed. It helps the image.''

Fees had been paid, clothes bought, and Tuilla cleaned up thoroughly. Now Maeve watched her new, smart-looking apprentice care for Cloudblue with a skilled hand. The girl had obviously been around horses. On that much, at least, she could set her mind at ease.

There remained the matter of some eggs.

Maeve scanned the teeming fairgrounds. Should she try the livestock dealers or booths where food was sold? Livestock dealers would have fresher eggs. She slipped a hand into her coat, weighing her purse. If she could meet the challenge, this fair would bring new patrons and fill her purse.

''Tuilla,'' she said, ''I am going now to buy eggs. While I am gone, you can set up.''

A hooded, cloaked figure came up behind her and touched her arm. She turned and looked into a painted face. ''I will return soon,'' she said to Tuilla.

The painted mouth moved in a grin, and the man said softly, ''I understand you seek eggs. Why spoil your pretty coat mucking around livestock, master? If you will walk with me, I can solve your problems.''

"Problems." Plural. And the face . . . painted, but so hauntingly familiar. A fair-ward she knew by sight, Marus, nodded at them, and Painted Face turned away, looking down, and said, "Let us walk away from here."

He went; she followed, wondering. When they had reached the booth of a busy dealer in old manuscripts, Painted Face stopped. "Now," he said, drawing an egg from his robe. "Take care not to act startled."

Startled? Over an egg? Maeve frowned, and Painted Face held the egg to Maeve's ear. She jumped back.

The egg was singing.

"Careful," said Painted Face. "Do not attract attention to us."

"What is this?" hissed Maeve. "Are you a priest, one who can sing things into existence?"

Painted Face only grinned. It made her skin crawl.

"Keep your magic eggs. I will go to the poulterer's for eggs that carry no blessing—or curse." She turned to go.

"Perhaps," said Painted Face, "what I have heard concerning the master Maeve is not true after all."

Maeve stopped, as he must have known she would.

"Perhaps the rumormongers are wrong, or I have heard amiss. Perhaps Master Maeve is not merely riding out her reputation as a great portrait painter. Perhaps she has her talent still. Perhaps at this fair she will have many new patrons."

Maeve looked over at the busy manuscript dealer. Her feet seemed rooted. She spied one familiar-looking youth with a telltale slouch. Well, it was no surprise that the wretched Gahr would be at the fair, no doubt now making some other master's life miserable.

When Gahr left she moved numbly to the table, picking up

a small scroll. She unrolled it, staring at the illuminations. Whoever did them had been very skilled. She became aware that the dealer spoke to her. "No," she mumbled. "No, thank you. I was only admiring it."

Painted Face was at her shoulder, patient.

Maeve replaced the scroll. The past had been sweet. Skill, talent, whatever one called it, lay dead. Well, she didn't have to *use* the eggs. Just have them. Just take them, to make Painted Face leave her alone. Once she had been at the pinnacle. When Piellao died, it had all seemed to evaporate, and she'd been powerless to stop it.

Maeve said at last, "How many eggs have you?"

Painted Face smiled and took her money.

The eggs lay in Maeve's basket, cushioned by a silk cloth the scarlet color of precious heartworthy. She heard Tuilla busily setting up. She listened to the bustle for a moment, then lifted the eggs to her ear and heard their strange harmony, at once eerie and seductive. Cloudblue snorted softly in postfeeding contentment.

These eggs will provide what you lack, he had said. None will be able to resist your portraiture now.

Maeve knew now who Painted Face was. Always a master of disguise. The son nearby. How could he be any other than Gohnd?

"Master Maeve?" Amazing how clean and well fed Tuilla looked now. She would be an industrious apprentice, perhaps one day even a fine artist. "We have a prospective patron."

With an effort, Maeve shook off her dismal thoughts and strode to the front of the setup.

The young lord awaiting her could have been Piellao's shadow. She smiled despite herself. And remembered that first fair, long ago, meeting Piellao much like this. Oh, yes—the same dark eyes and hair, the same cocked, quizzical brow. A face she could have painted in her sleep. Once upon a time, long ago.

He spoke first. "Ah, Maeve the master painter. I have been admiring several of your display pieces. Your charming little apprentice has been telling me that it is difficult to keep enough display pieces on hand, as your work is so very much sought after."

Maeve glanced quickly at Tuilla, who was suddenly very busy with some panels at the back of the tent.

"Thus I feel fortunate to have discovered you so early in the course of the fair. I wonder if your schedule is still free enough to render a portrait of Lord Vaten Staunce?"

Maeve played along. "Why, that would all depend on who this Lord Vaten Staunce is." He was no taller than she, and scarcely broader in his finery.

"Oh, you are looking at him," he said in mock innocence. "Have I neglected to introduce myself properly? For shame. Now I have entirely lost face, and you will have to paint me out of pity."

"When I paint you," said Maeve, "it will have nothing to do with pity." She decided quickly. "I will arrange my schedule to suit you, Lord Staunce. Tell me when it is convenient to sit to me."

He sparkled. "It is convenient at this very moment."

Maeve smiled. "As you can see, the light is fading, and I prefer not to work by candle or torch. Would tomorrow suit you just as well?"

"These technicalities are entirely beyond me! Lighting conditions, you say?" His smile was mesmerizing. "Well, in these matters I defer to your judgment. You are, after all, the master. I will arrive early tomorrow and will be quite content to sit for days if necessary. I bid you farewell, but only for the shortest of times.''

Maeve watched his splendidly attired back disappear in the crowd and sighed. Gradually she realized a bit to eat would come in useful at the moment. ''Tuilla,'' she said suddenly, ''fetch us some dinner, will you?'' She handed a few coins to the girl and retreated into the growing dark of her tent.

Alone except for Cloudblue and the eggs. Those cursed eggs. She should have gone at once to the poulterer.

Maeve bent forward and plucked an egg from the flaming silk, bringing it to her ear. The strange singing. Could they be, somehow, vestiges from the Three Lordly Ones? Or stolen from the great singing priests?

She should turn them in. Fling them to the ground. (Could they sing her skill back into being?)

Maeve turned to a small portrait, painted from memory, the only one remaining of Piellao. It showed him full face, in the bloom of health, before he had wasted away. That signature cocked brow. It was the one portrait she would never part with. It was how she would pose Lord Staunce.

She placed the egg carefully back on the silk. They looked like mere eggs, ordinary. From any distance at all, the song was silent.

She would destroy them. But first this one commission.

When Tuilla returned, Maeve took her meat pie and wandered the crowds alone.

''Ladies and gentlemen,'' said Tuilla. ''Unlike most of her contemporaries, the master portrait painter Maeve works in a spontaneous manner. You'll note that she uses no preliminary sketches, but rather works directly with brush and much diluted egg tempera from the first measure.''

Maeve smiled, not pausing in her work. The crowd was getting big, and Tuilla had learned well. She was a natural. Lord Staunce was arch and amused in his posing seat, eyes twinkling at her.

This morning she had broken three of the eggs, holding them well away in distaste, separating the yolks into a small glazed bowl. It had taken a moment or two to locate the basket of eggs. Mockingly she thought her inner self had deliberately misplaced it. Or maybe Tuilla had simply moved it, in the night.

''Master Maeve is the fastest contemporary portrait painter due to her unusual techniques. You will note her use of the sea sponge, cloth, reed, and fingers, as well as the more conventional brush, to achieve the finished portrait.''

Tuilla makes it sound as if I'm invincible, thought Maeve.

And today it was true. Her fingers were winged. They went right for the gold, flying over the panel, bringing out the likeness of Staunce as if by magic. (Magic. Yes.) It was a cloudy-bright day, one that cast no false and glaring shadows, her favorite light in which to work.

''I think I could grow to like all this sitting about.'' Lord Staunce sat close enough to be able to converse. ''If your rendering of me even approaches the works I have seen, I am sure my entire family will grow to like all this sitting about.''

''Are your family here at the fair?''

''Only my elder uncle, and he is so lean and ill favored that you will not wish to paint him, I am sure.'' Staunce laughed.

Maeve said, ''It is not mere beauty which inspires the

portrait. Only when the artist has captured the essence of her sitter's being can a portrait be called successful.''

"I was only teasing. My uncle is a fine man.''

"And for such teasing, you well deserved my lecture,'' she said, deftly applying touches of heartworthy to the young lord's costume. She forced her thoughts from the singing eggs.

And she went into the artist's trance, from which she carried on light conversations, checked proportions, mixed and applied pigments, all from another, mystical space in her mind. When she came to her full senses she was staring at the finished portrait of Lord Vaten Staunce, and the sun was only beginning its final bow toward the horizon.

She blinked. It was clearly the best thing she had ever done. She spoke, rather flatly. "Lord Staunce, it is finished now, if you wish to inspect it.''

Only then did the shooting pains in her back and shoulders make themselves known, the product of long hours in one position. "Carefully,'' she said. "The paint film will be tender for months to come, although it is dry to the touch at once. Do not handle it.''

"Oh,'' breathed Lord Vaten Staunce. "Oh!''

Maeve sat exhausted, limp. Yet a thrill hummed along her aching bones. It was back. She had it again. The eggs had given it to her.

Lord Staunce turned to her. "You shall immortalize my family indeed! And in addition to your fee, you must have something extra. You shall come to my quarters and pick something. Or choose anything you wish from the goods at the fair.''

So like Piellao. "I am humbly grateful, Lord Staunce.'' She pulled her crackling shoulders back. "But if it please you, let me come tomorrow. I am a little weary just now, and—"

"But of course, how thoughtless of me. This superhuman effort. You must rest. And this was a lightning-quick rendering, even for you. By all means call on me tomorrow. My people will look for you. Give your hands a rest, but let me have one of them, for a moment, before I take my leave."

Again she watched him go off. And Tuilla set to work cleaning her brushes, paint cups, sponges. With a groan, Maeve flopped onto her cot and stared at the tent ceiling.

She must have dozed off. Tuilla tapped her gently in the dark. "Excuse me, master. What shall I fetch you to eat?"

"Oh." She sighed. "Anything at all. Take some coins, and take some time as well. See a bit of the fair if you like. You have done well today."

Tuilla skipped away. Maeve closed her eyes again and eased back into the cot.

"Well, look who it is, laid out like the dead."

Maeve jumped up to face Gahr and Gohnd.

She collected herself. "What more do you want from me? You already have my gold for those filthy bewitched stolen eggs. You have been happy to know that after I dismissed your son, work and power have dwindled. And that I owe to you, I think."

"Oh," said Gohnd, "you owe me more than you know. Poor Lord Piellao. He went so fast." The painted face glistened with glee.

Maeve went numb. "You?" she said dumbly. "Why? How?"

"Why"—Gahr grinned—"is 'cause you liked him, and you was so stupid to get rid of me. How is 'cause you was

308

also so stupid to make all the images of him that we used to—''

''Enough.'' Gohnd cut him off.

A good portrait captures the essence of the sitter. . . .

''And now?'' said Maeve dully. ''And now?''

''And now the same will happen to your new favorite, for you used the eggs I sold you in the making of it. And the song of my eggs, with your imagery, binds your sitter to me for as long as I care to hold him. I will not say whether I cast a spell on the eggs or found them or took what did not belong to me.''

''Then why tell me this? Why not sit back and enjoy my bewilderment and suffering?''

''Because you will be prosperous, for my eggs have helped you to make a great portrait. All the nobles and great merchants and captains will seek you. And you will use my eggs, and give me gold—and their souls.''

''And if you is so stupid to refuse,'' said Gahr, ''we denounces you to the fair-court, and you will be nothing.'' This seemed to please him greatly. He giggled and spat.

''Tomorrow you will be busy,'' said Gohnd. ''We will see you then.'' They left her tent, and she sank back on the cot.

She stared at the tent opening, seeing nothing. Slowly she drew her artist's knife, ran her thumb over the point, stopped. Took it in her right hand, poised, felt the weight of it, pushed it gently against her left wrist.

Crimson drops oozed from the tiny wound, no more than a pinprick. Maeve held her breath, gripped the knife knuckle white, swept it back to slash.

And stood trembling, and dropped the knife. No. That would not stop them. Nothing she did to herself would stop them. She caught a jagged, rough half sob, fell to her knees to retrieve the knife, closed it, and walked out of the tent like a ghost.

She brushed past milling people, turned, and bumped gently from here to there in the torchlight. She went her tortuous path with no purpose and no destination. Now and then someone called to her. She could no more answer than she could stop her feet from moving.

She caught sight of Gahr and Gohnd, and they seemed to move toward her, pushing through the swarms of people. She went stumbling and collided with Marus, the fair-ward.

"Well, master painter," he said, steadying her. "Have you been in your cups tonight?" He smiled down at her.

She gripped his forearms, looking past him at the two figures moving closer with each stride. "No," she said softly. She took a breath and looked up into his steady hazel eyes. "Bring me before the fair-court," she said.

"You did what?" The magistrate glared at her.

"I knowingly used enchanted eggs to mix with my pigments, hoping they would boost my abilities, and used the resulting egg tempera to render a portrait of Lord Vaten Staunce. He who sold me the eggs is the wizard Gohnd." Maeve felt light-headed and serene.

"She lies," said Gohnd evenly. "She pleaded with me to cast a spell to bolster her fading talents. When I refused, she threatened to harm me. Why, you can see how much larger than I she is. She put her artist's knife to my throat. It's small, I grant, and legal, but the throat! I had no choice but to lie, and sell her some harmless eggs, which I told her were enchanted."

"He came to me earlier," countered Maeve, "and told me that by using his eggs I had subjugated my sitter's soul to him.

That he could cause Lord Staunce's death as long ago he caused that of Lord Piellao. That I must do as he told me.''

"She lies," insisted Gohnd.

The magistrate scowled from Gohnd to Maeve. "It is a great temptation to cast you *both* out. But we must see the eggs. Some, go and fetch these eggs from the portrait painter's tent."

"No!" Gohnd flung himself away but was caught on every side by sturdy fair-wards. By the time he had been subdued, a runner had returned with the eggs and Tuilla. She looked a bit wide-eyed, but not frightened. Maeve hurt for her. She was a fast study, a good apprentice. She must be provided for.

"Let me listen to the singing eggs." The magistrate held one to his ear, frowned, and did so with all the eggs. He rose, slowly, threateningly.

"These eggs make no noise."

Gohnd looked a little strange. "I said as much," he cried, brightening.

Maeve's mouth opened. And then a small voice piped up. "May I address the court, please?" Tuilla!

The magistrate hesitated, then gave assent.

"Those are not the eggs Master Maeve bought." When the hubbub abated, she went on. "Last night when my master was out enjoying the fair, I heard something at the back of our tent. I ran in to see a little beast, its mouth full of dripping egg.

"It was not at all afraid of me, and easy to capture. I took it to the poulterer's and traded it for fresh hen's eggs, not wanting to anger the master with my incompetence." Then Tuilla slowly reached into her pocket. "One egg remained untouched. Here, Your Honor, you take it, for if it is as you say, and the eggs are enchanted, I want nothing to do with them.''

The magistrate put Tuilla's egg to his ear. With an astonished look, he snatched it away again. "These eggs indeed sing! This is unlawful magic!" He drew himself up again.

"If it please Your Honor," began Tuilla, "I can see clearly now that Master Maeve was setting a trap for this dishonest wizard Gohnd. She told me nothing, however, and I am sorry if I ruined her plan."

"You have not ruined anything," said Maeve. She was wise enough to press her advantage. "The outcome will be the same."

The rest passed in a blur. Maeve rested a hand on the child's shoulder while sentence was carried out against the wizard, and she dismissed with a stern warning to leave such matters to the officials from now on. Maeve suspected that Marus's favorable words had much to do with this.

It was near dawn when they walked into the open air. Maeve stretched against the coolness. It would be good to sleep with the knowledge that her portrait of Lord Staunce had come from ordinary eggs. And from her own ability, which had lived dormant all the while.

But first things first. "Tuilla, take me to where you traded the beast."

It did not take long. The poulterer rose with his hens, and Maeve was glad they did not have to wake him.

"There." Tuilla pointed.

And there it was indeed. The same bright-eyed little beast who had stolen her eggs on the road to Ithkar Fair.

She picked it up, and it chirped at her. She gave Tuilla coins to pay for it, along with a good supply of eggs for both of them.

Maeve hugged the little beast to her. Its wet black nose explored her neck, and she laughed. It started a kind of high musical purring, in which Maeve thought she heard a hint of the exotic egg song, now rendered harmless. "You sly thing," she told it as its whiskers tickled her lips. "I will call you Piellao. You and Tuilla and myself. We will make quite a team."

"Come," she said to Tuilla. "Back to our tent. It is already tomorrow, and I have a notion it will be a busy day."

BIOGRAPHICAL NOTES

Gareth Bloodwine has written verse and short stories since his junior high school days. He also worked eight years in the theater, acting in over fifty plays as well as directing and writing scripts, of which two were produced. Fascination with music has led to a part-time career in that field also. He has earned a Knighthood as well as a regional award for bardic skills in the Society for Creative Anachronism, a game he has enjoyed for the past ten years. When not otherwise occupied, Mr. Bloodwine lives and practices medicine in the Southwest.

Living in Tucson Ann R. Brown and her British husband run Incahoots Decorative Rubber Stamps. Secretly, however, they dwell in the realms of Ann's novels and stories: a world in which a wren's feather sends a ghost back to his grave, and various other wonders are accepted as only a fair part of living. From that far country Ann and David invoke this Gaelic prayer for you: BEANNACHD DO T'ANAM IS BUDIDH. "A blessing to thy soul and victory!"

The son of a career air force man, James Clark from earliest childhood traveled extensively in this country and abroad. For the past fifteen years he has been employed by the *Orlando Sentinel*. He now shares his home with two dogs and a cat. He says that having been born on Friday the thirteenth, he has never been sure whether his current luck is good or bad. "The Magic Carpet" is his first step into the fantasy field.

A. C. Crispin is the author of the very popular Star Trek novel *Yesterday's Son*, as well as *V* (the novelization of the TV miniseries). In addition, she coauthored *Gryphon's Eyrie* with André Norton. "The Amiable Assassin" is her first published short story. She lives in Maryland with her husband, her six-year-old son, three cats, and two horses. When not occupied with any of the foregoing, she is usually reading or writing.

Monika Conroy was born, raised, and educated in Germany, where she spent her teenage years visiting castles, museums, and ancient monasteries, avidly reading legends. Having moved to the United States, she began writing in English, as well as doing such odd jobs as repairing TV and radio equipment and becoming an auto mechanic. For the past four years she has worked in a bank and taken college courses at night. She is currently at work on a fantasy novel.

* * *

Ginger Curry has earned a BA in psychology and has received the Independent Artist in Literature Award from the Florida Arts Council for her fiction. She is at present the fiction chairperson for the Florida Freelance Writers Association. With her husband and two sons, she relaxes by snorkeling in South Florida waters to add to a family collection of unusual fish.

Gene DeWeese is the author of thirty books, including several in which cats play major roles. *Adventures of a Two-Minute Werewolf*, one of his juveniles, was recently the "ABC Weekend Special" presentation. He lives with his wife and three cats in Milwaukee.

M. Coleman Easton's stories, some of which were published under the byline "Coleman Brax," have been appearing since 1980 in *The Magazine of Fantasy and Science Fiction* and in *Isaac Asimov's Science Fiction Magazine*. His story "Impersonations" was adapted for television as part of the syndicated series *Tales from the Darkside*. More recently, Easton has written two novels dealing with unusual forms of magic. In *Masters of Glass* (Popular Library, 1985), a young woman enlists the powers of colored glass in a struggle with a blaspheming magician. In *Iskiir* (Popular Library, 1986), a former goatherd and a potter's daughter fight an ancient desert sorcery.

Born and raised in Brooklyn, New York, P. M. Griffin's Irish heritage is reinforced by yearly visits to that country. She wrote her first story before she was ten and her first novel at sixteen. One of the latter is now being considered for publication. Her knowledge of history and folklore runs deep.

* * *

Having studied for an Honors B.SC. in Forestry, T. S. Huff entered the Canadian Armed Forces (Maritime Command). After that she went to Los Angeles and then headed home. Three years later she had a degree in Radio and TV arts from Ryerson Polytechnical Institute. She says that she has sold everything from apples to zippers and has worked as a farmhand, a security dispatcher, a bartender, and the head of maintenance for the YWCA. At present she lives in Toronto with three very large cats and works part-time at Bakka, Canada's oldest sf bookstore.

Caralyn Inks is a longtime fantasy reader who is a graduate of the 1984 Clarion Workshop. At present she is designing fantasy books and games for children. She lives in California with three children and three cats.

Mercedes Lackey is a computer programmer for American Airlines and is also well known for her "filksong" lyrics. She writes short stories and has a novel under consideration. A member of the Society for Creative Anachronism for eight years, she has also won awards for her medieval wall hangings. Her household consists of a husband, eight cats, and two dogs.

Some writers seem able to evoke other times and places with such a sure touch as makes one ready to believe in time travel and personal exploration of the past. Morgan Llywelyn, of mixed Irish and Welsh parentage, may have been city born and bred, but her heritage drew her from those high walls wherein she was a model, a dancer, and followed other modern roles, to become an expert horsewoman and, at length, a writer able to draw different people of different times and cultures with infinite skill. Her horsewoman is as alive as the heroine in her recently very well received novel, *The Horse Goddess*.

Georgia Miller has been a professional writer for fifteen years. She attended the 1984 Clarion Workshop and is a member of the Science Fiction Writers of America and the Writers Guild. In 1970 she won the Oklahoma Writers Award for the best book by an Oklahoman—the novel entitled *Three Ships and Three Kings*. At present she lives in San Jose, California, with her family.

Being a professional astrologer, S. Lee Rouland chose to write about that calling in Ithkar. This is her first fiction sale, and she says she enjoyed visiting Ithkar and hopes to do so again in the future as a writer and definitely as a reader immersed in the wonders of Ithkar Fair.

Susan Shwartz, having earned a Ph.D. in medieval studies from Harvard, now reviewing and contributing to a number of fantasy anthologies and editing one of her own, is also information coordinator at a Manhattan investment firm.

Kiel Stuart is a member of the Authors Guild and the Science Fiction Writers of America. Like Maeve in "The Singing Eggs," she is also a portrait painter who has exhibited widely.

ANDRE NORTON
